"A gentleman would never..."

"I would never count myself one of those, lass." He leaned in closer. "So do not harbor hopes that I am anything but what you see before you." He held out his hands and motioned around them.

"A thieving ruffian who would take a woman's virtue without thought or concern!" Even she looked surprised by the words she'd spoken.

"I would not say there would not be thought or concern if I took yours, Fia," he said, moving forward until their faces were a scant few inches apart. "I would be very thoughtful." A becoming blush spread up her cheeks and she stammered something before speaking it clearly.

"Is that the boon you claim?" she asked.

A shudder trembled through her, making him realize that fear was taking hold. He lifted his hand and cupped her chin. Sliding his thumb across those tempting lips, he shook his head.

"Nay. Not that," he whispered. "Only a kiss."

Author Note

I am so thrilled to bring you the third book in my A Highland Feuding miniseries—*Kidnapped by the Highland Rogue*! I confess, I am finding such inspiration from the true history of these two Scottish families and their centuries-long feud.

If you've read the first two books, you've met the heroine, Fia Mackintosh. She was a young girl caught up in the dangerous feud in *Stolen by the Highlander*, and then we saw her as an insightful girl in *The Highlander's Runaway Bride*. Now Fia is a young woman who thinks that the stories and experiences of Lady Arabella and Lady Eva are sooo romantic. And she's dreamed of a handsome Highlander kidnapping her and sweeping her into a torrid love affair that would lead to a happily-ever-after of her own. But when it happens, it's not at all how she thought it would be, and yet it's so much more at the same time.

Using the disguise of Iain Dubh, Niall Corbett cannot help himself when he meets Fia in a dangerous situation—he kidnaps her believing it's the only way to protect her. As we romance readers know already, nothing is ever that simple or clear, and this situation goes from bad to worse quickly. This hero is much, much more than he appears, and there is simply no way that Fia Mackintosh can ever be his. Or is there a way for Fia to find her coveted happy ending with this enigmatic rogue?

A hint before you read this—my next hero appears in this book. If you've read the first book, you've met him, too, but now he's grown-up and in need of a heroine. When he entered this book, he acted quite heroically, so I just know he's ready for his own story.

Terri Brisbin

Kidnapped by the Highland Rogue

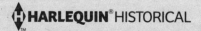

Recycling programs for this product may not exist in your area.

ISBN-13: 978-0-373-29902-7

Kidnapped by the Highland Rogue

Copyright © 2016 by Theresa S. Brisbin

Printed in U.S.A.

Terri Brisbin is wife to one, mother to three and dental hygienist to hundreds when not living the life of a glamorous romance author. She was born, raised and is still living in the southern New Jersey suburbs. Terri's love of history led her to write time-travel romances and historical romances set in Scotland and England.

Books by Terri Brisbin

Harlequin Historical
and Harlequin Historical *Undone!* ebooks

A Highland Feuding

Stolen by the Highlander
The Highlander's Runaway Bride
Kidnapped by the Highland Rogue

The MacLerie Clan

Taming the Highlander
Surrender to the Highlander
Possessed by the Highlander
The Highlander's Stolen Touch
At the Highlander's Mercy
The Highlander's Dangerous Temptation
Yield to the Highlander
Taming the Highland Rogue (Undone!)

The Knights of Brittany

The Conqueror's Lady
The Mercenary's Bride
His Enemy's Daughter
A Night for Her Pleasure (Undone!)

Visit the Author Profile page at Harlequin.com for more titles.

I've had the honor and pleasure of working with many editors while writing my thirty-nine novels, novellas and short stories over almost the past twenty years. Each one has taught me something about writing or my abilities. Each one has advised and suggested changes to strengthen my work. I'd like to dedicate this book to my first historical editor, Melissa Endlich, and to my current editor, Megan Haslam.

Melissa, your humor and gentle approach helped me through good and bad times of writing and life. Megan, your insightful comments helped me stay true to my stories, and I'm glad we got the chance to work together (and again). I am so glad I've had the chance to work with each of you, and thank you for your efforts in making my stories work!

Prologue

Brodie Mackintosh, chief of the mighty Chattan Confederation, smiled grimly at his cousin. The acrid smell of burning crops and dead animals made his eyes burn as he surveyed the damage.

'When?'

'Last night,' replied Rob, his cousin and the commander of all Mackintosh warriors.

'Any injuries?' Brodie waited for the worst. These incidents had escalated in recent days from simple mischief into unmistakable attacks. He waited for the inevitable.

'They chased most of the crofters out and away, but Old Angus would not leave.' Brodie cursed under his breath and Rob nodded in agreement. The old man was stubborn, so he'd stayed behind on purpose and not because of age or infirmity.

Brodie walked away then, examining some of the footprints on the soft ground. Crouching down, he stared off into the trees, thinking about the progression of the attacks.

This was the fourth incident in the last fortnight.

Each one in a different place across their lands. Each one destroying crops and livestock but very few of the crofts and never harming any of the villagers.

Until now.

Until Old Angus.

'What are you thinking, Rob?' he asked as he walked back to where his cousin waited. 'What or who is behind these?' When Rob didn't reply, Brodie met his gaze and saw the answer that neither of them wished to think let alone speak aloud.

Years, nay decades, of clan hostilities had ceased on his marriage to Arabella Cameron. Well, if truth be told, they had eased with that strategic marriage and ceased in the six years since. Part of their success had been due to skilful negotiation and monetary reward, but for many of the elders, weariness and loss had been the biggest and best motivation.

'Could it be, Brodie?' Rob asked. 'Would they be violating the peace?' Rob used his favourite words at the very thought of it and Brodie winced at his vehement choice. 'But, who among them would lead such an effort?'

'I know not, but I will seek out more information before making such an accusation to The Cameron.'

Brodie hated even the possibility that The Camerons were rising once more against them. Everything they'd accomplished in the time of peace between their clans and everything they'd suffered to attain that peace would be for naught.

'Send our trackers to see where they went.'

Rob nodded and went off to send the men on their assignment. Brodie walked back to edge of the forest and studied the perimeter. A small fragment of cloth clung to a broken branch where the path led away from the small cluster of cottages. He tugged it free and held it closer.

The colours and warp and weft were familiar to him for he'd seen his beloved Arabella wear it. In a shawl around her shoulders. In a sash across her bodice. In the blanket that lay at the bottom of their bed.

The pattern favoured by The Cameron's clan weavers.

Glancing at the piece of torn cloth, Brodie shook his head, partly in resignation and partly in regret. Nodding at Rob, he mounted up and rode back to the keep, still grasping the bit of wool in his hand.

He wanted to be the first one to reveal this to his wife. If her family was betraying their honour and their agreement, she needed to know it first. He owed her that much.

Chapter One

Fia Mackintosh tried to turn her glance away but failed. Oh, she would be the first to admit that her efforts to avoid staring at the intimate scene before her were not her best. But truly, the sight before her was one she would admit she wanted to experience for herself. Not with the man involved—God forbid!—but with a man who would look at her the way her cousin the laird looked at his wife.

Brodie towered over Arabella even more so than he towered over most of the men of the clan. The lady was petite and known throughout the Highlands of Scotland as the most genteel and beautiful woman who lived there. And yet, not for a moment did Arabella seem intimidated by the huge man standing so close to her, leaning down over her. When Brodie pressed his lips to Arabella's, Fia's own lips tingled. But that was not the worst thing.

The worst thing was when a loud sigh escaped her control and echoed in the silence of the chamber.

Loud enough to draw Brodie's attention from his wife. Loud enough to draw his attention to her instead. And even loud enough that Ailean, the lady's cousin and companion, laughed aloud. Thankfully, Aunt Devorgilla was not here to witness her embarrassment. Once again, Fia had broken the rule that servants were never to be seen or heard from when not being addressed. It was a lamentable failing that her mother had long bemoaned and, once more, it had gotten Fia into trouble.

'I beg your pardon, laird, my lady,' she began in a soft voice and without lifting her gaze towards him. 'I did not mean to intrude on a private moment.'

'If he wanted a private moment, my husband would have sought me in our chambers earlier, Fia,' Arabella said, laughing. She dared a peek now and watched as the lady pushed against her husband's chest, barely moving him an inch. Even so, he stepped back and crossed his arms over that chest. 'Brodie, I am well. You do not have to look in on me every hour of every day.'

Fia caught Ailean's gaze and the truth struck her from the knowing look there—the lady was carrying another bairn. Daring a glance at them, Fia realised the laird was being protective, now more than before, because of the lady's condition. Another sigh escaped as she hoped a man would hold her in such regard. Ailean laughed again at the sound and Fia felt the heat of a blush creep up her cheeks.

'Go on now,' Arabella said to her husband, who did not move a muscle in response. 'You have embarrassed our Fia and I need her attention on her tasks.' The mending lay forgotten on her lap. Fia grabbed for it to look busy and not lost in her thoughts which only made the laird laugh loudly.

'I think our Fia understands, my love.' Brodie leaned in and kissed Arabella's forehead. 'But I will leave you to your tasks.'

The wicked glint in his eyes warned Fia that he would not go quietly. So, when he reached out and pulled his wife into his arms and kissed her passionately, Fia had a moment to look away…

And she could not.

It was so romantic. So passionate. So…what she longed for in her own life. At least the next sigh that escaped went unnoticed by the others in the chamber.

'Good day, Arabella,' Brodie said as he set his wife back on her feet. 'Good day, Ailean. Fia.'

He nodded to both of them and left the chamber, his long legs crossing the floor quickly. When the door slammed, it startled all three of them. The lady smoothed her hands down her gown and then tucked a few loose strands of hair back in the braids that hung down past her hips. Ailean stood and filled a cup for the lady. Fia, well, all she could do was smile at the wonderful news she'd gleaned from this encounter. When Arabella caught sight of her expression, she smiled, too.

'I am not sharing the news yet,' the lady said softly, her hand sliding over her belly in a protective gesture. 'Not for a few more weeks, I think,' she added. 'But if Brodie continues his behaviour, everyone will realise it.' The last pregnancy had been too brief and ended sadly, so it did not surprise Fia that they would wait on any announcement.

'I will not speak of it, my lady,' she promised. Serving as the lady's maid often put Fia in situations where she would hear or see things not meant for others and she'd learned quickly how to keep confidences.

The remainder of the day moved quickly, as her days usually did, filled with tasks and duties, seeing to the lady's needs, accompanying her wherever she went through the keep and beyond. Fia could not help but smile as the laird seemed to appear out of the mist several times as Arabella walked in the village or saw to her duties around the keep or to her bairns cared for in the nursery. The anger or rather frustration in the lady's eyes always dissipated quickly as she gazed on her husband.

And each time that happened, Fia sighed.

Ailean and the lady took to laughing at the sound of it, but neither one took her to task over her naivety. The strange thing was that this was new to her. She'd worked for the lady for nigh on two years and, at first, took little notice of the goings-on of the romantic sort between Brodie and his wife. Only over the last several months had she begun to hear the whispered words and see the caresses and kisses.

Her mother had laughed the first time she'd witnessed Fia's reaction. According to her mother, it was because she was nearing the time to consider marriage and she was now noticing 'those matters.'

The truth was that Fia had noticed from her childhood days that there was something different…and lovely between Brodie Mackintosh and Arabella Cameron. Even when their clan suffered from the strife that divided them into two factions, forcing her and her family to live in exile in the mountains, Fia had watched the way her cousin treated the woman he'd kidnapped. Even having been only ten years at that time did not prevent her from seeing it.

In the years since, and especially since the lady kept her word and brought her to serve in the keep, it was so clear to Fia and everyone. And what woman in their right mind would not want such a match? Such a marriage? She sighed again. Such passion?

Now, as Fia helped the lady finish the last tasks of her day, before she would see to her bairns and husband, Arabella turned to both Ailean and her.

'On the morrow, I will accompany Brodie to Achnacarry to visit my cousin,' she said quietly. 'No announcement will be made of our journey and so neither of you will be required.'

'Arabella—' Ailean began. Fia watched as the inevitable test of wills played out. 'You are...'

'My husband will see to my comfort and my safety,' Arabella explained.

'But the attacks?' Ailean asked, wringing her hands together and shaking her head.

'There has been no sign of more attacks in weeks, Ailean.' Arabella smiled then and nodded to them both. 'Who would be foolish enough to attack the armed escort of the mighty Brodie Mackintosh? I am completely safe with him at my side.'

Fia waited for Ailean's next argument, for there were usually several. So, the quick capitulation was unexpected.

'Very well,' Ailean said softly as she nodded and looked away.

'I am certain your mother would enjoy it if you stayed with her while I am gone,' the lady suggested as she met Fia's gaze. 'I have put great demands on your time lately.' Realising the decision had been made, Fia did not object.

'You have not, my lady,' she said. 'But I appreciate your consideration.' Even servants who were not kin were treated as though they were here amongst Brodie's holdings. 'I will go to the village in the morn after you have departed.' Fia walked to the small dressing table and took up the brush there. 'But for now, shall I see to your hair?'

'I will see to that, Fia.' The deep voice of the laird echoed across the chamber. Fia blushed then, her cheeks filling with the heat of it.

'Very well, laird,' she tried to say without stammering as she put the brush in his hand. 'I will return in the morn then, my lady.'

She opened the door and allowed Ailean to precede her out. As Fia tugged the door closed, she heard the soft laughter of the lady within as Arabella chided her husband for embarrassing Fia once more.

Ailean walked down the corridor to her chambers and Fia made her way to the one she shared with several other maids. Moving quietly as she prepared for bed, she thought about asking Lady Eva if she required any help. Nessa, Lady Eva's maid from Durness, had recently left her service when she'd married and the new maid was still learning her duties. Surely she would be appreciative of some help?

As she climbed beneath the bedcovers of her pallet, Fia knew what going home would mean. It would give her mother endless hours to press her to accept the miller's son's marriage proposal. It was a good match for a girl such as she. The daughter of villagers could not expect to marry above her place and, truly, Fia did not wish that.

She wished and dreamed of a man who would make her blush the way Brodie made Arabella. Or the way Rob did Eva. Fia wanted the excitement of being swept off her feet by a strong man who was able to protect her and love her and desire her the way those men clearly did their wives. Another sigh escaped as she pulled the blankets high and closed her eyes. Marrying Dougal, the miller's son, would not give her what she sought.

As she dreamed that night, a man stood in the shadows holding out his hand to her. Fia walked towards him but hesitated, trying to see his face in the darkness there. Though she could see his black hair, all of his features remained out of her sight. He lifted his hand once more to her and she smiled, reaching out to him, to accept his offer.

She woke, tossing and turning, before anything else could happen.

Her mam believed in dreams, as did most of the old ones in the clan. Did this one mean she would meet the man of her dreams after all? That she should turn down Dougal's suit and wait for the black-haired man to enter her life and reveal himself?

The rising sun found her awake still, considering the proposal she'd received and deciding whether or not to accept it. By the time she had seen Lady Arabella off on her journey and made her way to her parents' cottage, she was nowhere closer to accepting that her future lay with Dougal, the miller's son.

* * *

'You should not tease her so, Brodie,' Arabella warned him.

Right now, as he slid his hands into the twisted braids of her hair and loosened them, he cared not for much else going on in the world. Arabella was his world and he enjoyed the feel of her silken tresses cascading over the skin of his hands and arms. Knowing it would caress another part of him very soon made that part of his flesh rise and ready.

'I did not do it to tease her, my love,' he said, burying his face in it now and inhaling the scent of the heather and honey soap she used. 'She is young and blushes at everything.'

'Our Fia is a young *woman*, Brodie,' his wife said, turning to face him now. 'And she has been infatuated with you since the day I met her.'

'Is that my fault? I assure you, I do nothing to encourage that.'

He slid his hands down to rest on her shoulders, drawing her closer to him. God, would the wanting never end? Six years together, two bairns and another on the way, and he needed to see her, to touch her, to hear her almost every hour of the day and night. Brodie leaned his head down and touched his mouth to hers. She opened to him as she always did and he tasted her deeply.

'I do not think it is you,' Arabella said as she leaned her face a scant bit away from his. Clearly she wished to speak more on this matter before seeing to his important matters.

'Then what is it?' Brodie dropped his hands and took a step back. Mayhap some distance would ease his need for her? He knew in an instant it would not make a difference.

'She wears the hope of a young woman seeking her first love in her eyes,' his wife said, letting out a sigh much as the girl did. 'She thinks that our beginning and Rob's with Eva are romantic.'

'I kidnapped you and held you against your will. Rob chased Eva, caught her and married her against her will. That is romantic?' Brodie asked, shaking his head. No matter how long he was married, no matter how much he thought he did, 'twas clear he did not and would not ever understand women. 'I cannot fathom it.'

Arabella stepped closer to him now and his body waited for her touch. She lifted her hand and touched his arm with only a finger, tracing up on to his shoulder and down on to his chest. He wished with all his might that his garments would drop away on their own so that her finger touched his flesh.

'You do not understand the appeal of being rescued by a handsome Highland warrior who becomes chieftain of his clan.' He tried to meet her gaze but he was caught by the movement of her finger as it slid lower and lower. 'Of being sought by a strong man who protects you against your enemies and reclaims a part of your soul you lost.' He was going to argue that point, for it had not happened quite that way between Rob and Eva, but when her finger crossed his belt and pressed against the fabric, he forgot how to think.

Another finger joined the first and then another until her hand cupped him, forcing a gasp from him. She paused, holding his sensitive flesh in her palm, and she met his gaze. Arabella was waiting for him to say something and Brodie struggled to remember the topic of their conversation. The girl. Her romantic dreams or some such thing.

'I…um…will try… Oh, hell, Arabella! I cannot put a thought together when you touch me like this!' Her laugh echoed around them both and lightened his heart.

'Be kind to her, Brodie. She is young and deserves to dream before she faces the reality of life.'

'Should I find someone to kidnap her? To sweep her off her feet as I did you, my love?' He did just that then, lifting his wife into his arms and carrying her to their bed. 'Then she can see how romantic it was for us.'

He followed her down and climbed between her thighs. Now she could feel the hard length of him— the one that she had caused with nothing more than a kiss and a caress. When she pushed against his chest, he lifted his weight from her.

'Brodie, she will find her own love, kidnapped or not. Just have a care for her tender feelings and sensitivities right now.'

'Fine! But now, my gentle wife, you should have a care for my tender feelings,' he teased. Sliding his hips, he watched her face as her body reacted on its own.

'Aye, my handsome Highland warrior,' she said, opening her legs so he could move closer to the place he knew would be ready for his touch. 'Come now, let me see to your tender feelings.'

The morning came too soon for his preference, but

he would hold her closely every night for the rest of their lives. He would discuss possible marriages for the girl when they returned from Achnacarry. He might not arrange a kidnapping but he could arrange a suitable marriage.

Chapter Two

A few days later...

Niall Corbett watched, arms crossed over his chest, as the motley group spread out over the area and claimed their places. As it did each time they found a spot in which to lay a camp, the fighting over the choicest bits began almost immediately. Though Anndra was the biggest fighter amongst them, Micheil was smaller, quicker and meaner.

While the shouting and brawling continued, Niall walked to a place that was on the perimeter of the clearing, higher than the surrounding ground and covered by a tree. It would do for now.

He dropped his belongings, few as they were, and seated himself on a nearby log to see the outcome of the fighting. As he expected, Micheil claimed victory once more and kicked Anndra's bags off the small patch of grass near the fire pit and placed his own there.

Lundie, Niall noticed, almost mirrored him. Arms crossed, watching the fight and resolution with thinly disguised contempt and resignation. No matter how many times Lundie had ordered the men not to fight amongst themselves, this small disruption happened at every new place where they camped. And over the six months that Niall had spent with these men that was a goodly number of fights. A few blackened eyes and cracked ribs were usually the result, so Lundie ignored it most of the time.

Niall walked through the area and realised it had been an organised camp some time ago. Caves into the mountainside held remnants of those who had lived here. With the mountain's forests and height to hide it, this would be an excellent place to hide for a long time. Lundie approached, so Niall stood.

'Someone used this place,' Lundie said. ''Tis too organised for another explanation.' Niall nodded.

'Nothing like the shielings the Highland clans use to watch their herds,' Niall added. 'The caves there show signs of having been used, too.'

'Do ye think 'tis safe for us to stay here?' Lundie, the man running this gang, had grown trusting of his opinion over the last months. A part of Niall's plan that was a success.

'With that old man's death on our last raid? I suspect no place will be safe for us for long.'

The Mackintosh was not known for his mercy but rather his strength and shrewdness. The death of one of his people would cause him to take notice and action against those responsible. Niall glanced once more across the clearing at just those men. He'd like to think it had just gotten out of control, but something niggled at him when he thought on how the whole raid had happened. If he had doubted it was planned, Lundie's next words confirmed it for him.

''Twas bound to happen,' the man said, shrugging his shoulders and looking away.

So, whoever was giving Lundie orders gave that one as well.

A line had been crossed with that death. What Niall was certain was meant only to be harassment was now much more serious. If a man's death was part of the bigger plan, what could be next?

'We will only be here for a few days. It should be safe enough for that,' Lundie said, his decision clearly made and the plan set in place. Niall could only nod as Lundie walked to the centre of the clearing and waited until he gained every man's attention.

He was not the leader who had a masterplan in mind, but only that leader's second-in-command. Someone else, someone more powerful, had designed these attacks and somehow benefitted from them. After each raid or attack, Lundie would disappear to meet with the one who gave the orders and then return with the orders for the next step. Niall needed to discover the identity of that one who had some plan to sow discord between the now allied Camerons and Mackintoshes.

Though his own orders gave him permission to do as he must, both to maintain his anonymity and to identify the leader of this plan, he did not countenance taking lives. Especially not innocent villagers who did not raise resistance but only protected themselves. But, from Lundie's comments, their activities had escalated and would again soon. Lundie pulled out a small sack and weighed it in his palm. Coins jingled within and the others smiled and moved closer. Niall watched and waited.

'Ye have done good work and yer reward has arrived.' Lundie tossed the bag to Iain Ruadh to distribute. Each man would get several gold pieces, more than any of them would have earned in years of honest toil. It took little more than that to gain compliance to whatever Lundie offered.

'Iain Dubh,' Lundie said, calling Niall by the name he'd used during his time with them, ''twill be yer turn for a reward on the next raid.' Though the others grumbled, they'd each earned the chance to claim something from their endeavour. 'Choose something ye like and 'tis yers.'

Niall nodded in acceptance and smiled as he received his gold. If their previous pattern held, Lundie would reveal their next target and they would attack on the morrow. Only the death of the old man had made them pause for any length of time. Tucking the coins into a small pocket in his leather jack, he waited for the rest of it.

'The Mackintosh has left his lands and gone to The Cameron,' Lundie revealed. 'On the morrow, we will make a small visit to Drumlui village.'

Niall forced himself to react as the others did. This was a huge challenge that the leader thought them ready for and the men listening smacked each other on the back and congratulated themselves for being given such a task. Niall's stomach roiled and clenched at the thought of such a foolhardy mission.

No matter that Brodie Mackintosh left his lands, his commander and others would be in charge of the security of the keep and the village. Formidable defences were in place and even more would be at the ready if the chieftain was not in residence. Good Christ! This called out disaster to him more than anything else they'd done.

'At nightfall, when the gates close, we will stir up a wee bit of trouble.' When the men cheered, Lundie waved at them. 'Nothing too much, ye ken. Just a little excitement that will surprise them.'

In other words, knock a few heads, toss a few cottages and get out. Niall shuddered at the thought of being that close to the main keep of The Mackintosh chieftain. He suspected that someone was trying to stir up trouble for the Mackintosh, but Niall did not want to be close enough to be caught when it happened.

'Seek yer rest. We ride hard before daybreak, taking different paths to Glenlui, and will enter the village separately.'

Lundie nodded at the men who sought their places and readied for the night. No fires would be built that could draw attention, even in this remote location. They followed the same pattern as they had for months, posting guards who would take turns through the night. Niall could see no good from this newest plan, so he decided to say something to Lundie.

'This is dangerous. You know that, Lundie,' he said quietly so only the other man could hear. 'Pricking at the man is one thing. Attacking his main village, at his keep, borders on madness.'

''Tis the order,' Lundie replied, with another shrug of his shoulders. 'Dinna worry. The pay will match the danger, Iain,' Lundie reassured him, believing that greed and gold drove him as it did the others.

'Well, then,' Niall said, nodding. Let Lundie think it was about the money then. On the morrow, Niall would be on his guard.

So, after sitting in the caves, dry at least, for a day they'd not planned on, they made their way down from the mountains and to the village. Niall made his way into the village, riding past the gateway of the keep without staring at the tall, stone walls around a taller stone keep. He dismounted, leaving his horse tied nearby, and went to the baker. After buying one of the man's last remaining loaves, he eased his way along the paths, observing the villagers who lived and worked here.

It did not take long to notice her.

A young woman, tall and lithe, walked past him and was trailed by a young man who he took little notice of. But, it took only one glance to assess this situation. The young man, awkward and lanky, wanted the woman. The woman who barely gave him a moment's attention. Until she stopped and turned, giving Niall his first good look at her.

Good God, she was a beauty!

She wore a plain gown, but that was the only unremarkable feature of hers. Green eyes the shade of the summer forest. A gently sloping nose that led his gaze down to the most perfect mouth and lips he'd ever seen on a woman. She said something to the man and he imagined how her lips would taste and feel against his own. How her voice would sound as she whispered his name....

Niall shook his head, trying to understand the strange wanting that this woman caused. Tossing the last bit of bread in his mouth, he chewed it slowly while sorting out the cause of his reaction to her. He was not an untrained, inexperienced lad with no history of involvement with willing women. Before, before he became Iain Dubh, he had had his share of lovers and even since becoming this rogue, women had sought him out for bed play.

Nay, inexperience did not explain it. So, he stepped into the shadows of the path where he would not be seen and watched the exchange between the two.

Even without being able to hear their words, he could decipher what was happening. The man was trying to convince the woman to accept his offer. He shuffled from side to side, unable to meet the beauty's gaze for more than a moment or two. Truly, Niall doubted he could have for much longer than that.

Then, the woman took the man's hand and was clearly attempting to be kind about her obvious refusal. Was the man making an offer of marriage? He was bolder than Niall thought him to be if that was happening,

'Dougal!' the beauty said louder now. Ah, the hapless lad was called Dougal. 'I have been as clear as I can about a match between us. I pray you to leave the matter now.'

Dougal, the hapless lad, opened and closed his mouth several times, trying to say something. The lad's rebuttal to the lass's refusal, Niall suspected. But the determined young woman—was she an Isabel or a Margaret?—did not give him the opportunity. She released his hand and stepped back, a clear message to one who had eyes to see it.

Niall let out a sigh and retrieved the apple he'd been carrying in his sack. Biting into it, he continued to watch this unexpected bit of entertainment to ease the waiting.

Bloody hell! He needed to get into position and realised the lass, and lad, would be in the middle of the coming disturbance. Glancing around, he wondered how to steer her away from it. Niall saw that his presence had not been noticed. Mayhap if they saw him, they would leave this area and go in some other direction?

He'd seen many other men and women in the months with this gang and had never thought of warning one of them, so why now? Why her? For it was the lass for whom he was concerned.

Without truly thinking on it more than that, he stepped out of the shadows, making enough noise to ensure she would hear him. And she did, stepping back even further now from young Dougal. She raised her eyes to his and Niall lost his breath with wanting and need for this perfect stranger.

Sucking in a breath, he nodded at her but remained where he stood. He wanted her to move down this pathway and away from the village well on his right. Tugging the reins of his horse, he slowly walked in front of her and she turned back to her companion and in the direction he wished her to go. After only a moment's contemplation of her choices, the beauty faced him once more, staring at his face as though deciding if they had a past introduction.

He would have remembered meeting this one but

could not. He'd never travelled to the lands of the Mackintosh and Cameron clans before this. If he'd seen her at court, his appearance would have been very different than it was now with dirt and grime covering most of his face and features and the worn and torn clothing of a band of men living on the road.

This close, he could see that her eyes were even more spectacular than at a distance, glimmering in this sun's light as though touched by fae magic. Her gaze narrowed and he felt the heat of arousal race through him. Wiping the back of his hand across his now sweaty forehead, Niall struggled with his control.

'Good day, sir,' she said quietly, still searching his face. 'Do you have need of something?'

Did she have to phrase her words so? His randy bits took a different meaning from them than the simple courteous one she meant. The sound of her voice, soft but with deep tones tracing through it, was as sensual as he'd thought it would be. Before he could reply, hapless Dougal walked to her side, and even took a step closer, positioning himself as her protector. The poor lad would never stand against what was coming.

'Good day to ye both,' he said, making his accent rougher to blend with the more common one of the gang. 'Nay, just travellin' on and stopped for a drink from the well there.' Niall nodded at the stone structure—a common reason and place for visitors to stop.

'The dipper sits in a bucket at its side,' the beauty replied. Hapless Dougal glared and crossed his arms over his meagre chest, mayhap able to read more in Niall's gaze at the young woman than she did.

Niall pulled his horse along, blocking the rest of the path, and feinted towards the well. The sound of stirring trouble began echoing into the clearing. The other two glanced to the source of the sounds and the woman took a step towards it. Without thinking, Niall grabbed her by the shoulders, ignoring her gasp, and pushed her in the other path.

'Go. Now. Away from here,' he whispered fiercely so that only she could hear his words.

She stumbled back a few steps and into hapless Dougal, who caught her. Niall could waste no more time here without exposing himself to the outlaws, so he did not spare another glance at her. Instead, he mounted and rode off towards the growing disturbance, knowing he must play his part.

The lass would have to see to herself, no matter how much his randy bits wanted him to do otherwise. That he had to force himself not to look back at her told Niall that she was more dangerous to him than any other challenge he'd encountered thus far. And these last months had presented him with many more than he'd ever thought to face.

The spreading chaos and noise drew his full attention now and he could give little more thought to the enticing, green-eyed temptress.

Chapter Three

At first, the stranger distracted her.

Fia was accustomed to meeting strangers in her duties to Lady Arabella, for many people came from all over Scotland and the world to visit the powerful chief of the Chattan Confederation. But this man was not of the same quality of those who called on Brodie Mackintosh. Oh, he met with villagers and farmers, but not those who had every appearance of living on the other side of the law.

This man stood as tall and was as muscular as Brodie himself. And though his garments were as soiled as he was, there was something about him that belied his condition. His blue eyes gleamed against his dark hair and the dirt that covered the masculine angles of his face. How long he'd remained in the shadows, listening to her conversation with Dougal over his proposal of marriage, she knew not.

And his strange words ordering her away. As though she would obey a stranger in her own village without reason.

But none of that mattered when she heard the

screams split the air. Glancing around, she realised that the gates of the keep would be closed by now for the night. With the setting sun, the village was isolated and unguarded, more so than the keep for its lack of warriors and weapons. And the sounds coming from the western edge of the village forced her to act.

'Dougal! You must run to the keep. Get help!' she said, as she turned once more to the growing disturbance. 'Now, Dougal!'

Fia did not wait for an answer. She ran down the path, past the well and through the rush of villagers escaping from whatever was happening. Reaching the split in the paths—one led to the fields, the other to other crofts and the mill—she watched in horror as the mayhem spread. Wagons were overturned. Fights broke out between some of the villagers and the men who seemed the cause of it all. When two galloped by her towards their cronies, Fia lost her breath.

In a moment, she was thrown back in her mind to the attack on the camp those years ago. Only ten years of age, she had been caught in the open as Caelan's men rode in, trampling anyone in their path. Glancing around this open area, with those two knocking down anyone they could and yelling all sorts of crude words and threats, Fia was that ten-year-old lass once more. The sights and sounds blended together in her thoughts, memories now feeling real and twisted with the events of the moment.

Until a child screamed out in fear.

Those years ago, it had been the lady Arabella who'd saved her, pulling Fia from the path of the attackers and pushing her to safety. Fia knew she must act or the child would be injured or worse by these uncaring fiends. Ducking low and running across the clearing, she sought the child and saw her crying in the midst of confusion. They were burning something and acrid clouds of smoke began to spread through the closely built cottages on the lane.

'Come, Meggy!' she called out to the girl as she ran to her side. Grabbing the lass's hand, she tugged her away from the fighting and into the woods around the crofts. 'Where is your mam?' she asked. All the girl could do was cry, so Fia hugged her for a moment and then placed her in a thick copse to hide her from sight. 'I will find her and bring her to you. Do not leave here until I return!'

Pulling branches around the girl, Fia ran back to find Meggy's mother. How they'd gotten separated, Fia could not imagine until she stumbled right over Anice where she lay unmoving in the path. Crouching down, she touched the woman's face and whispered her name. Anice stirred but did not wake. Thank the Almighty, she was alive! Rolling her on to her back, Fia checked quickly for injuries before trying to drag the woman into the trees. She'd barely gotten a good hold on her when two riders began circling them.

'What have we here?' one called out, coming so close that his horse nudged her back. Nearly losing her balance, Fia adjusted her hold on Anice and tried to move her.

'Here now, lass,' taunted the other, a man with a rat-like face. He pushed his horse against her until she lost her grip on Anice. She stood then, brushing her loosened hair from her face. She took a quick look towards the keep before facing them.

'Oh, they won't be here for some time, ye ken?' the

first one said as he swung his leg over the back of his mount and dropped down next to her. Now, standing on the ground, she realised he was a huge man. Fia could not prevent the shudder that made her stumble then. 'We made sure of that.'

Dougal? Had they caught Dougal on his way to the keep? Was he…? She backed away, slowly, step by step until she could go no further. Ratface was now behind her, trapping her between them. Fia tried not to panic but the terrifying lust in their gazes told her she would not escape.

'Ah, now, Anndra, ye hiv scared the lass,' Ratface said.

Aye, they had. Fia stood still, hoping not to cause them to take hold of her. If they did, her strength would do nothing against theirs.

The big man took another step closer and she could not breathe. He blocked her view of everything but his huge chest and meaty hands. Even though the noises around them grew, these two did not go back to their thievery and destruction. Nay, their gazes grew more intense and she feared now for her virtue and her life. When this Anndra nodded over her head at Ratface, she knew her time was at hand.

The large, strong hands grasping her shoulders now with a steel hold that hurt stopped her from getting away. She struggled against him, but it did no good. When she opened her mouth to scream, Ratface shoved a putrid scrap of cloth in her mouth and pulled her against him.

'Come now, lass. We just need a wee bit of time to show ye how a real man pleasures a woman. Ye will no' be sorry for it,' he whispered against her ear, sliding his tongue down her neck and biting her shoulder. Her cry muffled by the cloth seemed to excite them more.

'A real man now, Micheil?' Anndra laughed and sliced the laces of her gown with one motion. As he reached for the edge of her shift, she began to fight them in earnest. Twisting and pulling against their grasp, Fia tried to escape. The rag in her mouth made it hard to breathe and impossible to cry out. 'I will show her a real man and ye can watch and learn.'

The cloth of her shift was no match for his strength and she felt the cool air on her skin as he tore it open down to her waist. She pushed away from him, but that only forced her against the other man. The big one smiled, staring at her naked breasts as they grew taut, and he reached out to touch her. Fia held her breath, offering up a prayer for help. The sound of a sword being drawn behind them gave them pause.

'Why, thank ye, gentlemen,' someone called out from behind the huge man. 'Ye found her.'

Micheil cursed in her ear, a foul string of words she did not truly understand. Anndra turned, but kept her between them.

'Found who?' he called out.

'That lass ye hiv between ye there.'

Anndra shifted again and Fia took advantage of him not holding her to drop to her knees and scrabble away. She did not get far before Anndra grabbed her by her hair and dragged her to her feet. It took a moment of absolute silence before she realised that the men gaped at her now. As she tried to clutch the rent edges of her clothing, she finally saw the third man.

The stranger. He was one of them. Had he been

searching for her during the chaos? Confused and in pain, Fia struggled to free herself. The tall man walked closer, sword drawn, and she could not tell if he was friend or foe. He had warned her away, given her a chance to flee ahead of the danger, even if she had not heeded his words. Before any more could be said, a loud and shrill whistle pierced the air and the three all canted their heads at it.

'Weel, then,' the stranger said. ''Tis time to move on.'

''Twill take only a minute or two,' Anndra said, pulling her closer.

'She is mine,' Micheil said, tugging her to himself.

Fia managed to pull the gag from her mouth in the struggle and fought in earnest against them. Using a trick she'd learned from the boys in the village, she knocked her head back into Micheil's face, aiming for his rat-like, narrow nose. His howl of pain was satisfying, for a moment, until Anndra turned to grab her.

'Nay,' the stranger said, walking closer and holding his sword up. 'Lundie said I get my pick this time. And I picked her.'

Now he reached out and took her arm, pulling her away from the others. From their expressions, it would not be that simple. The stranger stared at her even while he spoke to the men.

'Lundie? Did ye no' give me my choice?'

'Aye.' A man she'd not seen before walked his horse forward from the shadows. 'If ye want to waste it on a piece of tail, fine though she may be, go on wi' ye then.'

Lundie looked at the other men and nodded, ordering them away. When they'd taken off running, he looked at the stranger and then tilted his head in her direction.

'Ye ken the problems it'll cause, dinna ye?' Then, this Lundie let his gaze move over her from her feet to her head, pausing at her belly and her breasts. She tugged the edges of torn cloth closer to cover her flesh. ''Twould be easier if ye just took her now and were done wi' her.'

The stranger walked up to her, lifting her chin even as she trembled. For some reason, she suspected any dirty fighting moves would be familiar to him. He'd wanted her away before and mayhap he would allow it now?

'Oh, I will take her,' he whispered just before his mouth touched her and told her the answer without words.

Fia was not prepared for the onslaught of sensations caused by this man's kiss. Oh, it was nothing like any kiss she'd received before. Those had been innocent. Those had been hesitant. This, this was searing and possessive. It was not long before she realised he had no plans to let her go.

He slid his hand into her hair, tangling his fingers in it and holding her mouth to his. Pressing with his tongue, he sought an opening and soon found it when she tried to speak. For a moment, just the slightest bit of time passing, she forgot her situation. She forgot herself and could only feel the growing heat pulsing through her.

For a moment. Then everything crashed down on her as she remembered. So, she bit him. He yelled but he pulled himself away as she'd wanted him to do.

'Damn ye!' he said, wiping the back of his hand across his mouth.

'A problem, I tell ye,' Lundie called out. Another whistle made them both look towards the keep. 'Take her or leave her, but do it now. We ride!' Lundie turned his horse and rode off.

'I pray you, please let me go,' she said, trying to step away from him. 'My friend needs help there.' She nodded to where Anice yet lay unconscious.

Without waiting for his reply, she slowly backed away and moved towards Anice. The sounds of the fighting were less but now the clamour rose in the direction of the keep. Warriors were coming.

'Go. Now. Away from here,' she said, knowing those words had been his own to her. She ran towards Anice only to be caught by the large man called Anndra who'd returned unnoticed. He wrapped his beefy arm around her waist and spun her to face the other man.

'If ye keep losing her, I think I wi' keep her for meself.'

Any thought that she would be released fled as the stranger strode across the clearing. His gaze was hard now with no sign of the desire that she'd seen there before. And no sign of relenting and letting her go.

'This is the way ye do it,' Anndra said quietly behind her.

Before she could turn around, her head exploded in pain and the whole village around her went black.

Niall cursed under his breath as the lass crumpled under the blow. Anndra held on to her and smiled grimly at him. Niall ran to his horse and mounted, riding to the two and reaching down to grab her and pull her over his legs.

As another whistle sounded, he understood there was little time left to do anything but get away. Taking her or leaving her was no longer a choice he could make, so he turned his horse and rode off to the west. He, Anndra and Lundie followed one path that would lead them across a stream, destroying their scent and their trail.

He tried to ignore the woman in his lap. Niall had to hold her in place there so she would not slip off. Riding with her dead weight was difficult but had to be done. From the feel of her body, she was alive though not awake. His true trouble would begin when she woke.

Lundie had said this would cause problems? Oh, aye, it already had and would continue to do so until he found a way to get rid of her. One woman in a gang of men was not a good thing. A glance at Anndra and he knew claim of her being his prize would only last so long and then go out of control.

They crossed the fields quickly, followed the stream away from Glenlui and into the deep thickness of the forest, always heading north and west. Their travel slowed with the full dark after the sun set, but Lundie picked his way along the rough path in the light of the rising moon. The lass had not stirred at all as they crossed the miles leading away from her village. When Lundie called a halt, Niall slowed at his side.

'Ye shoulda left her behind,' he said, spitting into the dirt. His words were low enough that Anndra could not hear.

'Anndra had other plans for her,' he admitted part of the truth.

'There is a soft spot in ye that will be yer death, Iain.'

Niall could not disagree about either of Lundie's suppositions. But, for so long, he'd been someone other than himself and, for the first time in that long time, his action to protect her felt like the man he used to be. A nobleman. Yet, Lundie was correct—acting like the nobleman he'd been raised to be would get him killed on this mission.

He watched as Lundie climbed down and tied his horse near a grassy patch off the path. Lundie ordered Anndra to the stream for water and then he walked to Niall's horse and reached up to take her. She did not react at all as he handed her down and then tied his own horse to graze. Niall pulled a rolled blanket from under his saddle and opened it on a dry area of ground. Lundie laid the woman on it and then lit a torch so they could see to setting up their meagre camp.

Her hair had come free from her braid and lay around her like a crown, gold strands in the brown reflecting the torch's light. Niall fought the urge to sift through its silkiness with his fingers and concentrated on his true task—check the back of her head where Anndra clubbed her. His hand came away with fresh blood.

Lundie walked to him and handed him the flask in his other hand. Niall took a deep swallow and passed it back. He waited on the man's words.

'A fortnight.'

'A fortnight?' he asked.

'I'll give ye a fortnight wi' her. If she's still alive then, ye find a way to rid yerself of her or I will.' Lundie met his gaze until Niall nodded, accepting the message given. 'Anndra's bringing water. Clean her up and get some rest. I will take the first watch.'

Everything was accomplished in a short time and, soon enough, the lass's head was bandaged and her gown tied together with some strips of cloth from her shift. Niall settled behind her still form as Lundie put out the torch. They would take no chances of being seen in the darkness by keeping it burning through the night. As the air began to chill and she shivered in his arms, he tugged the edge of the plaid he wore over his trews free and tossed it over both of them. He'd only just closed his eyes when she moaned. Though it was a soft sound, it drew his attention immediately.

'Hush now,' he whispered. 'No one will harm you now.'

Niall felt her sink back into unconsciousness and thought on his promise. Anndra shifted on his blanket nearby, making Niall wonder just how long he could or would keep her for himself in the ever-increasing danger of this mission.

But, he would do what he must because there was too much to lose otherwise.

Chapter Four

The pain in her head roused her.

Unlike anything she'd felt in the whole of her life, it made her stomach roll and the bile rise. Fia knew she must roll off her back, but the waves of agony stopped her. Her groan of misery echoed out before she could prevent it.

'Here now,' a voice whispered in the darkness.

Strong hands gently moved her to her side and, if she did nothing, she discovered the pain did not worsen with the movement. Her stomach did though, rebelling and causing her to retch. Now, those hands, and arms, lifted her to her knees and held her as her misery grew. When her body ceased its rebellion, the arms laid her back down slowly and carefully.

'The head wound, I'm afraid, is the cause of that.'

Fia lifted her hand to her head, searching for the cause of the pain and found an egg-size lump there on the left side of it. That injury. Her thoughts and memories were muddled as she tried to remember what had happened. All of it was in darkness, as she was now. Complete blackness surrounded her. Blinking, she tried to see anything and could not. Panic rose now within her, making it difficult to breathe.

'Let me light a torch,' the voice said as though it, he, knew what she was feeling.

She knew that voice. She did. But in the growing fear, she could not remember the person who'd spoken. Fia felt movement around her and then a flash and sparks as he used a flint to light a torch. The brightness hurt her eyes so she closed them until she became accustomed to it. Then, she looked at the man who'd helped her.

The same stranger who'd accosted her in the village during the attack. The same man who'd tried to warn her away from the coming danger. The same one who'd kissed her.

'Who are you?' she asked. She began to push herself up to sit and the pain and dizziness made her stop.

'I will clean that up first,' he said, nodding at the smelly mess near her.

Fia could only watch as he retrieved a shovel from outside and dealt with it. Her nausea lessened when the odour was gone. She also took the opportunity to look around the place where they were.

It looked very familiar to her, but its name and location escaped her. Only then she heard the voices outside the…cave! They were in a cave.

'Do ye think he means to kill her?' someone asked loud enough for her to hear.

'I had hopes he'd share her before that,' another replied.

'I didna think he was that kind,' a different voice added.

'What kind?' that first voice asked.

'Ye ken. The kind that resorts to killing a lass who willna…'

'Haud yer wheesht!' the man in question yelled. He dragged his free hand through his hair and looked back and forth between the shovel he yet carried and the opening of the cave. 'I amna killing her!'

'Will ye share her then?' the other man asked as though it was a reasonable request. Share her? Share her!

She moved then, pain or no damn pain. She pushed herself back, scrambling until she hit the wall. Looking for something she could use as a weapon, she found nothing. Fia found it difficult to even keep her eyes open, but she knew she must. When he stepped away from the opening and towards her, she put her hands out in front of her.

There were two of him, nay, three now. The watery shadows thrown off by the flickering torch made it impossible for her to tell what she saw. Fia rubbed her eyes and blinked several more times. He seemed closer now. As he crouched down before her, she pressed herself against the wall.

'I will not kill you, lass,' he said, dropping the shovel to the ground. Holding out empty hands, he nodded. 'And I have no intention of sharing your charms with them,' he added.

His tone reassured her but only until she realised what he'd said. Not killing her was a good thing. However, even in her muddled mind, she understood he'd only agreed not to share her with the outlaws sitting outside. He did not say he would not take her himself.

She followed his gaze and was horrified to see that her shredded gown exposed her legs to him. Pulling her legs up to her chest, she wrapped and tucked the gown's edges tightly around her. His expression did not change much—the lust was clear but now a touch of amusement entered his eyes.

'You were the ones who attacked the village.' Her words hung there between them and, as she watched, his gaze turned dark.

'"Attacked" is a strong word,' he said, sitting now and crossing his legs in front of him, dusting dirt off his hands. 'We simply had some fun.'

'Killing and attacking innocents in the village? Burning the cottages? Destroying their possessions? I call that despicable!'

Fia said it with such force that her head ached even more. She closed her eyes for a moment and opened them to find him only inches from her. She'd neither heard nor saw him move, he'd done it so quickly. He leaned in even closer until she could feel the heat of his breath on her face.

'Considering your situation, I would suggest you not be making such accusations loud enough to be heard. My friends out there will not take kindly to such things,' he began. He smiled then, one that would have been devastating if under different circumstances, and she waited for the rest of the threat she knew was coming. 'And, since I am the only one standing between you and the lads who want to be sharing your favours, I suggest you keep such words to yourself.'

Fia nodded and he stood and moved away, gathering some items from around the cave. She had been stupid and she knew it. Better to say nothing than to risk insulting or inflaming those who held her prisoner. Fia vowed to remain silent, as much as she could, until she understood what was happening. He approached once more, this time slowly, and held out a skin and a sack to her.

'You likely do not feel like eating or drinking right now, but this is watered ale and some bannocks. Bland enough on even an unsettled belly.' When she hesitated, he placed them next to her. 'There's also a bucket there for…your needs.'

He was seeing to her comfort, such as it was. Why? When she did not respond, he shrugged and stepped back.

'I would think you would soon be hungry after two days without.'

'Two days?' she asked. 'I have been here two days?' So much for her vow of silence.

'Nay. We were on the road for most of that time. Here, just lately.'

Her thoughts filled with dozens of questions. So many they overwhelmed her and what little strength she had. All she could do for now was to nod. Part of her struggled to keep control while the other part wanted to begin crying and ranting at this stranger before her.

'I have to see to something. I will return in a while.'

Had he seen her struggle? Did he know how close to falling apart she was? Whether or not he had, it made no difference to her in this moment. She appreciated being given some time to sort things out. As she sat there, confused and dizzy from pain, she heard him call out to the others as he left the cave.

'I've never had to force a lass afore,' he said. 'Wi' this pretty face and my soft words, I wi' have her beneath me, panting, afore she kens I've tasted her charms!' The men laughed loudly.

Stunned by such a claim, she could only listen to his boldness.

'On her back. Agin' the wall. It matters no' to me, lads,' he called out. 'The lass wi' have Iain Dubh plundering between her legs afore she can say my name!'

'Iain Dubh!' the others called out. 'Iain Dubh!' It became a chant to them and a challenge to her.

The man was a scoundrel of the worst kind. These outlaws saw this all as some kind of game and now she, or her virtue, was their quarry. As the anger rose, something else played in her thoughts. Listening now to the chatter, she heard this Iain Dubh speak to the others in the rough accent of those uneducated. Though she had learned the more cultured way of speaking necessary for service to the wife of the chieftain, clearly these ruffians had not.

But Iain Dubh had.

When he spoke to her, when others could not hear, his rough accent disappeared and he spoke as someone educated would speak. Like a nobleman.

She had lost her mind if she thought him a nobleman. A desperate laugh bubbled up within her at such a thought. Fia blamed it on being caught by outlaws, kidnapped and attacked and brought here to this damp and dismal place.

A nobleman amongst a gang of thieves and criminals?

When her head calmed and she could move without pain and dizziness, she saw to her needs and managed to turn her shift so it did not open in the front. She put the gown back on and tied the strips of her linen shift around her to keep it closed as best she could. A needle and thread would be helpful, but what kind of outlaws carried such things with them?

It was as ludicrous as thinking she'd heard someone of noble birth here.

He'd adopted the look and ways of common criminals.

He'd adopted a new name.

He'd pretended to be this other man, a rogue in the company of outlaws, robbing and plundering, drinking and swiving their way across the Highlands in search of riches.

But when he was with her, all of that fell aside and he wanted to be the other one. And saying what he'd said to the rest of them had been the most difficult acting of his life.

He had no intention of forcing himself on an unwilling woman, but the others did not need to know that. He, whether Iain Dubh or Lord Niall Corbett, was good—very good—at seduction. Niall had saved her life and if he eased her fears and she wanted to show him some soft gratitude, he would accept it.

For now, he needed to remain in his disguise and keep the others from suspecting he was anything or anyone but the man he portrayed. The only thing he would commit to was trying to keep her alive until he could arrange to release her somewhere. As long as she went along with him and did not know their location, he was certain Lundie would not care.

Niall sought out some ale and drank it as the others spoke in great detail about what they'd like to do with the young woman in the cave, reinforcing his suspicions. Good Christ, but he did not need this complication now! It had taken all his wits and intelligence to stay ahead of the very suspicious gaze of Lundie for these last months. He was close now, so close to finishing his task and regaining everything meaningful in his life. He would let no one, including himself, get in the way of his success.

And especially not some woman who simply crossed his path and made his cock stand. Silence surrounded him and he realised that he was staring at the cave…and the others were staring at him. Anndra, the huge fighter, stood, grabbed him by the arm, pulled him to his feet and thrust him towards the cave.

'Go on wi' ye now!' he shouted. 'The faster ye' tire of her, the faster I get my turn, ye ken!' Anndra grabbed his crotch in a crude gesture and the rest of them laughed boisterously at it. No doubt they were thinking of the same manner of things.

They expected him to avail himself of the woman within, so Niall bowed and saluted them and walked to the cave. He had spoken loudly enough for her to hear everything. But, the look of pain and exhaustion on her face when he'd left gave no surety that she was even awake. In a way, he hoped not. He leaned down and entered quietly, waving off several offers to help.

She sat where he'd left her, but something was different about her. She leaned against the wall, her head leaning to one side. Her braid was back in place and the bandage on her head looked fresh.

And she slept, sitting up like that, back against the wall. He walked closer and spied a knife clutched in one hand. Where had she found that? Glancing at his boot, he realised he must have lost it in carrying her in and settling her down. Since it was not his *sgian-dubh*, he worried not over it.

As Niall watched her slow, even breaths, he realised that he had no idea of her name. Not once in their interaction had hapless Dougal spoken it. No one in the village had called out to her. That might be the first thing he asked her after he woke her. And, hearing those rude comments outside, Niall knew he must put on a show for them or risk their entrance into the cave. Letting out an exasperated breath, he stood and put his hands on his hips.

'Well, lass,' he said loudly. 'Are ye ready for me?' From the guffaws outside, he knew they were listening. She startled awake, even now still confused by the head injury and fear, from the dark expression that filled her gaze.

'Nay!' she yelled. Scrambling against the wall, when she could go no further she lifted her hand and held the knife between them. Her hands shook more with each step he took closer.

'Ah, lass,' he said, holding out his hand. 'If I want ye, that little sticker willna stop me.' He laughed then, forcing it out. 'And I have a blade I will use.' The raucous laughter meant he'd been heard.

'I will use it,' she threatened, even as her grip loosened and her head tilted. 'I will…' The knife dropped and she fell to one side.

Niall quickly laid her down on the blankets and tossed another over her, drawing her body away from the cold, damp cave wall. He tucked the knife into her hand and closed her fingers around it. Though he was not at present a danger to her, there were many others who might be. The knife would give some pause.

Then, he walked out of the cave and approached the fire there, and, with a flair, placed his hands over his heart.

'She has, alas, been overtaken by my charms,' he said. He poured some whisky into a battered cup and raised it. 'May she have more stamina on the morrow!'

'Ye are too squeamish, Iain,' Micheil called out. 'She canna fight if she is not awake.'

'And now we ken why Micheil is so popular with the lasses,' Niall said in a droll tone. Raising his cup once more in the man's direction, he continued, 'May Micheil discover that tupping a lass who is awake is much more fun than his way!'

As Niall had hoped, the others continued to drink and the banter went on for some time. When the time came and the fire was put out, he only hoped that he could find some way through this on the morrow. To add to his difficulties, he now had two weeks to find a way to save this woman who had stumbled into his path.

God help them both!

Achnacarry Castle

Brodie Mackintosh listened to the messenger's grim news and nodded. The man bowed and stepped out of the chamber, leaving Brodie to face Arabella and her cousin. When the door shut, he walked to Arabella's side and took her hand.

'There's been another attack, but this time it was Drumlui village.' He'd discovered that his wife did not like prevarication when it came to distressing news, so he shared the rest of it. 'Some damage. A number of injuries.' He paused and took a breath. 'Fia has been taken.'

'Fia?' Arabella said as she stood and shook her head in denial.

'She was in the village when it happened. Just after the gates closed at sunset three days ago. Rob has sent out searchers and trackers. We will find her, Bella.'

'She's just a lass,' she whispered. Ever since Arabella had met Fia in their camp, she had taken to her as though the girl was their own daughter. 'What will happen to her, Brodie? We must find her.'

'We will, Bella.' Brodie faced Bella's cousin who now sat in the chieftain's chair of the Clan Cameron. In spite of Gilbert's denials, Brodie still suspected some involvement. The man was greedy in a way that hearkened back to the original of their clans' feud. In a way that even ruthless Euan never had been. 'I would appreciate your help in this matter, Gilbert. The girl is kin.'

Though Gilbert nodded, Brodie sensed there was something more going on here.

'Certainly,' Gilbert said, nodding to his servant. 'Send for Alan.'

Alan was The Cameron responsible for Brodie's acquittal of charges of murdering Malcolm, Arabella's brother and the man who was intended to be chieftain. He could find anything and anyone and Brodie had no one among his own kith and kin who was better.

'My lord, he is away at Tor Castle now. He should return in two days,' the servant replied.

'Send word for him to go immediately to Drumlui Keep. The Mackintosh's man will give him further instructions on his arrival.'

Brodie nodded at Gilbert. Arabella's eyes were filled with fear over the girl's fate. No one needed to speak of the possibilities.

'We will return home at first light,' he said. 'Better to be closer when she is found and returned.'

He hoped his voice sounded more confident than he felt. In truth, if the girl was found, 'twas most likely she would be dead. And, if not dead, then…

'Brodie, why would they take her?' Arabella asked, her voice trembling.

She already knew the answer, but he could see it was her fear and worry that made her ask it. And, truly, what could he say? Gilbert's snort of derision made his blood boil. If he had not been committed to keeping the peace between their clans, Brodie would have punched him in the face to remove the sneer that went with the sound.

'We will find her, Bella,' he vowed.

'And then?' his wife asked.

'We will bring her home.'

They ate in silence that evening, no one offered any chatter or gossip when all knew of the situation and the seriousness of it. The hours crawled by and neither he nor Bella slept a wink.

Barely had the first glimmer of sun brightened the sky when they bade Gilbert farewell and rode out of the castle's yard on to the road that would take them south to Drumlui.

These attacks were well planned and escalating to the point where it would be expected for him to take action. Brodie doubted not that some sign of The Camerons had been found at the site of the attack in the village. So, someone was trying to stir up trouble in a very large manner. As they rode towards Drumlui, Brodie thought on who would benefit from an escalation in hostilities between his family and Arabella's.

Chapter Five

A bright light cut through the darkness.

Her head hurt but so did her neck and her back. She struggled to remember why. Had she been sick? Had she been…?

It all flooded back to her in a moment and she groaned as the memories of the attack and the stranger filled her mind. Reaching up, she tried to feel the back of her head and was surprised to see the knife in her grasp.

Fia knew Iain had returned to the cave and could remember the bawdy calls from the others. She could see him standing before her, expecting her to…to… And then she could not remember. Sitting up, she placed the knife on the ground close by and rearranged her clothing. With a cautious pressure, she tested the size and tenderness of the lump on her head and discovered it seemed a bit less than the last time she remembered checking it.

As she climbed to her feet, Fia realised the dizziness was gone as well. Wobbling as she stood, she waited for her knees to stop shaking before walking to the bucket there. When she'd sorted herself out, she noticed that it was quiet outside the cave. Creeping to the opening, she leaned down and peeked outside.

She could see only as far along the path as the turn in it just a few yards away. Even kneeling down did not make it possible to see more. Dare she leave the cave? Would they have left her here alone? Had they moved on without her?

Without any idea of where she was, Fia suspected she would have to escape on her own and try to get back to Mackintosh lands if they had left them. But the memories of Brodie speaking to Arabella about the recent attacks across his lands made her think that she might still be near Glenlui and their village of Drumlui.

Fia retrieved the knife and took one of the blankets. If it had taken them two or more days of riding to reach this place, it would take her many more than that to return home. So, she grabbed the skin of ale and the oatcakes she'd not touched. Glancing around, she found a larger sack and emptied it, placing the skin and oatcakes and blanket inside. It would be easier to make her way carrying the one thing. Prepared now, she crept out of the cave and waited until her eyes were accustomed to the brightness.

Any other time she loved a sunny day, but this day a little grey sky and cloudiness might have helped hide her movements. With the sun shining as it was, she would be in plain sight of anyone looking. Fia stayed close to the cave wall and then crept through the bushes, looking and listening for sounds of the others. From the laughter and voices last night, she thought there were four or five men. When the sound of branches crackled behind her, none of that mattered. Only escaping did, so she ran like the devil was on her heels.

'Bloody hell!' a man called out loudly. 'She is gettin' away again, Iain.'

Fia ran in the opposite direction she'd planned and realised that the path felt somehow familiar to her. That was not possible. She pushed thinking away and simply followed her instincts now.

And those instincts led her to a clearing. The man stalking her was getting closer, she could hear his laboured breathing right behind her. The sight before her forced her to stop and then the shock at what she remembered kept her from moving again. The one chasing her nearly slammed into her back and then grabbed her by the shoulders.

This was the centre of their camp.

Nay, not the outlaws who now stood here, but the Mackintoshes who had sought refuge all those years ago. This was where they'd hidden themselves while their cousin Caelan tried to destroy them all and control the clan. There had been dozens and dozens of men, women and children here, living as they could, keeping their faith in Brodie's right to inherit and lead them.

She had lived in this very place for almost a year before Brodie succeeded and they returned to Drumlui. Fia knew where this place was.

And now she was back.

In the middle of the band of outlaws who had kidnapped her during their attack.

Six men of various shapes and sizes and temperaments stood before her, all holding some weapon or another. But, those weapons were not the terrifying thing in this situation. Their gazes filled with desire, plain lust and need and danger.

Terror filled her then, sheer, utter terror, making it impossible to draw a breath or think her way out of this. The tight grasping hold on her shoulders would not let her move much until he began shoving her forward, ever closer to the danger before her.

Her fear spurred them on now and they began calling out threats and…promises. She searched for the one who'd helped her before and could not see him. The wind shifted then, bringing the smoke of the fire at her. Her eyes teared and her nose burned at the smell. The villain at her back pushed her closer and now the scent of sweat and dirt reached her.

'She looks awake and ready now, Iain Dubh,' the giant man called out. She'd not seen him approach but Iain shoved the man holding her aside and grabbed her by the wrist to hold her there. 'If ye canna swive her now, I really will need to show ye the right way of it.'

'I hiv told ye—I amna sharing her,' he replied. The men hissed and guffawed their disappointment. 'But,' he began, turning her to face him, 'I am no' opposed to letting her do other things for ye scoundrels.'

Yelling and clapping, the men grew louder and more boisterous over this. Fia stared in horror at Iain Dubh, wondering if he would do this to her.

'Nay! Nay, do no' mistake my kindness,' he called out to them. 'She can cook for us. 'twould be better than the burnt mess ye call porridge, Martainn!' he said, meeting her gaze now. 'Can ye cook, lass?'

Fia did not say a word, fear yet held her in its control. All she could do was give a slight nod in reply.

'There ye go! Finally, a decent meal is to be had,' he said. With a grip that did not relent, he tugged her closer. 'And I would no' mind if she washed my trews and shirt,' he said. 'They are close to standin' on their own.' He laughed then and pointed at one of the others. 'Lundie, will we be here long enough for her to do some laundry?'

'Aye,' a tall man off to one side said. She'd seen him before. In the village when Iain Dubh had claimed her. He must be in charge of this ruthless group. 'A few days.'

'There ye go, friends,' Iain Dubh said, smiling at them. 'Ye can hiv a hot meal in yer bellies and clothes on yer backs that dinna smell as bad as Micheil does.'

The mood of the men had changed from dangerous to something less so. Oh, she did not doubt that any one of them would seize her and do those things they'd said, but, for now, they seemed calmed from their worst. Calmed by Iain Dubh. With only words, he'd eased their demand for her and given them something else to please them. When he pulled her closer, wrapping his arms around her and resting one of his hands on her buttocks, all good thoughts about his abilities and his intention scattered.

'And when she is tired of cooking and laundry, I wi' keep her busy with other…chores!' The men laughed then and Iain leaned his face down to hers. In that last moment, as she planned to bite him again if he tried that disgusting thing with his tongue, he whispered so only she could hear. 'If ye naysay me, lass, I will give ye over to them.'

Though she expected the kiss, the gentleness of it surprised her. As did the feel of his hand in its intimate caress. Trapped between his strong chest and his embrace, Fia tried not to fight him. His tone gave no indication that he was jesting or did not mean what he'd said.

So, instead, to keep panic away and not struggle in his arms, Fia did what she did when trying to distract herself—she began counting the number of cousins in The Mackintosh Clan. She managed to count the first fifteen, by name and age, before the kiss changed and drew her attention back to him and his mouth. He had slanted his mouth against hers and was rubbing his tongue over her lips.

Mayhap because she'd not been paying attention, it was not as abhorrent as that first time? Now, though, he slid his other hand into her hair, holding her head close as he managed to get his tongue inside her mouth and…taste her! The hand on her bottom caressed her there and pressed her against the obvious hardness in his groin. When she shifted in his embrace, he lifted his head and laughed aloud.

'I think the lass is interested after all,' he said so everyone could hear. 'But, ye hiv a meal to make, love. See to that and then I wi' see to ye.'

Before she could speak, he spun her around to face the fire and swatted her on her bottom, sending her in that direction. Fia let out a squeak and she stumbled away from him. Making porridge would be easy and preferable to what the scoundrel had planned for her. Gathering the edges of her torn gown, she tightened the belt and linen strips holding it all closed.

'Where are your supplies?' she asked, looking at Lundie. He was in charge of this motley group, so she would give him his due.

He led her over to a tarp-covered pile and tugged one edge of it loose. Wooden crates and sacks of all sorts and sizes lay there. Whether bought or stolen, she knew not, but most staples needed to feed the gang were here. And in adequate amounts.

Glancing around, she found a large iron pot that could be used. As she lifted it, she saw and smelled the burned-on layers of many previous uses. As Fia was about to ask if she could take it to the stream and wash it out she realised she held knowledge about this encampment that they most likely did not.

She knew where the stream led. She knew which caves connected. And, she remembered where the secret tunnels were. Brodie had insisted that everyone in their camp—be they man, woman or child—know an escape route from it. Fia did not remember any talk that those pathways had been closed or filled in when they all moved back to Drumlui, so that knowledge could be the means of her escape.

'Is there a place to wash this out and get water?' she asked.

'Aye, down that path, but 'tis a good mile.'

'Is that where I'm to launder their clothing?' she asked.

'Aye.' Lundie nodded and then whistled. A few seconds later, one of the men broke through the trees and approached. 'Take her to the stream, Martainn.'

'Isn't she Iain Dubh's?' he asked, rubbing the back of his hand across his grimy forehead.

'I did not tell you to swive her at the stream. I said take her there so she can clean that and get water,' Lundie explained. 'Only that, do you understand?'

For a moment, it looked as though Martainn would

object again, but he held his words behind his teeth. With a nod, he pointed to the path leading off to the left. And down the mountain she knew. Grabbing the pot and an empty bucket, she followed his directions to the stream. Fia could have gotten there faster using a different route or even one of the tunnels, but she kept that knowledge tucked away.

For the first time since this terrifying ordeal had begun, she felt a sense of relief and hope. As long as she was alive, she could escape here. No matter what happened, she could get home.

The walk down took much less time and effort than climbing the steep incline of their path back. In spite of Martainn's initial reluctance, he was not such a bad overseer. He kept his distance as she knelt at the stream and scrubbed out the pot. He even told her what supplies remained in the boxes and sacks. Clearly, he had tired of being in charge of meals and was glad to pass it over to someone else.

When she'd managed to find a stone with a flat end, Fia used it as a way to scrape the coated grime off the pot's bottom and sides. She noticed that Martainn's attention drifted and she used that few moments to clean her hands and face, tighten her garments and remake the braid from which her hair threatened constantly to escape. Once done, she filled both the pot and the bucket with water and stood. To her surprise, Martainn took them from her and motioned for her to go ahead of him. In a short time, they entered the centre of the camp and found the others there waiting.

With no interference other than a few rude comments whenever she bent over, Fia gathered the oats and a few other ingredients and soon had the porridge cooking over the fire. Keeping a close watch on it and adding more water as was needed, it took little time before the smell of it spread through the area. Before she knew it, the men were standing with bowls and spoons in hand, waiting for her to finish.

As she scooped out porridge for each of them, a few whispered words of thanks and Fia found herself surprised by it. Martainn's was the loudest and she almost laughed at it. After she'd served all of them, Fia moved away from the pot and sat down on a log. No one stopped her or said much for they were too busy filling their bellies. Then a bowl was shoved under her nose and she looked up at Iain Dubh.

'Ye didna eat, lass,' he said, holding it before her. She took it with a nod. A spoon followed and her stomach growled loudly enough for him to hear it.

'In truth, I was not sure there would be enough,' she said. She only then remembered the sack with the bannocks in it and could not remember where she dropped it.

'Is it cooked well enough?' she asked, eating her first spoonful. It was blander than she was accustomed to, preferring to add fresh cream and nuts and even a wee bit of the *uisge beatha* made by the Mackintosh's brewers to it at home.

'Och, aye,' he said. When she raised her gaze to his, he was staring at her. That bit of amusement glinted in his deep-blue eyes and she waited on the rest. 'So much so that I canna wait to discover yer other talents.'

His attempt at humour over such a matter soured her stomach and she put the bowl down and looked away. Only Anndra's approach broke the tension between them.

'Is there more?' he asked, holding out his bowl. Fia nodded and rose to give him the rest of it. She scraped the bottom of the pot, filling his bowl as much as she could.

Unwilling to return to the matter between her and Iain, she reached for the bucket of water and added some into the iron cooking pot to loosen the remainder of the porridge so it would not burn on the surface. In spite of trying to ignore him and the looming danger, she was aware of his presence as soon as he approached.

'I dinna ken yer name, lass. What are ye called?'

She hesitated in answering him. Was she safer as Fia, Lady Arabella's maid, or as an unknown villager they'd kidnapped? Before she could decide, he nodded.

'I see then. Keeping yer identity secret? Weel, I wi' give ye a name so we all ken what to call ye when we need ye. For cooking and cleaning and the like,' he added with a wink. He stood there with his arms crossed over his chest and his blue eyes gleaming with mischief now. A lock of his black hair fell across his brow, making him look like the scoundrel he was. 'What do ye think, lads? Is she an Isobel or mayhap a Margaret?'

It brought their attention to her once more, making her very nervous. They stared and studied her for several minutes in silence before Martainn spoke. Fia fought to keep her mouth shut, remembering that silence might be more helpful than speaking out.

'My auntie Agneis cooked well. Mayhap Agneis?' he suggested.

'Yer Aunt Aggie was ugly as sin,' Anndra called out. 'This one isna that. Let's call her… Cora.'

The men all shook their heads and complained about both of those names. Another one, a man with bright red hair and a long beard, one she'd not spoken to, stepped forward. 'I think Sile is a good name for her.'

Fia watched and listened as they each offered suggestion after suggestion without ever coming close to her true name. 'twas interesting though to watch their manners and hear the comments about the kith or kin with the names they said. And, she learned the names of her captors and began to figure out who led this group and who followed. The years of observing the laird and lady were of some use in assessing people.

Lundie was in charge and everyone followed his orders.

Iain Dubh seemed respected, though begrudgingly, by the rest of the group. Even now he used humour to defuse the tension.

Anndra, Micheil, Martainn, Iain Ruadh and Conall all followed orders. Though there seemed to be a sense of comradery among them, she did not doubt for a moment that they would turn on each other if the right reason came along.

'So, Iain Dubh, what's she to be called?' Micheil called out, clearly tiring of this matter. But, by asking Iain, Micheil confirmed Iain's claim on her.

Iain seemed to think on it and then smiled. She could not even guess which suggestion he would choose.

'I think Lundie had the best one. We wi' call her "Ilysa".'

The name echoed through the clearing as each man tried it out. Fia noticed it had been Lundie's second suggestion. A smart decision to use their leader's choice, she thought.

'Come, Ilysa. We will stroll down to the stream to clean up the cooking pot.' The men did not mistake his meaning or his intention.

Nor did she.

'Twas yet early in the day. The weather was clear and warm for a spring morning here. There were hours and hours before night would fall, but Fia doubted that her efforts to protect herself would wait that long. As he lifted the now-cooled pot and held out a hand to her, the very devil sparkled in his eyes. Deciding she must reserve her strength for when the time came, she accepted his hand and walked at his side.

Fia kept thinking about the various paths and hidden places in the camp. The cooking pot might make a fine weapon if she needed it. Then she could hide until these outlaws moved on or help arrived.

Chapter Six

Ilysa.

She was no more Ilysa than he was Iain Dubh, but both names would have to work for now. As she walked at his side, quietly and with her attention elsewhere, Niall wondered what she was thinking. Was she worried about losing her virtue to him? Or that she was facing an attack of some kind when they reached the stream?

Her expression remained empty as they walked, even when he drew to a halt before the opening of the cave. A slight frown and gathering of her eyebrows were the only sign of concern from her.

'I hiv need of a few things,' he said. 'Ye wi' wait here?'

Surprise that he phrased it as a question showed for a moment before she nodded in reply.

'I do not think I have a choice.'

'Och, aye, la… Ilysa, you always have a choice.' If her glance showed surprise or confusion, he did not let it stop him.

Niall did not give her a chance to get into mischief

or try to escape—even if it would have been impossible. He grabbed the sack that held his clothing, meagre as it was, and a small jar from another sack and put them together in one. Ducking to leave the cave, he thought of one more item and put it in, too.

He did not take her hand again, but she walked at his side in silence. She'd already taken this path down with Martainn so he did not need to tell her this way or that. About halfway down, he took the cooking pot from her and carried it. The sun broke through the gathering clouds just as they reached the stream.

'I will wash that out,' she said, holding out her hand.

Niall gave it to her and sat in a spot where the sun warmed the ground. As she walked to the edge of the rushing water, he realised that it must have been the same place she'd used before for she moved directly to it. It was only as she knelt there that he got a clear look at her.

She looked worse for the wear. Even though he could see she'd tried to clean herself up, dried blood yet remained on her head and down the back of her gown. But that was not what drew his eye. Nay, what caught his attention was the sheer and utter whiteness of her complexion. Her face had little colour in it at all, making those eerie green eyes appear even bigger. Her hands, with those graceful fingers, trembled as she struggled to complete her chore. And her body shook as she leaned down to dip the pot in the water.

And, though she most likely did not know he saw it, he watched her eyes drifting closed several times as she saw to her task. He'd been so busy trying to keep up his façade that he'd never noticed her weakening condition. But now he had. Niall stood and strode over to her and took the pot from her hands, tossing it on the ground next to them.

'I will clean it,' she said, wiping her hands on her torn and ragged gown. When she met his gaze, she threw her hands up between them. In fear. He could see it in her exhausted eyes. 'I will…'

'Stop,' he said, shaking his head. 'I will not hurt you.'

'You will,' she whispered. 'If not you, then the others.'

She thought he would take his pleasure on her here and now.

'You need to wash and rest, Ilysa or whatever the hell your name is!' he said sharply. 'In my bag are some clean trews and a tunic. Wash your hair and the rest of you and come to me when you are finished.'

'Come to you?' She blinked several times at him and shook her head.

'I will wait for you where the path rises. Do not do anything rash. Wash. Dress. I will be waiting for you,' he said, pointing as he reached for his bag and tossed it to her.

He dared one look behind him as he strode away and she sat clutching the leather bag to her chest and staring at him. Niall ignored all the things going through his mind and walked until he could not see her any longer. After kicking at the dirt for several minutes, he leaned against a tree and waited.

Daft woman! Why had he seen her in the village? Why had he interceded for her? He'd seen a number of women involved in their attacks, most were simply shoved about in the mayhem. So what had drawn him? And why now?

Niall was so close to discovering the true identity of the person behind this plan of aggression meant to cause strife once more between two of the most powerful clans in the Highlands. The King had made it clear he wished an enduring peace between them. So, someone was trying to cause problems for not only the Mackintoshes and Camerons but also for the King.

Lundie almost trusted him. The man had made the quiet suggestion that Niall might be introduced to their sponsor soon. So, any misstep or mistake or anything that raised suspicions about him would jeopardise all of his work. And place his family and everything he had been promised in danger as well.

He kicked the dirt again.

Niall thought on how to manage this, how to manage her and keep his plan moving forward. Lundie would leave in a day or two to get new orders. He'd placed Niall in charge the last two times and hopefully, if the woman caused no problems, he would again. He'd been gauging the time it took Lundie to go and to return to try to figure out where the threat was coming from. If only…

The winds shifted then and a chill entered the air. Turning towards the stream, Niall realised that some time, or rather too much time, had passed since he'd left Ilysa there alone. With growing alarm, he raced back to the stream, searching for her.

At first glance, he did not see her. Though he wanted to call out, he feared it would bring the others' attentions, too. He crossed the distance from the path to the water's edge in a few hurried strides.

Had she run? Was she already a mile or more away from here?

He stopped and stared when he saw her, his breath caught in his chest. She lay in the long grass there asleep. Though she was curled into a ball, her damp hair was unbound and lay loosely around her head, drying in the sun there. She'd donned his clothes as he'd told her to do and her own were washed and tossed over branches nearby. Niall stood over her, completely confused about why he was relieved to find her…safe.

Minutes later he was no closer to understanding than he had been before.

Niall should wake her but it took only a glance to know she needed sleep. Once they returned to the camp, they would expect her to do other chores and cook again. So, he gave her this time to recover her strength. And to give him time to plan how to deal with her.

If the others thought they were gone for too long, they did not show it by seeking them out. No one came down the path. So, Niall waited. And waited.

He never knew he'd fallen asleep until the crunching of dried grass underfoot roused him. He'd dozed off in the patch of sunlit ground waiting for Ilysa to wake and now someone approached. Barely opening his eyes, he peered across the clearing and saw her approach. At first he thought she was simply walking up to him, but with a more careful look Niall realised she held the empty pot like a weapon, ready to bash it over someone's head.

And his head was her obvious target.

Niall waited until she was close enough and swung his leg out in one motion, knocking her feet from under her. As she fell, the pot went flying off in one direction and he moved to catch her. She came down on him and he rolled until she was beneath him.

She'd been biddable until now so this surprised him. She struck out against him, aiming her nails for his face even while she tried to force her knee up between his legs. As he tried to protect the randy lad there, Niall grabbed her hands and pressed them back over her head on the ground.

'Get off me!' she said through clenched jaws, her body bucking under his. Unfortunately, his body had the opposite reaction to the one she was hoping for and the result was clear to her. 'Let me go, you brigand!'

'Stop trying to scratch me,' he said, using his legs to capture hers and force her still. One of her legs broke free and she forced her knee up. Niall stopped it a scant few inches from his privy bits. 'And stop that!' he ordered.

His words did no good at all, she squirmed and twisted beneath him in spite of the differences in their strength and size. She had not yet realised she could not win this kind of a fight once she'd lost the benefit of surprise.

'Lundie wants to ken if yer done tupping the lass yet, Iain?'

Her body stilled and her gaze moved to his at the sound of another's approach and the reminder of the ever-present danger to her. He recognised Conall's voice and lifted his head to look at him. The youngest in their gang, Conall was probably the least of his worries.

'Almost, Conall,' he called out, narrowing his gaze in warning at Ilysa. 'We wi' be along presently.'

'Lundie said to fill the pot. There are rabbits to cook for our supper.'

'Very weel.'

Niall did not move other than to nod at the boy and watch as he retreated up the hill. Then he made the mistake of glancing back at the woman he held prisoner there. A tiny glimmer of tears gathered in her green eyes and, though she tried to blink them away, he'd seen them.

'I pray you, let me go,' she whispered.

'Lass, I cannot let you go now,' he said. 'You can lead people directly back to us and we cannot allow that to happen right now.' Niall released her hands and climbed to his feet. 'Bide your time and I will see you released when I can.'

He made the very serious mistake of watching her rise from the ground. In his clothing. In his trews that now outlined the curves of her hips and legs. Nay, that hugged those curves. It mattered not that she'd rolled up the extra length of them. His trews were touching her skin.

And those legs were glorious to watch as she gained her balance. She was taller than most women and her legs were as long and lithe as she was. Now, as she faced him, anger filled her gaze and her eyes glowed green.

'And you expect that I will submit to your…?' She waved her hand as she thought about her words. He'd come up with several before she did but held them. 'Your baser needs?'

His mouth went dry at the thought of what his baser

needs would like to do with her. He stared at her, sliding his gaze over his tunic and trews, watching the way her hair swung as her breathing laboured. It was as glorious as she was. Niall only knew he'd stepped towards her because she stepped away.

'Surely Dougal has baser needs?' he asked. 'You must have seen to those for him.' Had she seen to hapless Dougal? Did hapless Dougal even have any idea of how to handle or what to do with a woman like this one? He thought not. Her horrified expression and gasp told him what he wanted to know—she was a virgin.

'Dougal? How did you know about him?' she asked, glaring at him as she thought. 'You were listening! In the village. Before the attack.'

'You were quite entertaining, the two of you discussing marriage. Hapless Dougal trying to convince you to accept his offer.'

'Hapless? How dare you insult him,' she said, striding to him in only three paces. 'He is kind and loyal and…'

'He sounds like a faithful hound to me, lass,' Niall retorted. 'Not a red-blooded man who knows what to do with a woman like you.' When she raised her hand to slap him, Niall grabbed it and pulled her into his arms. 'Dougal would not know what to do with you if you were in his arms like this.' He slid his hand into the length of her hair and wrapped it over and over until he held her head close. 'Dougal would not kiss you like this.'

He took her mouth in a searing, possessive kiss, wanting to show her the pleasure that could be had in exploring those baser needs of his. With her height, her body moulded to his at just the right places. He felt her breasts pressing against his chest and envied his tunic then. With her head in his hand, he tilted her face and fit their mouths together more intimately and kissed her over and over until she opened to him.

His traced the edges of her lips with the tip of his tongue and slipped inside to taste her. Though he could feel her struggle against him, her body tense and rigid, Niall also felt the one moment when she did not. When she just accepted his kiss. He smiled against her mouth and gently rubbed his lips across hers. It was all he needed for now.

Just knowing that, for one scant second, she did not fight it. Niall stepped away from her and saw the confusion in her eyes.

She'd expected him to press, nay, push for much more than the kiss.

She'd expected his 'baser needs' to overrun his control.

She'd expected to be taken, her virtue torn from her by the rogue before her.

'Fix yourself,' he said, nodding at her wild, loose hair. 'And get your things while I fill the pot. There is nothing more impatient than a gang of hungry men waiting for their supper.'

At first she stood watching him with that enticing expression of hers that combined innocence, confusion and surprise. He would like to be the man who saw that expression in her eyes as she reached the peak of pleasure for the first time. And to hear her moan out in soft sighs and gasps would be wondrous indeed. If she continued to gaze on him so, he might find his control and common sense slip after all.

'Now, Ilysa.'

She startled and then ran to the bushes where her garments lay strewn and drying. He watched her out of the corner of his eyes as she ran her fingers through her hair, untangling it as best she could. A wince at one place told him she'd touched the injury there. Then with the speed of experience, she wove a long braid and tied it off with a strip of leather.

He filled the pot and waited for her. She rolled her garments, now somewhat clean, and tucked them under her arm. Then, she turned and began to walk down the other path.

'Ilysa? This way,' he said, motioning to the correct way. As he watched, she shrugged and followed him up the path. Something niggled Niall's suspicions as he waited for her to go in the correct direction.

Though her legs were long, he slowed his pace so she could walk at his side. He could not help but notice the colour in her cheeks and the well-kissed look of her lips. From the brighter light in her eyes, he thought the rest might have done her some real good.

They walked wordlessly back to the camp and he accepted the jibing of the men now that he had clearly taken his pleasure of her. Interestingly, the men did not harass her as much as they did him, for she had begun making their next meal. Martainn helped her, getting the various ingredients she asked for from their supplies and doing anything that required a knife.

But the one thing that kept his attention, the thing that made him smile throughout the meal's preparation and consumption—the way she would touch her finger to her lips. She seemed unaware that she was doing it and unaware that he watched her so closely.

Several times, as she was tending the pot of rabbit stew or watching the oatcakes on the girdle, she would reach up and stroke her lip and a hint of a smile would curve the edges of her mouth.

She was remembering his mouth there. He was certain of it.

Feeling smug over that realisation, Niall looked forward to repeating it on their next encounter.

Chapter Seven

Stupid.

Stupid and daft.

Stupid and daft and witless.

Fia would blame it on the head injury which had muddled her thoughts and her good sense. As she sat away from the fire, eating her portion of stew and oatcakes, she tried to focus on making a plan to escape. And she tried valiantly though unsuccessfully not to think about the kiss.

And she especially tried not to think of that one moment—small though it was—when she not only allowed his kiss but had nearly kissed him back.

Stupid and daft and witless.

Then, she had nearly exposed her knowledge of the area by taking the other way, the one he did not know about, away from the stream. For the moment, she did not think he was suspicious about it.

She was never going to survive let alone escape if she did not pay heed to her situation and less attention to her captor's attempts to take liberties with her. That he'd had ample time and opportunities to do his worst to her and had not only served to confuse her more than she already was.

Fia dipped the last bit of bannock into the stew and scooped it into her mouth. Never in her imaginings could she have seen this happening to her. Cooking for outlaws hidden in the Mackintosh's camp. She stopped herself just a second away from laughing aloud at it.

All those times she'd dreamt of being kidnapped and saw it as a romantic escapade now seemed so childish. Brodie and Arabella had fallen in love right here in this place, she remembered. Glancing around the clearing, she could see where their tents had stood. For a moment, Fia could almost see those who'd lived here, making their way around the encampment. Her parents, their kin and others who'd gone into hiding with them.

In spite of the terrible danger, those months had, in some ways, been among the best for her. For in that time and place, she learned about loyalty and honour and commitment in a way that most wee ones never know.

And about love.

Several relationships, other than Brodie and Arabella's, had begun in the camp. Margaret and Magnus were married now after discovering their attraction to each other here. Only a lass of ten, Fia had not understood everything, but the unbreakable bonds formed here taught her to wish for the same in her life.

Letting out a sigh, she closed her eyes against the inevitable truth of her current visit to this place. She had gotten what she'd always wished for and it was nothing like what she'd thought it would be. She might not even survive it.

The sun began its downward slide to dusk and the winds kicked up dust in the clearing. Fia stood then and felt the chill air on her face. A storm was coming and coming quickly. The mountains here seemed to funnel the storms around them, but this one would not pass them by. The fact that winter was over would not protect them from the ravages of spring storms here that could suddenly move in with strong winds and heavy rain or snow that could last for days.

'Iain,' she called out. He'd been speaking to Lundie and surprise filled his eyes when she spoke his name. 'A storm comes.'

Iain and Lundie and the others seemed to take notice now of the shift in the winds. Were none of them from this area or from the Highlands? Only strangers or outlanders would not know what to watch for as the seasons changed and the skies could be turbulent and unpredictable.

'I have seen this before, Iain. A spring storm comes and we must take cover,' she explained as the men turned their attention to her. 'The supplies should be moved inside…the cave.' She'd almost given away her one advantage then. She must be cautious. 'The horses should be sheltered, too,' she urged.

Neither man nor beast would be able to withstand what could be heading at them now. Iain approached and took her by the shoulders, as though staring at her would reveal some truth.

'Is this an attempt to escape again?' he asked.

'Escape is not a choice now. Not with the coming storm.'

The silence around them only magnified the growing strength of the winds. The men grumbled a bit amongst themselves and looked to Lundie for his orders.

'Martainn and Anndra, gather the supplies. Conran and Micheil, secure the horses in the break there. Iain Dubh, have ye found a cave larger than the one ye put her in?'

'Aye,' Iain said, pointing to a familiar place. 'The one that opens behind these trees is larger. It should fit all of ye.' Lucky for her, Iain had looked around the area. Otherwise, she'd have been in the difficult situation of whether or not to reveal how much she knew about this place.

With a few shouted orders and a little time, everyone had moved their belongings and supplies inside. She noticed that they were very adept at closing up and moving their camp when need be. Essentials like buckets of water and dry wood were brought in as well. By the time the first thick, wet snowflakes fell, everything and everyone had been settled inside one cave or the other.

Fia helped as she could until Iain grabbed her by the hand and took her to the smaller cave he'd claimed as his. They ran faster as the snow came down thicker every moment and she was out of breath when they entered. Although she had not seen it being done, some of the supplies had been brought here as well.

'So, Ilysa,' Iain asked as she sat on a wooden box, 'how long will this storm last?'

She shrugged and shook her head. Storms now were the most unpredictable of the whole year. And she did not watch and study the weather as the farmers and others did.

'Hours to days, I would guess,' she said.

As he began to ask another question, the truth struck her—none of them were from the Highlands. If they had been, one or more of them would have understood the changeable weather and dangerous storms here. And, if none were from the Highlands, then none of them could be Camerons.

At every attack there had been a sign of The Camerons left behind. Pieces of wool tartan usually caught on a branch or underfoot marked the attacks as their work. She'd heard Brodie discussing it several times with his counsellors and with his wife—a Cameron herself. The reason they'd left Drumlui was to travel to Achnacarry and discuss the matter with the newest chief of the Clan Cameron.

None of them were Camerons.

So who was behind these attacks? Her gaze moved to Iain and she realised he was staring at her, waiting for something.

'Well?' he asked.

'Pray, repeat your question,' she said softly, now listening to him.

'I said 'twill be a long few hours to days if you sit in silence.'

He walked over to a lantern she'd not seen before and lit it, the flame sending shifting shadows against the stone walls. Fia waited for him to ask his question again, trying to gather her thoughts and not say the wrong thing in reply.

'I asked how you know so much about the weather.' He stood now directly across the cave from her, watching her closely.

'I have lived in this area all my life. My parents worked the land and knew how to watch for the changes that signalled storm or snow.' She brushed her loosened hair out of her face. 'They learned to listen and watch so that their crops and herds could survive.'

'And the Mackintoshes have been fruitful on their lands,' he said.

'Is that why you attack us? Are your people jealous of our success?' she asked. Now it was her chance to observe him. 'Or do you want something we have?'

Fia did not put a name to his people. Let him think what he willed. She had a care since no one outside of Brodie and his closest counsellors and wife—and his wife's maids—knew about the connection between the attacks and The Camerons. He'd made certain to keep that a secret from everyone but the few people who must know it.

He met her gaze then and the edge of his left eyebrow seemed to twitch. Only the tiniest bit and only for a bare moment. But she'd seen it.

'Mayhap we are only looking for a bit of fun?' he asked. He shrugged now. 'Mayhap we were bored and sought some entertainment?'

He was lying. The twitch in his brow told her that. Fia wondered if he knew of it. She supposed that she'd been watching the people surrounding Brodie, both kith and kin and the many strangers who visited him, that she had noticed those kinds of revealing gestures and expressions before. A question came to her, but she did not want to pry…yet. So, she shrugged.

'Mayhap you were.' She nodded at the lantern, changing their topic of discussion. 'Where did you find that?'

'In one of the other caves. This area is riddled with them. And 'tis clear that they have been used before.'

'Places like this exist all over the area,' she said. 'Further north, there are shielings that are used during the summer while the cattle graze but they've saved many a life when a storm moves in unexpectedly.'

'Just so,' he said, looking away. Had she irritated him with her knowledge? Had he ever travelled the drovers' roads and seen the shielings?

'Now that we have hours ahead and a bit of privacy,' he said, turning back to her once more, 'what will we do to fill the time?' His words and tone were not particularly lewd, but Fia doubted not his intentions.

'If I had a needle and thread, it would be a fine time to repair my gown,' she said.

She'd spoken the truth and answered his question—though from his surprised expression, he'd not expected it. So when he leaned his head back and laughed loud and long, she could not help but smile in return.

His appearance changed so much when he smiled that way. His eyes lightened and he looked younger, though she had no idea of his age. His unruly hair moved as he laughed and she wanted to reach out and push it from his eyes. Instead, she slid her hands under her and watched his reaction.

'Do you not wish to wear my trews any longer then? I can always help you off with them,' he said. He was back to innuendo and suggestive language. She knew men in Drumlui who teased the laundry maids and other servants with such talk. It had never impressed her. Not when the young men in attendance to Brodie tried it and not when strangers or courtiers visited and thought to make connections with her as a way to get to the lord and lady.

'Does that work?' she asked. 'Speaking words with double meanings like that.' He stopped laughing and looked at her in a shocked kind of silence. She guessed that no one had ever asked him such a thing. 'Do women fall into your waiting arms when you say such things?' He seemed to think about her question and then nodded slowly at her.

'Well, in truth, aye, it does usually work,' he said. 'Many of them do.'

His words now were filled with a masculine smugness that told her he did win over the affections of women like that. Not that his appearance did not help—with those wicked blue eyes and his tall, muscular build. Well, she suspected he would fare so much better with a good wash and some clean garments.

Which made her realise she was sitting there with her legs on full view to a man who was neither kith nor kin. Worse, he was a man intent on having his way with her and his gaze thoroughly examined her legs and every other bit of her.

But he'd not yet. And that puzzled her. Even more so, she wondered why he had not retaliated for her attempt to knock him witless earlier at the stream. He had knocked her to the ground and wrestled her until he…kissed her in that possessive way. She swore her lips tingled even now. As she reached up to touch them, she noticed he was watching her closely. Worse, the smile that lifted the edges of his lips told her he knew she was thinking on it now.

'So, do you have a needle and thread?' she asked,

trying to ease the growing tension between them. 'I could mend your garments, too,' she offered.

'Would it surprise you to find out I do indeed have such things?'

A needle and some sturdy thread would also be used to repair injuries received during fights and attacks, she thought. Fia glanced at the supplies that lay strewn around the cave and remembered the rest of them in the other cave. They did seem to be well supplied and would need to be able to see to themselves.

'I would suppose not, considering what I have seen already.'

He got up and searched for a small wooden box, no bigger than her hand. Handing it to her, he brought the lantern closer, too. She pried the tight lid off and found sewing needles and several spools of thread inside. All she needed were...

'If you promise not to use them on me,' he said, holding out a pair of shears. He had not forgotten about her using the pot as a weapon and his words told her he would not underestimate her again.

She nodded acceptance of his terms and took the shears. Without new laces for the front of her gown, she could cut narrow strips of fabric from the hem, twist them tightly and use them to tie up the front of it. Though this was not the first time she'd worn trews, the thought of wearing his bothered her.

A blast of cold air shoved its way into the cave, past the canvas flap that served as a makeshift door, making her shiver. The flame in the lantern flickered but remained burning. He got up again, pacing around the cave until he searched in another sack and pulled out a cloak. Her cloak. She'd thought it lost until now. Iain walked to her side and dropped it over her shoulders.

'My thanks,' she said quietly. She adjusted it around her, keeping her hands free to work on her gown.

She lost herself in the task, letting go of her fears for the moment and concentrating only on the fabric on her lap. Even in the inadequate light thrown off by the lantern, her hands moved quickly and accurately. Most of the time she could do it without watching or paying heed—a talent developed because she wanted to watch or listen to whatever was going on around her. But some of the time, like this moment and in this situation, she let the mending pull her in so she would not think about what she could not fix.

With the winds howling, the snow falling and her captor at her side, watching her every move, she knew she could not change this. She glanced at the canvas flap when another strong burst sent it fluttering and considered what actions she could take and when.

The weather could be a help to her efforts to escape.

If she could get out of the cave, she could use the snow or rain and winds to mask her as she sought out the secret tunnels that would lead her off the mountain.

But, if she left now, she would never discover their true purpose.

If she escaped they would no doubt ride away rather than get caught if she brought Brodie and others back to hunt them down. And their identities and the true reasons for the attacks would remain unknown. She let out a sigh then, which drew his attention. Shaking her head, she bent to her task once more.

However, she was no fool to think she was safe here. She faced many dangers, including the seven outlaws now sheltering among the caves. Any one of them could harm her or worse. So, the sooner she got away, the better. Just telling Brodie what she'd discovered about them would help him find the true culprit or culprits behind this campaign of attacks.

The more she thought about it, the more she realised that if The Camerons were not guilty, then someone was trying to make them look it. And the reason she could come up with for someone to do that would be to stir up trouble between clans who'd long been enemies and only recently settled their feud.

Who would want to make trouble for Brodie and Arabella's families? Who would benefit from such strike and feuding? Unfortunately, she did not know a wide enough circle of those powerful enough to want this or make it happen. But Brodie would. If she could get back to Drumlui…

'You are thinking so hard I can almost hear your thoughts, lass,' Iain said from across the cave. He'd leaned against the wall, with his long legs stretched out before him and crossed at the ankles. 'Mayhap you can share your thoughts with me and I can help you solve whatever problem is vexing you?'

Once more, he was playing the rogue. The sensual undertones in his voice were extremely tempting. No wonder women fell into his arms and into his bed.

'I am but concentrating on my task, sir,' she answered without lifting her gaze to his. She knew that she would see the icy depths of his blue eyes blaze with wicked amusement if she did look. 'If I do not prove myself able to mend garments, you might find another more onerous chore for me to carry out.'

Damn and hell, what a foolish thing to do!

She had responded in words that came dangerously close to sounding like his own. When he stood and walked the few paces to where she sat, Fia felt the tension grow. He knelt before her, took the gown with the needle and thread still in it from her hands and tossed it aside. Then he grabbed the shears and pushed them far enough away from her that she could not reach them.

'Enough cooking and cleaning and mending, Ilysa. You owe me a boon,' he said. With one finger, he lifted her chin until she could not avoid looking into his eyes.

'A boon?' she asked in a whisper. Was it now? Would he...would they...now?

'For not revealing your murderous intent to Lundie and the others.' His finger slid along her jaw and on to her neck, making her tremble. From fear? From anticipation? She knew not which.

'For controlling myself when other lesser men would have taken full advantage of having a woman like you within reach.' Now his finger traced the edge of the tunic she wore. She could not breathe. She could not look away as he slid that one finger up the other side of her neck, teasing the edge of her ear before stroking along her jaw.

'So tell me, Ilysa,' he whispered as he leaned in closer. Only a scant inch separated their mouths and when he spoke again, Fia could feel his heated breath against her lips. 'Must I take my boon or will you give it freely?'

Chapter Eight

Niall had never been indecisive in his life. Once committed to something, he remained that way until the need for it was past. If asked to make choices, he made them without whining or bemoaning. When the King, his godfather, had offered him everything he'd lost in exchange for finding out the true culprit behind the growing hostilities, Niall had agreed in less than a minute.

Yet, kneeling here before this woman, he could not make up his mind whether he wanted to have her or to walk away completely. Oh, his randy bits had made their decision, but all of the consequences and ramifications of becoming intimate with her confused and delayed him.

His rational mind told him to claim a boon of truthfulness and discover more about this woman and her place in The Mackintosh clan. More about The Mackintosh himself. More about The Camerons. He needed facts to seek the one he needed to find for the King. He needed to complete this mission and report back to the King. He needed his mother and sister freed and his lands and titles and wealth returned to him.

But after watching that mouth of hers while she worked, worrying her teeth over her lower lip and then touching it with the tip of her tongue, his randy bits wanted…her. Desire so strong it would have brought him to his knees had he not already been on them flooded him, heating his blood and making his flesh even harder.

He'd sensed an innocent's curiosity in their last kiss and so Niall knew that tupping her would not make her amiable and willing to give him anything. So, tupping was not a choice in this. Knowing it and even accepting that decision did not make it easier to control the growing need within him for her. Of course, if tupping were her idea, he would be amenable to that, but from the expression in her eyes, one of both fear and curiosity, that would not happen soon.

The wind whipped up outside just then and the snow fell even harder, reminding him that they had hours or possibly days here together. Niall smiled at her then.

'So, what is this boon you intend to claim?' she asked.

'This time…' he began.

'This time?' She pushed back, falling off the wooden box beneath her and rolling on to her knees. 'What do you mean "this time"?'

'Each time I must protect you or hide your behaviour,' he said, 'or answer your questions I will claim a boon.'

He lifted the box and moved it away so there were no impediments between them. He crawled closer, watching her eyes darken as he did. He suspected that her curiosity would get the better of her. Niall also guessed from her narrowed gaze that she had as many questions about him and the others as he did about her. This exchange of boons might work in his favour in so many ways that he smiled.

'Only a rogue would...'

'I never claimed to be otherwise.'

'A gentleman would never...'

'I would never count myself one of those, lass.' He leaned in closer. 'So do not harbour hopes that I am anything but what you see before you.' He held out his hands and motioned around them.

'A thieving ruffian who would take a woman's virtue without thought or concern!' Even she looked surprised by the words she'd spoken.

'I would not say there would not be thought or concern if I took yours, Ilysa,' he said, moving forward until their faces were a scant few inches apart. 'I would be very thoughtful.' A becoming blush spread up her cheeks and she stammered something before speaking it clearly.

'Is that the boon you claim?' she asked.

A shudder trembled through her, making him realise that fear was taking hold. He lifted his hand and cupped her chin. Sliding his thumb across those tempting lips, he shook his head.

'Nay. Not that,' he whispered. 'Only a kiss.' Surprise flitted over her features for a moment. Then she leaned away from his touch.

'And will you use your tongue to do that...that?' she asked.

Niall could not help but chuckle at her naivety.

She was so different, so fresh and unaffected than the women he'd known or shared his bed with. At the court, they were connivers, all seeking their own fortune and trampling anyone who stood in their way. They shared their favours with anyone who could benefit their position or standing. As the King's godson, albeit disinherited, he'd been used as much as he'd used.

But this one…she could steal a man's heart with her innocence and he would have to guard his if they were together for long.

'Aye, I will use my tongue,' he promised. 'And, as long as you do not move away, I promise that my hands will stay at my side. You, however, may touch me as you wish.'

'I would never do such a thing,' she said. Then she swore under her breath, in some of the most crude words he'd heard in a while. Another surprise about her he would never have expected—the lass could curse like a common thief.

Niall did not want to point out the obvious to her— he could have her beneath him so fast that she would not even have the chance to take a breath to scream. Right now though, he wanted her to allow him his way in this. He needed to taste her fully, without interruption and without argument.

Now.

As he leaned in, she scrunched her eyes closed tightly and clenched her fists as though she expected something utterly terrible to happen. The challenge made, Niall accepted it and touched his lips to hers.

He kissed her slowly, rubbing his mouth over hers, coaxing her capitulation. First, he touched their lips together and then he pressed his against her mouth. Her tightly pursed mouth softened after a bit and he smiled against her.

'That's the way now,' he urged. Canting his head, he moved in closer and touched his tongue to her lips. Over and over, he outlined the fullness of them, teasing them until she opened to let him in to do...*that*.

And he did *that*, stroking her mouth, tasting her and trying to convince her to participate in this kiss. Her body shifted, but did not move away, so he counted that a battle won. He shifted his own, leaning in until he could feel the heat of her body, never using his hands to hold her.

Niall felt the sigh against his mouth. A signal louder than the skirl of the pipes, he sought her tongue and stroked it. Once, twice and a third time before she responded in like. He wanted to shout out in victory as she hesitantly slid her tongue along his. His body reacted as though struck by lightning at the innocent's caress. Hard as rock, his flesh surged as she sucked on his tongue, drawing it into her mouth. When he felt her hands clutch at his tunic, Niall was dumbfounded.

He'd taunted her with that very action and never dreamed she would touch him of her own choice. His desire for her flared then, nearly overwhelming the control he was exerting over himself...and, most especially, his hands. He thought she would withdraw now and yet she remained there as she'd agreed to. Now it was his turn to pull back from her.

He eased his tongue from her mouth and kissed her several more times, each one softer than the last, until he released her lips. Their reddened, swollen, well-kissed appearance made him smile. The fact that

her hands still held him pleased him more. He'd recognised that she was a canny, bold lass though he'd
truly never expected this much from her in spite of
his teasing words.

She would indeed be the death of him. Her with
her innocent-temptress ways of looking at him. Now
this kiss had shaken him as much as it must have dis-
turbed her. Her eyes drifted open and she caught sight
of her hands on his tunic. He could not help but smile,
which made her frown in return.

The kiss done, she jumped to her feet and walked
as far from him as she could. His body, the randy bits,
wanted him to follow her and to taste her again. Niall
knew it was his time to bide, so he needed to put some
distance between them. The canvas flap on the cave
lifted as the winds swirled once more, giving him the
perfect excuse. And the snow would cool the heated
blood that even now raced through his veins.

'See to yourself. I have to see to the horses.'

Niall forced himself out into the cold, wet night,
wrapping his cloak tightly around him to keep off the
worst of it. Even when his skin cooled as the snow
found a way through to it, the rest of him did not. He
trudged through the muddy mess of a path down to
the cave where the horses were and did check on them.
The hardy creatures were huddled close together, bearing up well under the onslaught of the storm from
what he could see.

He strode back up the hill and paused to listen,
his head tilted in the direction of the other cave. An
occasional voice or laugh told him they were awake
within, so he walked on to the smaller cave where she
waited. Bending down, he pushed the flap out of his

way and entered, praying for the strength to resist the urge within him to have her.

If he had thought that the kiss they'd shared would ease the need, he had been wrong. So very wrong. And it only took a glance at her to know the danger he faced.

He'd kissed her as she'd seen Brodie kiss Arabella.

With lust and longing and desire. 'twas the kind of kiss that led to another and another and then on to something else. The kind that ended up with the lord and lady hidden away in their chambers for hours.

And though Fia would like to proclaim that she had been unmoved by his blatant attempt to seduce her, she would be lying. The feeling of his lips on hers and his tongue tasting her deeply had caused an ache, a swirling, heated ache, deep within her body. One that wanted…wanted more and wanted relief. Even now her hand slid down to the lower part of her belly where it still throbbed deep inside.

She wanted to laugh at her continued stupidity. Truly she was.

Fia thought that his promise not to touch her would keep her safe. She thought his promise to use his tongue would be something she could simply ignore and tolerate. Sweet Jesus, why had no one warned her? And damn her weakness, she had touched him when she'd sworn she would not.

His chest was hard and muscular. Heat poured off his body under her hands and she'd been tempted to slide her hands under his garments to feel his skin. Then, her lips ached from his kisses and she was lost. It was only a kiss, but, oh, what damage it wrought!

How could she look at him and meet his gaze knowing she'd fallen so badly towards sinning with him? And worse, he'd mocked her with a smug expression in those blue eyes at her vow not to touch him, all the while knowing the truth of his wicked plans. So, she finished her ablutions and wrapped her cloak around her, tightly, leaving nothing exposed for him to see or, God forbid, touch.

Then, when she heard his approach, Fia tucked herself back against the far wall, gathering her legs up close and wrapping her hands around her knees. He pushed against the flap and entered, surrounded by a blast of frigid, wet wind. She watched him in spite of her bowed head and held her breath when he stopped before her and tossed his cloak aside. Her face flamed even though she did not look up at him.

Just the memories of his mouth on hers and her allowing such shameful liberties kept her head down. The sigh escaped and echoed across the cave. She heard a short, sharp exhalation sound as he turned away and began sorting through the supplies. He said nothing to her as he pulled this and that from the various sacks and boxes. Soon he'd collected a pile of blankets and another canvas tarp.

The brigand went about his business without speaking to her. So, she watched his every move without ever speaking to him. Soon, with the canvas to prevent wetness under him, he was ensconced in what looked to be a comfortable, warm, dry pallet. Worse, he stretched out under several layers of wool and put his hands behind his head. For a short while, the only sound within the cave was the storm outside.

'Ah…' He shifted on to his side and stared at her.

The cold stone wall was sticking in her back even as he settled more comfortably in his makeshift bed for the night. 'I know you can see me, lass. 'twill do you no good to pretend otherwise.'

'I see you,' she admitted, still not meeting his gaze. It would be filled with smugness and mocking and she cared not to see it.

'There is plenty of room for you here,' he offered, probably in the same way the devil offered Eve a bite of that apple in the Garden.

'I am fine and well here,' she said. Unfortunately, when she pushed back against the wall, a sharp part dug into her back more and made her gasp.

'I suspect that the cold and the dampness will seep into your bones and leave you unable to sleep and unable to move on the morrow.'

'Could you burn some peat?' she asked.

They'd used braziers to burn logs of peat and keep warm those years ago. The opening high up on the cave's wall to allow the smoke to escape was probably just plugged up with growth. Then she realised she could not point it out to him without revealing her knowledge.

'So you will let your stubbornness keep you from accepting my offer then?' he asked, rolling back to lie flat. 'Dougal has no idea what I saved him from by kidnapping you,' he boasted.

His words stung and she blinked against them. She had not thought about how Dougal and her family would react to her experiences since being kidnapped. She knew they would be concerned, her parents heartbroken, but what about the others in Drumlui?

His taunt only served to remind her of one indisputable fact—whatever had been possible with Dougal before would never be again. Even though Iain was teasing, he'd brought up one terrible facet of being kidnapped—she would be considered ruined by everyone in Drumlui. Unable to make a good marriage now. Possibly unworthy of serving the clan's lady and tending to her children, too, for she would now be thought of as soiled.

Mayhap if she explained what had happened and that she'd kept her honour and virtue, Brodie would understand. Arabella would understand. Her family would be pleased by her safe return. But every day, she would face those who'd heard the story and would never believe that men such as Iain Dubh and his ilk had not used her for their pleasure. Her life and reputation were ruined.

She needed to get away now. She needed to get home. Panic filled her as the need to run grew to an uncontrollable level within her.

Now. Run. Anywhere.

Fia jumped to her feet, tangled in her cloak and stumbled her way free. Heading for the opening of the cave, she did not think about what she would need or even where she could go. She just needed to be away from here. As she reached for the flap, he wrapped his arms around her and lifted her from her feet. Before she could fight him off, he'd swaddled her with her cloak and laid her on the pallet.

'Hush now,' he whispered softly. 'I do not know what I said to cause such a reaction, but I apologise for teasing you so.'

Fia twisted and turned only to find herself held

securely in his arms. In his very strong arms against his muscular chest.

'Let me go, I pray you,' she begged. 'I must get home now.'

'Even without the storms, you are not going back there now, lass.'

'I have to. I need to tell them. I need them to know…' He pulled her closer and tucked her head beneath his chin and she fought against the warmth and comfort of it…of him.

'Tell them what?' he asked.

'I am not ruined. I can marry Dougal. I am not… unworthy.'

He said nothing, but his body began to rock slightly, back and forth, taking her with it. His strong hands rubbed the length of her back, up and down, slowly. Without words, he'd acknowledged the truth of her situation—whether or not she succumbed to their wicked pleasures, Fia Mackintosh was well and truly ruined and her life would never be the same again.

She tried to struggle against his hold and against the truth, but each time, he simply held her tighter until she ceased. Then he would rub her back, warming her and soothing her. As she felt the pull of sleep on her weary body and broken spirit, Fia refused to believe that this could be the way her life changed. And worse was the realisation that in attaining her childish, ignorant desires and getting the things she'd only dreamt of, she would have to lose everything and everyone that was important to her.

There had to be a way out of this for her that did not destroy her life and her family. There had to be.

As she drifted to sleep, even the sounds of the storm seemed to mock her naive stupidity.

'What do you need?' Brodie Mackintosh asked him.

Standing in the privacy of the lady's solar with only a few of the chieftain's closest kin and advisors, Alan Cameron knew that Brodie understood the situation about Fia. Alan's cousin Arabella seemed to be avoiding the stark truth of it all.

'A few supplies,' Alan said, shrugging. When he went tracking, he lived mostly on what he could find to eat. But some oats and dried meat would be helpful. His flask needed to be filled and a skin of ale, but otherwise he would travel light in order to travel fast.

'Do you want someone to accompany you?' Rob Mackintosh asked now. The man in command of Chattan Confederation warriors did not like to stand back while others acted.

'Nay, Rob,' Alan said, shaking his head. 'I work best alone.' Rob stared grimly at Brodie, clearly not happy over this decision of his chieftain's.

'Brodie, I still think we should send more men out,' Rob said. 'Even Alan cannot cover all the lands around here.'

'Nay, Rob,' Brodie said. 'For now, I do not wish to draw more attention to this than is necessary.' More attention, especially others looking in at the clan's business, meant more problems and more pressure to take one action or another. Brodie, as usual, did not want his hand forced in this.

And the fewer people who knew about Fia's kidnapping, the better. The ones involved had already beaten several others and killed the old man in the last attack, from what Brodie had revealed to him. What the lass's condition would be, no one could guess. If she yet lived, they might have done any number of things to her. While he could, Brodie was trying to protect her reputation while determining if he could save her life.

'Get her back, Alan. Send word to me if you need anything or anyone,' Brodie said. Rob nodded and stepped back, accepting his choice of action.

'Aye, Brodie.' Alan nodded and then turned to face Arabella.

All those years ago, he'd been the one to track her down when she'd been kidnapped. It was then that Alan had met Fia, a young girl living among the outlawed men and women of the Clan Mackintosh. And then that he'd saved Brodie from execution by The Cameron, his uncle.

'I will find her, Bella,' he said. 'I promise.'

'No matter what, Alan, bring her home. Bring her home to us and her parents.' Her words spoken so softly nearly broke his heart.

With a nod at the Mackintosh, Alan left the chamber and rode to the village to use the last hours of light to gather what traces and clues he could. She'd been taken nearly five days ago from the centre of a busy village, so it would make tracking them almost impossible.

As he crouched down, studying some tracks left in the mud at the edge of the village, he knew they had split into smaller groups and ridden off in several directions. He looked out into the distance, deciding which path he should follow first.

If he was trying to throw off someone following

him, he would use the rivers and streams to lose them. There were still markings of three horses heading towards the stream to the west. Three horses, three men, matched the description given by two who'd witnessed Fia being taken. Standing now, he walked to the very edge of the fields, listening to the winds.

They would all meet up in one place. There had been no sign of them ahead of the attack which came at nightfall. To the east and south were the lands of not only the Mackintoshes but also The Camerons. To the west and the north lay the mountains and then the coast. Not many hospitable places in those directions…except…

Could they have found or had knowledge of the hideaway Brodie had used years ago to keep his family safe? He'd lived in exile for months, avoiding his cousin's and Alan's own family's attempts to capture and kill him for his role in the death of The Cameron's heir. It was high enough in the mountains to make a great refuge and was defensible by even a small number of men.

Had they taken Fia there?

Turning back towards Drumlui Keep, Alan planned his search. On the morrow, he would head west and search out signs of their destination. By the time the keep settled for the night, he was packed and ready to leave at first light.

He rode west away from Glenlui until signs of them disappeared. That led him to the far side of the mountains where the entrance to the camp lay hidden. But, before he could follow the secret path on to the mountain, the winds shifted and a storm arrived out of nowhere. From the intensity of the change in direction and from the coldness that now blew across the land, Alan knew he needed to find or make a place to sit this out.

He came upon the shieling just as the snow and wild winds made travelling impossible. Once he'd tied his horse inside the shelter of the dwelling's back wall, he tugged off the blanket and saddle and dragged all his supplies and such into the meagre hut. Not much more than four walls and sod roof, it would still give him some refuge from the dangerous weather.

Alan pushed the layers of tartan off his head and looked around the small space. A wooden pallet would keep him off the ground and somewhat dry. When he opened the small chest in the corner, a few sacks of staple foods were revealed, along with a jar of honey and a heavy girdle on which to cook. A stack of peat along with some logs lay in the corner.

The Mackintosh made certain these shelters could keep someone who needed them alive for some time. Which was practical in these remote areas where they grazed their cattle before taking them to market. It meant that a man could stay here and oversee the herd. And now, in the time of the change of the seasons, it meant surviving when the winds turned against you.

Though the snow had changed to rain two days later, the winds whipped it across the land, making it foolhardy to fight. Then, with another two days of torrential rains, the road back to Glenlui as well as the one up the mountainside were unpassable. Oh, he tried, but sank into the mud that seemed almost knee-deep in places.

Any signs left behind were gone for ever, so Alan simply bided his time while the spring storm blew itself out. He was not worried, for, if he could not travel in this, neither could those holding Fia.

Chapter Nine

When she finally had given up fighting his hold on her, Niall felt all the tightness in her disappear at once. As quickly as the panic and fear had begun, it finished with her collapse. He did not release her then, choosing to hold her close. To keep her warm, he told himself even though he knew there was another reason.

He wanted her. He wanted to have her.

She surprised him with every word she spoke and action she took. Even this emotional torrent that came out of nowhere like the storm that still raged outside was unexpected in its timing and strength. He thought she would have fought him off or tried to escape much sooner than this. But his rather cross tease about her Dougal had triggered it.

She'd been struggling to keep going and had probably not even thought about the repercussions that would face her if she returned home. She was correct—a woman would be counted ruined by his, their, actions even if he did not touch her again. Even though the only thing she had given up was a searing kiss. It mattered not to their common laws or the Church.

If this had happened when he was Lord Niall Corbett, certain behaviours would be expected.

Well, first, he would not dally with a virgin who worked in service to him or his family. Oh, no one would question his right to do so, but he'd never been one to pursue any woman who did know what she was doing in the bedchamber. If she had been gently or nobly born, he would be expected to marry her. Whether he'd actually taken her virtue or not, keeping her in his intimate company for as long as he had and sleeping with her every night would have forced a marriage contract.

But he was Iain Dubh, thief and ransacker of villages, secret agent for the King, in the company of rogues who were being paid to bring trouble to the lands of Brodie Mackintosh. And she gave no sign of being anything other than a common villager with hopes of marrying hapless Dougal.

It was a harsh assessment, but one he needed to make to keep him on task in spite of the temptation she was. If, when this was all sorted out to his satisfaction, he—Lord Niall—could do something to ease her way, he would.

Aye, 'twas his fault that she was involved at all. If he'd been paying attention to his role in the attack on Drumlui, he would never have noticed the brown-haired, green-eyed beauty walk by him. And he would not have dawdled watching her discussion with hapless Dougal. Things might have gone differently and the young man might have convinced her of his worth and they might have been kissing in the shadows instead of her running into the thick of things.

Whom was he trying to convince of this foolery?

He would have noticed her anywhere and she, with her stubborn bravery, would always run into trouble instead of away from it. Even now, when she should still be resisting him, she turned to him in sleep and accepted his comfort.

Though the winds and rain had lulled him into sleep, he did not remain there. When morning, or this day's excuse for it, arrived, he lay awake trying to see his way out of this. When the weather cleared, Lundie would leave and seek out their sponsor for the next target and for their payment for the last. By the time he returned, Niall would have reached the end of the fortnight Lundie had ordered.

What could he do with her? He could not leave here now to take her to safety. Knowing the Mackintosh, there would be men out searching for the ones responsible for the attacks…and for the lass. The man was relentless in protecting his lands and his people. Only with their stealth and speed and with the guidance of the man pulling their strings had they managed to stay ahead of his retaliation.

The lass had changed that. And the storms.

As though his thoughts had wakened her, Niall felt her body tense as she came awake. Her indrawn breath warned him of her fear.

'Good morrow,' he said, easing his arms from around her. 'I wish I could tell you the storm has moved on, but alas, it has not.' He kept his tone even and calm, giving her a chance to get her bearings.

Faster than he would have thought possible, she rolled from his side, tugged her cloak free and jumped to her feet. Backing away, she stumbled until she hit the wall.

'Have a care for your...'

Too late, for she bumped her head against the stone and winced. He pushed back the rest of the blankets that she had not dragged free and stood. She reached up and touched the side of her head where she'd been hit. Nodding, she seemed to gather her wits and walked around the cave, setting this and that to rights. Without a word being spoken, she gathered up her mended gown and folded it neatly, placing the needle and thread back in the wooden box now.

'So, how long can this last?' he asked.

'Spring storms are the most unpredictable here in the Highlands,' she said without looking away from the task she'd set for herself.

She seemed to do anything that would keep her from his immediate area or that would have her pass him by, as though she thought he would reach out and grab hold of her and force another 'boon' from her. He would not mind another searing kiss but from the way she avoided him, it had not affected her in the same way.

Or it had and she was trying to ignore or deny it.

He thought the latter.

Thinking on it, he knew it was the latter. She had melted into him, leaning against him, sighing against him and even touching him in spite of her claim she would never do such a thing.

'So, a few more hours? Days? What would your guess be if you made one about this particular storm?'

She stopped and stood, tilting her head to one side and listening. Another loud crack signalled more damage from the powerful winds. She closed her eyes and he fought the urge to kiss that tempting mouth once more. But, more kisses would simply bring more danger to an already perilous situation between them. Lucky for him, she opened her eyes then, ending the dreamy expression she wore with a frown aimed at him.

'When the winds shift to the other direction, it's a sign of the coming end. From the feel of this one, another day, two at most,' she said. 'The good thing is that 'tis rain now instead of snow. If the snows continued, we could have been trapped here for weeks.'

He would not mind a few weeks with her, peeling back the layers of stubborn innocence to reveal the truth beneath. She spared him one glance as though his thoughts were apparent. Well, if she looked lower than his belt, they would be.

Even two more days would require something more than the few strips of dried meat among their supplies. Niall leaned against the wall, observing her very methodical approach to cleaning. She searched through the sacks and boxes there and separated the foodstuffs from the other sacks, placing them away from the opening of the cave. When she realised he was watching her every move and action, she pushed her hair back and shrugged.

''Twill keep them dry and from drawing the attention of creatures who might seek shelter from this storm, too.'

Practical. Eminently practical and experienced, too.

Niall realised now that this was their weakness—not a man among them was from this area of Scotland. If their plan had involved one or two short attacks, quickly done, then that would not matter. But on a longer undertaking, having someone who knew the area and, by God, the storms, would have been helpful.

He also understood the reasons for hiring men without ties to the area—no loyalty to those they targeted, dependence on their leader, easily dispensable for there would be no one to notice their absence. The last one worried him, though he knew it would be part of any endeavour like this—witnesses, anyone with knowledge who could tie the attacks to someone other than The Camerons as was the plan, would need to disappear when all this was done.

His companions might not have figured that out yet. They did not think ahead or above the basic arrangement they'd agreed to. Attacks for gold. They mayhap even thought they would walk away with that gold when all this was done. Niall knew better, for anyone powerful enough to manipulate these two Highland clans would not leave witnesses. Lundie would survive only if his connection to their puppet master was one of strong kinship.

Did Lundie know the way this would go? Niall suspected he did. Lost in his thoughts about the coming weeks and his quest, he'd not noticed that she'd stopped moving about. She stood now studying one corner of the cave where a small niche was formed out of the rock from ground to ceiling.

'What is it?' he asked, coming to her side. Examining the unnoticed alcove now, Niall found traces of black soot coating the wall, surely a sign of past fires.

'Does it not look as though fires may have burned there?' She voiced his very suspicion.

Niall reached up and followed the stone until he

found the softer patch of soil. Pushing against it, the dirt and roots finally gave way and fell apart, showering mud and leaves down on to the floor of the recess. A small opening would vent the smoke from a fire now. And it was cleverly placed to angle to the side, so the rains did not enter so easily.

'With such a thing, you can cook in here while the storm rages outside,' he said. ''Tis clear that people have lived here and used these caves in the past.'

His observation did not seem to surprise her. Not at all. Niall crossed his arms over his chest and narrowed his gaze. If he had not been watching closely, he would have missed the tiny flinching in her own gaze at his words.

'Aye, some of the Mackintoshes lived here for several months years ago,' she said softly. 'My mam told me stories about those terrible times in our clan.'

'If I fill the pot with water, you will be able to make some porridge. Can you make twice as much as you made before?' It would feed them until they could leave the caves and seek some fresh game.

When she did not refuse, he bade her to see to herself before lifting the flap and going out into the storm. Niall stood for a moment there at the entrance and saw the fallen trees across the clearing. The heavy snow of last night had turned to rain now and it flowed in torrents, down from the highest point in the camp towards the stream at the bottom. The force of the rushing water cut deeply into the existing paths, leaving them to look like slashed scars all along the ground.

He'd set the cooking pot out to gather water and it was overflowing from the night's snow and rains. They would have to build a fire and he needed the metal girdle pan as a support. After he carried the pot inside, he made his way, buffeted by the strong winds, to the other cave. He lost his way once, struggling to see while the winds blew branches and rain at him.

Lundie stood watching him as he approached.

'Did ye see the damage there? And the trees down over there?' Niall asked, roughening up the way he spoke. 'And the water is tearing up the path down to the stream.'

He needed to crouch low in order to make it in without hitting his head, but once inside, the space there allowed even Anndra to stand at ease. The men were sitting around the walls, leaning back, whiling away these hours when they could do nothing else. He nodded to them.

'There is a cooking place in the cave, so the lass is making porridge,' he said. The others cheered at his news.

'I need to see to things,' Lundie said. That meant leave to visit their benefactor. 'I canna wait much longer or I will miss him.'

'The lass said once the winds turn, the storm will blow itself out.'

'I mayn't be able to wait for that. Otherwise, no gold. And no gold…' Lundie glanced over at the others. No gold meant they would become as unpredictable as the storm outside. Niall nodded his understanding.

'How long will ye be gone?' Niall asked. He had a good understanding of where they were now and which lord owned what lands around them. If he knew where Lundie was headed, it would give him the clue he needed.

'Three days, I think,' he replied.

That was more than he'd told Niall in the past. From here, Lundie could reach the western coast and return. He could make it to Inverness in the north, Inverary in the south and over to Skye in the west and back in three days. He could even reach the eastern edges of the Highlands towards Edinburgh. Too large an area with too many possible lairds and chieftains to sort it out…without something more to go on.

'Tell me what ye need.' Niall let the words remain there without saying more. Then he turned to leave. 'I wi' bring the porridge when 'tis ready.'

'Will she be a problem if I leave ye in charge?' The others had heard the question and turned their attentions to the conversation.

'I'm certain the lads know their gold depends on following yer orders, Lundie.'

'When I return, we wi' visit a village I ken,' Lundie said. 'And we'll see to some entertainment for all of us.' The promise of pleasure from females of a particular nature made them all smile.

'If she keeps cooking for us,' Martainn called out, 'we can leave her be.' The man hated that the chore of cooking for them had been thrust on him, so this made him happy enough.

Niall retrieved the metal rack that would hold the pot up off the fire and the iron girdle pan and made his way back along the now-flooded path. If the rains continued at such a pace, the entire top of this mountain would wash away. Finally, after slipping and nearly sliding halfway down the mountainside, covered in mud, he arrived back at the other cave.

Although more dirt would not matter to the cave,

Niall did not wish to get the pallet he'd made wet or muddy. So, before entering, he let the rains rinse most of the muck off his boots and his trews. It mattered little for he was well and truly soaked in the time it had taken him to walk back and forth. He finished and pushed the flap back to enter.

Niall thought he'd been loud enough to wake the dead. Her reaction—she jumped up and moved quickly to the other side of the cave—spoke of suspicious behaviour to him. Then, he spied his own small leather satchel. Where she'd dropped it.

'What are you doing, lass?' he asked, stalking across to stand before her.

Chapter Ten

The usual sense of merriment in his gaze was gone now. Fia backed up and away from his belongings. She pushed her hair behind her ears and watched as he came towards her now. Taking her shoulders, he pulled her up so that her feet did not touch the ground and their faces nearly touched.

Nearly.

Anger poured off him in waves, much as the cold did from his wet clothing and hair.

'I asked you what you were doing.' He shook her a bit, staring at her eyes as she tried to speak. 'Tell me,' he said roughly, his voice louder than she'd heard before.

'I was…seeking a way to start…' she stammered out. 'To start the fire.' She tried to point to it, but he held her shoulders so tightly that she could not move her arms. 'I thought…'

'You thought what?'

'There was not one in the sewing box or anywhere else,' she finally said. 'I thought you might have one in that.'

He did not move or look away for several seconds and, for the first time since he'd kidnapped her, Fia felt herself in danger…from him.

'Truly, Iain,' she whispered. 'I only sought the flint to light the fire.'

The anger that controlled him in those few, tense moments seeped away and he nodded at her. Lowering her until her feet touched the ground, he took in a breath and exhaled it quickly.

'I keep it here,' he said, taking a step back and reaching to his belt. He took the stone and a small piece of metal out of the small pouch and held it out.

Her hands shook when she accepted it from him. Clutching it, she waited and watched to see what he would do next. Granted, no one liked their belongings rummaged through, but she'd had a good reason. And it was going to take some time to heat the water and cook the porridge on the small fire that they could build there.

First he found his satchel and put it back inside a larger sack where she'd found it, shoving it into a corner behind several other bags and boxes. If she meant to look in it again, he'd made it as difficult as possible for her. Then, he walked to the entrance and picked something up. Two things actually. She'd been so frightened that she'd not noticed before. Holding them out to her, he motioned to the alcove.

'This will hold the pot over the fire and give you a level surface.'

She recognised the metal girdle and rack from yesterday's cooking. He must have retrieved it from the other cave and their supplies. Fia stood back and let him place it over the blocks of peat she'd placed there.

Once balanced, she put the pot on to boil and prepared the oats and flour for it.

At home, the hearth would never be allowed to go out completely, so it was easy enough to get the fire hot enough to make bannocks or prepare the pot for a stew or porridge. Here, beginning anew, it would take some time before the fire or the water was ready.

Time enough for her to finish mending her gown.

Fia turned around, intending to get the sewing box, and found a half-naked Iain Dubh.

Her first thought was that the black hair that caused him to be called 'Dubh' extended down over his chest, across his belly and disappeared beneath the belt at his waist.

The second thing that occurred to her was that she'd seen her share of bare-chested men in spite of her rather sheltered existence, but not many could compare with the masculine beauty of this one.

Just before she turned quickly away, as a God-fearing maiden should, Fia thought that she really would like to touch his skin and run her fingers through those black curls on his chest.

Trying to hide both her curiosity and her embarrassment, Fia took hold of her gown, sat near the lantern and began to work. Leaning her head down, she tried to keep her gaze on her work and not on him. Mayhap he had not noticed her reaction? Mayhap he did not see the burning blush in her cheeks caused by the sight of his bare chest? She hoped for both and discovered that he was well aware of both.

'Here, lass,' he said, approaching so quietly she did not hear him until he spoke from right beside her. 'It might work better if you turn it *this* way instead of the other.' His scent reminded her of leather and fresh rain. His skin, glistening with water from his soaked tunic, now gave off heat as he reached across her to turn the gown in her grasp. Heat she could feel because of his nearness.

Foolishly distracted by his display, she'd been trying to sew the back of her gown rather than the front of it. Fia tried to calm herself by counting each breath slowly and evenly, a surely unsuccessful attempt to show him that she was not affected.

But, oh, she was. Her skin felt tight and her mouth tingled. Her palms itched, ached, to rub against the muscular chest and over his shoulders and—God forbid!—down the flat, hard belly where the curls disappeared. She began counting cousins once more in an effort to ignore him and to regain her control.

It might have worked, too, if he had just moved away and covered himself. But, nay, he did not do that. Instead, he walked two paces away and then undermined her control and her resolve not to watch his every movement completely. If only he'd kept those trews in place!

Out of the corner of her eyes, she could see him loosen his belt and tug it free. The needle slipped in her grasp now as her fingers and palms grew sweaty. Then he worked the laces until the garment sagged down low on his hips. Fia fought the urge to gasp loudly as more skin was exposed to her. She closed her eyes now and whispered a prayer to whichever saint in heaven would listen to aid her in this moment of weakness.

She'd thought herself a good woman. A chaste woman. A prayerful woman at times. It had taken but two, three, of his kisses to prove all of her life was a sham. The blood of a loose woman raced through her veins and, now tempted, seemed to increase with every encounter with this wicked man.

Mayhap this was what ruination was about? The act or acts mattered not, but the awareness and desire to sin did? The need to turn and watch him? The need to touch him?

She daren't move or look or breathe right now. 'twas a sin to want to do those things, but a venial one, for certain. Acting on those urges must surely be a more serious, even mortal, sin. When he pushed the trews down and off, Fia could not think. Every bit of her strength was being used to not look, to not turn around, to not…want to do those things.

'I slid down part of the pathway when I lost my footing,' he explained as he now walked to his bag and sought another pair. His voice did not tremble as hers did when she attempted a simple reply.

'Ohhhh?' The single word was elongated into a much longer sound than she wished. Mayhap he would not notice? Fia could not help but see his fine form as he passed near her. His body seemed sculpted like a statue she'd once seen in one on her travels with the laird and lady for it narrowed from that strong chest and back to a narrower waist and hips and…arse. If his chest was muscular, his long legs were even more impressive.

Men had little or no reticence or embarrassment about their bodies. The warriors who trained at Drumlui Keep would fight in only trews and would wash in the nearby river without worrying over whether or not they were seen. Not that she went a-looking. Fia was now trying desperately to adopt such a calm attitude and it was not working at all.

She could bear no more of this, so she placed the gown on the floor next to her and climbed to her feet. Walking to the alcove, she crouched there, as close to the fire as she could safely, and paid great attention to it. Since the water was not even near to boiling—the pot was yet cold—there was little to do it. But the heat of the growing fire and the heat within her as her body reacted to the sight of him combined to make it overwhelming and uncomfortable.

Without turning to face him, she walked to the opening and lifted the flap, stepping just far enough out to be able to drop it behind her. She had no intention of going further or running away. Fia just needed a few moments to gather the wits she seemed to lose every minute she was near him.

'Lass?' he asked from behind her. The canvas flap yet separated them. 'Do not run.' She could hear him moving about the cave, cursing as he did. When he lifted the flap and stepped out, he had his trews on and his boots and was fighting his way back into a tunic.

'The fire,' she said, 'the heat…'

She really could not explain the rest, so she held her cupped hands out into the rain and caught some of it. Splashing it on her face, she repeated that until she felt some relief. He remained there, standing behind her without saying another word. Fia guessed that as long as he knew she was not trying to escape, he would allow her this small freedom.

He went back inside and returned a few moments later after she could hear more rummaging happening. All her sorting would be for naught if he continued that. Right now though, she was unwilling to meet his intense and wicked stare after seeing so much of him. Knowing now what was under those garments would change for ever the way she looked at him. His arm soon appeared from behind her, holding two of the leftover bannocks.

'Here,' he said, 'you should eat.' She dared a glance at him before taking the food. 'You did not eat as much as the rest of us did and you worked long and hard. With your head injury…' His explanation drifted off as he lifted his hand again. 'Eat.'

Tempted to refuse, her belly answered for her with a long, low growl of emptiness. She accepted one of the flat cakes and nodded to him to keep the other. She stood there, just under enough of a ledge of stone so as to not get soaked with the rain and ate the bannock in silence. As the winds rose once more, the rain began to pelt them, so she followed Iain back inside.

Instead of letting the flap close, blocking all of the possible light from outside, he tugged one edge of it up and tucked it so it would remain open. The day's light, meagre though it was, did its best to brighten the darkness of the cave and it succeeded somewhat. Fia picked up her gown and the wooden box she'd used as a stool and moved closer to the fire to finish it while watching the pot. When the water in the pot reached a boil, she added the oats and the flour along with a bit of salt. Once it bubbled again, she covered it with the flat girdle pan.

Iain, now dressed, wrung out as much water as he could from his clothes and laid them over boxes that would not be bothered by the wetness of them. Glancing down, she realised that she wore his only other garments. Hurriedly, she pushed the twisted and stitched length of fabric in and out of the holes along the front of her gown, replacing the laces that had been cut.

She had time now to put her gown on. Somehow it meant regaining herself a bit, so Fia gathered the gown and sought a place of some privacy…which did not exist in the cave. Though some of the others had several smaller chambers that went back into the side of the mountain, this one did not. She decided there was only one thing to do.

'If you would give me a moment of privacy,' she began.

A bright flash lit the whole cave and thunder rumbled right behind it. The storm had taken a turn for the worse and at the worst moment. No one should be out in this kind of weather.

'Go on now, lass,' he said with a shrug. 'I will not look.' Since he'd admitted he was nothing but a rogue, she doubted his sincerity. Her face must have shown that disbelief, for he laughed. 'Well, I will try not to look.' Fia was willing to give him a chance until he spoke again. 'Much as you did not look when I changed my trews.'

The burn of embarrassment filled her face and she turned away. He spoke the name they'd chosen for her. Even as he said it, she wished she could hear him say her true name instead, but she stifled the urge to reveal herself to him.

'Ilysa, go about it,' he urged. 'I will check on the porridge.'

Iain walked towards the alcove, the same place as where she'd been while he was undressing. If she stood in the centre of the cave, immediately behind him, she knew he would not see much of her at all. And she wore her shift even now under the borrowed tunic and trews. Fia positioned herself and untied the laces at the neckline of the tunic, tugging it quickly over her head and pulling her gown on.

'Ah, lass. Could you not have given me a wee peek?' he asked without moving.

He could not see her, she was certain of it. He was goading her, teasing her because he could and she did not argue with him. Fia tugged the gown down and decided to keep the trews on beneath it. She'd never considered how warm they could be on cold days but now she envied men for wearing them. When she approached him and the fire, he turned and studied her.

'You look like the Norse women of old, who rode and fought at their men's sides.' His words and tone echoed of admiration rather than sarcasm or insult and Fia's heart warmed at hearing it. 'All you need is a sword or battleaxe.'

Who was this man who knew of Norse customs and legends and yet rode with outlaws? Who spoke in the cultured accent of the nobly born to her while speaking in a common one to the brigands? Who had saved her from certain assault and possible death and made certain she was fed?

Who had held her while she fell apart…?

This comfort she felt in his presence was perplexing to her. Any sane person in her situation would be terrified of his nearness and his attentions. The way he held her at night, at his side, close enough to feel the heat of his body.

And his almost-kind treatment and consideration

towards her puzzled her as well. Though she had no experience with rogues and outlaws, surely his care of her was not the norm?

The loud sizzle of porridge boiling over into the fire tore her attention away from the questions about the man. She ran to the pot and used the length of her gown to protect her hands from the heat. Lifting it was difficult for the pot itself weighed almost a stone empty. As she felt it slipping from her grasp, strong arms encircled hers and took hold of it.

'Here now,' he said, his mouth near her ear. So near that his breath tickled the sensitive spot. 'Let me help.' His body wrapped around hers, supporting her hold on the heavy pot.

He eased them back, step by step, until they were away from the fire and could put it down. He let go, but his hands and arms released her slowly. She stood and unwrapped her hands.

'My thanks for your help,' she said softly. The entire pot could have been lost if not for his quick actions.

'I confess my actions were more about filling my belly and the others than out of kindness,' he said. A glance at his face said he did not believe that lie either.

He stood there as she slid the girdle and stirred the porridge. Placing the flat cast-iron pan over half the opening of the larger pot, she turned to him to ask if he'd carry it back. Before she could, he reached down and did exactly that.

The next hour or so passed in a companionable silence as she tended the fire and food and he watched her work. After a bit, he walked over and knelt with his back to her, but she knew he had retrieved his leather bag and was looking through it.

From his reaction earlier, 'twas clear to her that something of importance was in that bag. More than a simple thing like gold or coins. Less likely to be something of a personal nature. Whatever it was, it would reveal things about Iain Dubh that he did not wish revealed. Once he'd checked on whatever he was protecting, he replaced all the contents, tied the bag and shoved it back inside another one.

Fia knew she needed to discover what the item was. She knew without a doubt that it was tied to this whole endeavour. Her hours and days of observing people at Arabella's side had taught her much about understanding motives and actions. She'd learned more in those quiet moments of observation than in her lessons to read and write. Brodie was a masterful strategist and he taught without even knowing he was doing so. His men learned from him as she had.

And it was that experience that told her this was all connected. The secret in his satchel was part of it. It might even be the link between all the parts. The attacks. This gang of outlaws. Brodie and The Camerons. But, what part Iain Dubh played and how this would conclude was the thing that terrified her the most.

She must find a time to search through that bag. Though, with his constant presence and now his suspicions of her, Fia knew it would be difficult at best. Her mother bemoaned her stubbornness and so had Iain Dubh.

He had no idea just how stubborn and tenacious she could be.

* * *

The lass was driving him mad. Utterly and completely daft.

He would and could not allow her to be a hindrance to his mission, for too much and too many people would be affected by it. Just as he'd settled that argument in his own thoughts, she would do something that would make him question his resolve. She was quick-witted, funny, skilled at cooking and sewing, and intelligent.

Niall knew she was keeping secrets from him, just as he was from her. But his secrets involved King and Country and were too important to disclose. Hers? He suspected, from the way she shoved strips of dried meat and a few bannocks into what seemed to be an opening in the edge of her cloak when she thought him not looking, that it involved escape and an attempt to return to her village. Well, if his plan worked, he would know the truth very soon.

With the porridge cooked and a large number of bannocks baked on the girdle, they took advantage of a brief lull in the storm to make their way to the other cave. The men's behaviour surprised even him, for they did not call out one insult or threat to the lass. Not even when she bent over and showed the lovely outline of her fine arse to them as she served the porridge.

Amazing, he thought, what an empty belly and hunger would do to a man's self-control.

As the men sat and ate, she carried her bowl with her as she walked the perimeter of the larger cave. Though he could not see them clearly, the shadows revealed that there were smaller chambers that led back into the mountain. She seemed very interested in those chambers. Only by watching her closely did he notice the momentary pauses in her route and her observations. Niall noticed it again on their way back to the cave he'd claimed.

They reached the place where the path turned and headed up the mountain a bit and she stopped, tugging on the length of her gown as though it had gotten caught on a bush or rock. Niall watched as she kept pulling on the fabric, seeming to be loosening it, while her gaze moved in a different direction—towards another small path that split off several yards further up. If the rains had not returned just then, stronger than they had before, he thought she might have paused longer to study the path. As they ran the final yards to the cave, all the bits and clues fit together.

The lass knew the encampment!

She did not get her knowledge from her mother as she'd claimed, she knew it because she had been here.

By the time they closed the flap against the increasing winds and lit the lantern, Niall understood her plan—gather supplies and then escape using some secret passageway or path known now only to her. She walked to the box she used as a seat and sat down. Her cloak remained around her shoulders, hiding her secret hoard.

'Are you cold?' he asked, moving towards the alcove and its banked fire.

'A bit,' she said with a nod. 'It will pass now that we are back inside.' He tossed another brick of peat into the fire. Lundie's coins had bought supplies of all sorts for their time here.

The warmth increased and spread throughout the

cave. Granted, there would always be a certain damp coolness within its stone walls, but the fire helped. If she grew warm, she would need to remove the cloak. If she did that, her hidden supplies would be revealed. And what would she say?

'So,' he began, walking back to where she sat, 'what should we do while we wait?'

She moved so quickly that she stumbled over the box and had to put her arm out to stop herself from falling. He grabbed for her and managed to get a hold on her cloak. Though it did not come loose, the food-stuffs she'd shoved into her cloak did, dropping to the floor at her feet. For a moment neither of them moved nor spoke. Then, when he could hold it in no longer, Niall laughed aloud.

'Going somewhere or are you just hungry?' he asked, scooping up some of the bannocks and holding them out to her. Would she lie?

She grabbed them and, without uttering a word, shoved them back inside her cloak. Tugging it back into place, she watched him as closely as he did her.

'Food for your journey home,' he said. 'And with your knowledge of the camp, I suspect you know a way out of here that will keep you from sight as you escape.' She gasped, telling him what he wanted to know. 'Will the pot be your weapon of choice once more when you decide to leave?'

All the colour drained from her face in a moment and she swayed on her feet then. When he reached out to steady her, she backed away, putting as much of the cave between them as she could. It mattered not to him, for it was time for her to share her knowledge of this place. And more so, to tell him who she was.

Niall realised, as he prepared to confront her, that one part he needed to know and the other he desperately needed to know. Damn his soul, but he feared the desire more than the need.

Chapter Eleven

'Sit.' When she did not act, he repeated his order, pointing to the makeshift stool. 'Sit there now.'

Niall had come to dislike seeing fear on her face, but if that's what he needed to get the truth from her now, that's what he would use. His tone made her move and she crossed to the box a few paces away.

'So, there are other ways, secret ways, in and out of this place and you know them.' Crossing his arms over his chest, he stood in front of her and watched her as he spoke. 'You lived here when you were a child during the conflict between The Mackintosh and his dead cousin.'

He let the silence stand between them until she twitched. Well, her left eye did, giving him the sign he needed. Niall crouched down so she would have difficulty avoiding his gaze.

'A boon for a boon mayhap? To loosen your words?' he asked. Her body reacted quickly and Niall didn't think she realised it at first. Those lips opened and her tongue slid along them. He could not help the smile on his own face. Her demeanour changed in an instant to one like the warrior woman he'd called her earlier. Ilysa crossed her arms over her own chest, mirroring his stance, and then she met his gaze with a glare.

'I will not let you kiss me again,' she said. Her words were spoken quietly yet he heard the strong vow in them.

Niall leaned in towards her then, wanting to prove her newest lie, and stared at her mouth. Moving slowly, he stopped when only a few inches separated them, when he could feel the heat of her open-mouthed breathing against him. Then, as she leaned the tiniest bit closer, he closed the space and his mouth almost touched hers.

Almost. His point proven, Niall leaned away.

'I do not think I would have to force you to accept my kiss, lass.' He smiled as she shook her head at him. 'That is not the boon I speak of now. I wish some information in exchange for granting you the same.'

Though her disgruntled expression over the kiss had not eased, her green eyes showed interest in this new offer. She tilted her head and studied him.

'A question for a question?' she asked. Niall sat back on his heels and nodded. 'And if I will not answer?'

'The other boon will be required.' His pleasure that she did not scream and run from him was somewhat dimmed when she spoke.

'And if you will not?'

'Then a boon of your choosing,' he offered. 'Though letting you go is not going to happen.'

'Very well,' she said. 'I suppose you will go first?'

He needed to concentrate on the questions he chose, for he knew she would play this well. An ill-chosen word or phrase and she would wheedle her way out of giving him the information he wanted. He stood and took a couple of paces away from her. His body had been protesting ever since he leaned out of her kiss and parts of him would like nothing more than to take what had been offered.

'How many ways out of this place are there?' She stood now and paced around the cave before answering him. 'Not counting the ones I know about.'

'Which are those?' She glanced over and waited for his clarification.

'The main one in from the west. And the one along the stream.'

'Then three others.'

'Three?'

'Aye, three.' She nodded, confirming her answer.

She began to explain and then she stopped, smiling at him as she did. Aye, the lass would play this game well. He motioned for her to take her turn, preparing himself to dissemble and limit his answers as best he could. What would the lass want to know about him?

'Where are you from?' she asked, remaining in the far shadows as she spoke.

'Twas not the first or second or even subsequent question he'd expected from her. He thought about how to answer and what possible reason she had for knowing that. Giving his place of birth would not reveal too much. He thought. He hoped.

'I was born in a small town in the Borders near Kelso,' he said.

Niall watched as she thought about his words. A few silent minutes passed before he asked his next query. Each one, he knew, would bring more risk with the possibility of more information.

'Another?' he offered.

He could almost feel her curiosity stirring from across the chamber. Niall had a number of questions he'd like answered and it might give him insight into who would want the mighty Mackintosh clan and chief to suffer. Her nod of acceptance made him feel a strange elation.

How closely did she know the Mackintosh? Would Brodie Mackintosh send a troop of men out to find her? What did she know of the feud that threatened to explode between the two powerful families? How many knew of this place? Did he believe The Camerons were behind the attacks?

All of them good questions. Questions to which he wanted answers and to which he would get them…in time. For now, he needed to ask but one.

'Will The Mackintosh send his warriors to find you?' He settled on that one. It would give him information that he could use with Lundie and the others.

'Brodie Mackintosh would not leave his kith or kin to fight his battles or take his punishments. He will not abandon me.'

Her words ended in a quivering voice, in spite of the faith she expressed for her chieftain. Her certainty sounded very, very personal to him. Was she…?

Nay! She was an innocent, he was sure of it. But her knowledge made it seem like she knew the chieftain well. So, if not his leman, what were her ties to him? Too late to ask that question now.

The lass stopped pacing then and faced him. She was waiting for her chance to ask her question.

She started and stopped a number of times, clearly unsure of which question to ask. Finally, she let out a breath and the words flowed with it.

'What are you?'

She watched his eyes widen then before he spoke. He'd not expected this question or her first. In trying to decide whether or not she was in danger and, if so, how much, Fia needed more information about this man who stood between her and the rest of the men there.

His first answer revealed that he was not from the Highlands. She suspected he was more than what he seemed so his second reply would fill in the unknowns about that. If he answered. He could decline and offer her a boon of her choosing instead. As she stood there waiting, she thought about what she could ask him for her boon.

Her gaze went to his mouth. Memories of the way he possessed her mouth during those kisses made her ache for another. She took in and let out a deep breath, trying to keep herself in control and trying not to ask for another of those kisses. He'd been staring off at the shadows in the back of the cave and thankfully had not witnessed her wanton display.

'I am a man who had sold his honour to the one who will pay the most.' He'd whispered the words so softly, she thought she might have imagined them. The pain as he said them made her heart hurt. Then he cleared his throat, smiled that wicked smile and spoke loud enough that there was no mistake of his claim. 'I am Iain Dubh, lately of the west of Scotland.

A sacker of villages. A kidnapper of fair maidens. A thief among thieves.'

Though she had thought part of this exchange between them meant she needed to answer truthfully, Iain had not thought it necessary to follow that assumption. He'd lied then, even as he'd revealed a painful truth with the first words. She thought to take him to task over it and realised it would change naught. He would lie when he wanted and share the truth if he thought that was needed.

A liar among liars.

'What is wrong?' he asked. Turning towards her, he took a step in her direction. Only the voice calling from outside stopped him.

'Iain Dubh,' Lundie said, summoning him. 'The winds have changed like the lass said.'

Iain waved with his hand for her to stay where she was rather than join him at the opening as he lifted the flap. Lundie stood there waiting. The rains still poured down, but the winds had changed their direction, blowing in now from the east and south rather than north and west. Though it might be hours more, or even a whole day before the storm ceased, this was a good sign.

Think what he might, Fia planned to escape. There would come a moment of distraction or inattention and she would use it to get away. Or to get into the shelter that lay buried in the side of the mountain. If she disappeared, these men would search for her at first. But with what she'd told Iain about Brodie, she thought they might decide that their own escape was more important than staying around for Brodie's arrival.

Oh, he would come. Or he would send his men to

find her. These outlaws might have hidden their destination at first, however that would not prevent the leader of the Chattan Confederation from using all the resources at hand from seeking her return. From what she'd overheard, they'd ridden west before turning back north through the mountains. It would only be a matter of time until Brodie or someone thought to search here.

While Iain was outside with Lundie, she retrieved and wrapped the bannocks and dried venison and beef strips. Tucking them carefully back into the lining of her cloak, she folded it and laid it out of the way. Then she walked as quietly as possible over to the entrance and, staying out of view, listened to the two men talking there.

'At first light,' Lundie said.

'Ye said three days?' Iain asked him.

'Aye, depending on the roads after this storm. But that is my plan.'

'And when ye return? We leave?' he asked.

''Tis what I was told. The men'll be paid and go off in their own ways. If'n ye be wanting more work, I can speak to…him and ask him.'

'Aye,' Iain said.

So, he meant to continue his lying, thieving, pillaging ways if there was gold left to be earned? Even the sadness in his voice when he spoke of selling his honour was a lie.

That he lied truly did not surprise her, but her own sense of pain in hearing him offer his honour up again did. Shaking her head, she listened on.

'Do ye think The Mackintosh wi' be sending out

after us?' Lundie asked. 'After her?' Fia listened for
what Iain would say. Would he warn them off?

'I think we wi' be safe here until yer return. Once
yer back, we can set things to right and be on our way.'
She heard shuffling feet and knew Lundie was leaving. *Set things to right?* Did that mean her?

'Wi' ye tell the rest of them?' Iain asked as Lundie moved away.

'Aye. I wi' give them orders, but ye wi' hiv to deal
wi' problems because of the lass,' Lundie said. 'If ye
expect me to back ye with *him*, show me ye can handle this.'

Iain grunted in reply. Though she expected him to
enter the cave, he did not. Instead, as she peeked from
behind the flap, she watched him walk a short distance
away, taking shelter under the thick and interwoven
branches of an ancient tree. In that moment, Fia knew
she must be prepared and ready to go as soon as the
opportunity presented itself.

For, these men would never leave a witness alive to
tell of their guilt. Even if it was not The Mackintosh
chasing them. No matter who followed or if none did,
they could not take the risk that someone's words, her
words, could connect them to their crimes.

So, though she'd thought that the danger she faced
was to her virtue, Fia now realised that her life was
at stake.

She spent the next hours as the storm blew itself
out considering her plan and her choices in silence
for he did not try to engage her in conversation. He
was as lost in his thoughts as she in hers. Fia had
told him of the three paths out and yet never told him

where they were. Now, she prayed that each of them remained open and usable after all the passing years. She would have to get to whichever one was closest when her chance came.

He watched her throughout the rest of the day. She could not look at him without wanting to scream at him. He played the appealing rogue so well, even while planning her demise. Well, she could play her role just as well. She waited as the rains finally ceased and the men began to clear the centre of the camp from most of the downed branches. She obeyed orders and made a meal. She even followed Iain Dubh back to the cave when he called to her.

Lundie gave his final orders to the group, promising them gold and other rewards before they sought their rest that night. None of them wanted to risk their payment, so begrudging acceptance was given. As Anndra said to her, soon they would have enough gold to buy any number of women for their use.

Iain followed her into the cave after giving her a few minutes to take care of herself. She avoided the pallet he'd made up there, for she did not wish to be anywhere near him. When he arrived, he closed the flap and checked the banked fire in the alcove. It yet gave off a fair amount of heat and would make it more comfortable than the last night had been in there.

Fia planned to sleep sitting against the wall, wrapped in her cloak and ready to run. All of that changed when he lifted the blankets and lay down on the side closest the entrance. He placed his sword at his side and then beckoned her in. When she shook her head and began explaining that she would prefer to sleep elsewhere, he got that angry expression in his gaze that worried her.

Within minutes, she lay next to him, with as much distance between their bodies as she could manage. Unfortunately he had other plans and soon, she lay on her side with him close behind her. His breath on her neck taunted her. When she tried to get up once, he took her braid and wrapped in several times around his fist, chaining her securely to him for the rest of the night.

Alan remained in the shieling for those first nights, watching the snows change to rain and back again several times before the rains won control of the storm. The main road up the mountainside remained impassable and would most likely remain so for some time. He ventured out to attempt it every few hours while the sun was up and on the third day he made it further up than before.

He changed his route, remembering how he'd found his way in the last time and crept in silence and under cover until he reached the encampment. Six men worked to clear a place in the centre of the camp. One man was their leader for it was obvious from his behaviour and from the way the others acquiesced to his every order. None of them sounded as though they came from the Highlands and none of them wore plaids, choosing instead the lowlanders' mode of dress.

Alan smiled. None of them were Camerons. The scraps left behind at each attack were truly to throw the blame where they wanted it to land.

Most of the damage from the storm he could see

were from broken branches and downed trees. As he watched they carried supplies and such out of one of the caves and set up a fire, for cooking he thought. Keeping a watch for any sign of where they might be keeping Fia —if she was still with them—he remembered his time here and knew there were several caves up along the paths. Mayhap he would need to look there?

Then he saw her, walking down the pathway to the left, followed by a tall, black-haired man. As they approached, he could see that she looked well. Or better than he'd expected in a situation like this. Shifting his position and leaning to the other side of the tree that gave him shelter, he also saw the mutinous expression on her face that foretold of trouble.

Yet, she walked freely among the men, not one of them abused or mistreated her. Indeed, she cooked something for them and they stood in an orderly line waiting for their portion. Each spoke to her as they passed and she did not cower or seem in fear of her life. But… There was something different in the way the black-haired man treated her.

And something different in the way she responded to every word he spoke and glance given. It reminded him…it reminded him of the way Brodie and Arabella were, here, in this place, all those years ago. Alan put that aside when the older man, the leader, began to speak to the group. With their attention turned to him, Alan took advantage of it to skirt his way to the other side of the clearing. Staying far enough away that his movements were not seen, he positioned himself nearer to the caves and listened.

Their leader, Lundie as he was called, would leave

in the morning. He would meet with the one behind this whole plan, the attacks and more, Alan suspected. As he spoke, Alan's thoughts tumbled about, sorting through the details and coming up with an idea. An idea, a plan that conflicted with his orders from Brodie.

The meal done and the instructions and orders given, the men sought their rest. The black-haired one took Fia by the arm and guided her back up the path towards the caves. Alan watched for any sign of force or fight and saw none. The man released her and let her go to the cave alone, waiting a short while before entering it himself. Alan took note of each man's position around the fire and other places before he moved closer to the cave where Fia was.

Listening with care, he heard no sounds of a struggle within. And no sounds he would associate with unwanted attentions. If a man was forcing himself on a woman, there would be some sounds. Indeed, soft snoring echoed from the cave shortly after the flap was closed. So, Fia was safe? The black-haired man some kind of protector?

He had dozed as the night passed. Considering his choices, he made his decision and, by the time the first faint light of dawn began to inch its way into the sky, he had made it back down the mountain. With his horse readied and supplies packed, Alan watched from the other side of the shieling as Lundie rode slowly along the muddy road. He waited some time before mounting and following, staying just within the cover of the trees and off the road.

As Lundie had said he would be gone for three

days at the most and now Alan knew his direction—north and west. Alan thought of which enemies of The Mackintosh and Cameron clans lived north and west of their lands.

Alan would follow him to his meeting, identify the one behind this plot and return to the camp before Lundie would. If possible, he would send word to Brodie, but if not, he would rescue Fia from the camp and have her out of there before it all went to hell.

A sound plan. A sensible plan.

So, two days later, with proof of treachery in his grasp from a different direction than the one Lundie had headed in at first, Alan rode hard to reach the camp so he could free Fia and get her the hell out of there.

He found disarray and confusion. He found blood and many signs of struggle. He found a camp emptied and left in a hurry.

But he did not find Fia.

Chapter Twelve

Niall woke from a dream to a dream.

He had dreamt of a green-eyed temptress who warmed his bed with the wonderful touch of her hands and mouth. Opening his eyes then, he found the very same woman in his arms. Niall dared not move for fear of ending it.

He remembered going to bed and fearing she would try to escape in the night while he slept. So, he'd wrapped the length of her hair around his hand and held it, and her, there. That much was clear.

When she had turned to him, when they had begun kissing and caressing, he did not remember. Nor did he care. In sleep she gave to him what she refused him in her wakefulness. So, as any warm-blooded man would do, he let her.

Once. Twice. Thrice more she opened her mouth to him and he tasted her deeply. Her body eased against him and the softness of her breasts pushed against his chest. He slid his hands around her, stroking her back and pressing her hips against his hard flesh. Her hands were busy as well, slipping inside his tunic and touching the black curls and skin of his chest there.

He was not a fool. He knew she would wake at any moment and it would be over, but for now, Niall enjoyed the touch of her hands and mouth on his skin and the feel of her filling his arms. For an impossible minute, he let himself truly dream that she was his.

Then her eyes opened.

He could tell the exact moment when she knew where she was for she stilled in his embrace, her hand yet within his tunic, and her fingers stopped swirling in the hair there. He mourned the loss of her closeness even before she moved away. A crude curse escaped in a whisper but her mouth was near enough to his ear that he heard it. He heard every word of it.

'I am no such thing,' he said, releasing her before she even protested his hold. 'I assure you my parents were not that closely related and were indeed married at the time of my birth.' Niall paused and then shrugged. 'And, though I like sheep, I am not overly affectionate towards them either.'

She squealed and rolled away then, the cold of the cave quickly filling the space between them. He unrolled his hand from the length of her hair as she moved.

'What did you do?' she asked, standing and smoothing her gown down. He noticed that she continued to wear his trews under her gown. Right now, after having her so close, he envied those damned breeches. 'Did you decide to take another boon?' she asked.

Then, she looked at her hand and at him, or rather his chest now exposed by the loose ties at his neck, and then back again. He smiled, remembering her fingers on his skin.

'I went to sleep,' he said, sitting up then and tying the laces at his neck. 'Little did I expect that my prisoner would accost me in such a personal way.' He nodded at her hand. She gathered her fingers tightly into a fist and dropped her hand to her side.

'I was asleep...I do not remember doing such a thing.'

The words were a falsehood that they both recognised. He did not argue it with her for he was more intrigued by this second use of profanity. Not so much its use, but the colourfully correct way in which she used it.

'Where did you learn to curse so well? I've heard outlaws who did not use it as you just did.' She blushed, the becoming pink spreading up her cheeks and making her green eyes appear darker then. Her embarrassment distracted her and she answered him.

'From a cousin,' she admitted.

'And you were permitted to listen to and use such language?'

Young women of her age would not usually be exposed to such a thing. At least not among his family. His mother would have punished anyone who spoke thusly in front of his sister... His sister Elizabeth was about Ilysa's age. He looked away and imagined for a moment how she would look now. Turning back to the lass, he listened.

'Anyone who knows my cousin hears it. He mastered the art of profanity early on. Some look on it as his weakness and some consider it a skill. Most care not which.' She smiled then as though remembering this cousin. 'To ease your concerns, nay, I was not to listen and Rob did his best to control it when others who might be offended by such words were present.' She sighed then. 'My mother washed my mouth out with soap when I repeated Rob's words before her.'

They stood there, each lost in thoughts of kith and kin, when noises from outside revealed the other men were also awake. Lundie would be leaving and Niall needed to speak to him first.

'Stay here until I return,' he said. Then he remembered her intention to escape. 'Or must I bind you hand and foot to ensure you remain?' She sighed then, a soft exhalation of breath that made him uneasy somehow.

'I will remain because you owe me a boon now and I expect to collect it,' she said.

He laughed at her words and her expression as he left. It was only as he walked away, Lundie in his sights ahead, that he realised what she'd revealed.

Her cousin Rob.

Robbie Mackintosh, second in command to his cousin Brodie. The man who oversaw the vast number of warriors in the clan and in the confederation formed by several others. A Mackintosh always led that powerful group. Several things worse than what the lass had said passed over his lips at this realisation.

If she was close enough to her cousin Rob, it went then that she was close to Brodie. How close akin would determine a number of things. Such as how soon he and the others would be exterminated for having kidnapped her. Such as how painful a death he would face for having ruined her.

Niall stopped and went back to her. He strode over and grabbed her by the shoulders, studying her face.

He'd been given the names of those closest to Brodie and to The Cameron. He wanted to know whom he might encounter or hear about in preparation for this assignment. Thinking on the list he'd received from the King's man who knew them best, Niall remembered Brodie's closest counsellors and their wives' names. And the lady's companion and her…maid.

'Are you Fia Mackintosh?' he whispered. 'Are you?' He gave a little shake. 'Tell me true.'

The shock on her face confirmed her identity to him. This young woman was a favourite of the laird and lady. She was trusted with their persons, their children and their safety and comfort.

One of the trusted few who had access to every part of their lives.

She would never be left in the custody of outlaws. Not for long. They truly were in more danger than she was.

'Give me the rest of the day and I will come up with a way to get you out of here,' he whispered. 'But say nothing to anyone else.'

His thoughts spun wildly as he left the cave. Lundie had gone and would not return for two, mayhap three days. Somehow he would need to convince the others to leave here, without their gold, before the Mackintosh's men arrived. And to leave without harming the lass. All of that without revealing how he knew of it and without exposing his role further.

Fia. Fia Mackintosh.

'Aye,' she whispered back.

'Just go about things as you would,' he said. 'Stay out of their way as much as possible,' he urged. She nodded and watched him closely. He felt like his wits had flown. Niall walked to the entrance of the cave and turned back to her before stepping outside.

'We came in from the west,' he explained. 'In which direction should we expect The Mackintosh to enter the encampment?' He knew two and she'd mentioned three more.

At first, he doubted she would answer. She had no reason to trust him. None at all, for he'd not given her anything but lies since they met. Well, other than the area of his birth. Every word he spoke to her was filled with lies. Then, when she did speak, he wished she had not.

'All of them,' she said.

He'd looked truly shaken by the knowledge of her identity. And yet, that he knew her name surprised her. She was a maid in service to the chieftain's wife. Certainly, she travelled quite a bit with Arabella and would have been seen by others outside the clan.

She was quite visible at Drumlui Keep, having duties to both the lady and at times to her children and, even on rare occasion, to the laird himself.

But none of that explained how this lowlander knew of her and knew her name.

Well, he had ordered her to stay here and she would. Fia smiled then. Glancing around, she lost no time in finding his satchel and bags. Untying them, she dumped out the contents and searched through them.

There was something here he did not wish discovered and she needed to find it. An icy shiver traced its way up her spine, giving Fia a very bad feeling about what was coming. Listening for the sounds of approaching steps, she tugged open several smaller pouches and discovered coins, some gold, some silver or copper, in them.

Leaving one, she ran and brought her cloak over and shoved the smaller one into the lining. She might have need of coins, she told herself.

A wrapped bundle at the bottom of the sack drew her attention next. She tugged the string holding it closed free and discovered a small book of hours within the canvas covering. The edges of the pages showed use, constant use as though read daily over the years. So, he could read. An outlaw, a man for hire, would not have that skill. She opened the book, the kind made for women and very costly, and found a name written there.

Elizabeth Corbett. The last name was unfamiliar to her. Not a Highland family, for certain. Who was she?

A sick feeling rolled in her stomach and threatened to make her heave then. His wife mayhap? Mother? Why else would he carry such a personal and precious thing as a book with him?

Voices carried into the cave as Iain called out orders to the men, reminding her to hasten her search.

Fia dug deeper inside and pulled out more garments and a small, sharp dagger that would fit in her palm. After secreting it with her other hidden cache, she reached in and felt something small tucked or secured in a pocket within the bag itself. Turning it inside out, she untied the knotted leather strips and freed it.

A ring. Not a wedding ring as she first thought, this was a man's signet ring with a round, carved bevel on it. She held it up, trying to use what light streamed into the cave to see the image carved there. Letters. A name. In Latin. A crown.

She nearly dropped it when she recognised the symbol of royalty.

Rings like this one were not simply passed around freely. It spoke of someone close to the King. It spoke of protection by the King. Only nobles and the very wealthy or very important got close enough to the King to even kiss one of these rings.

How had this self-professed outlaw gotten this ring? Surely he could not have stolen it and had that go unnoticed. Rings like these were created for express reasons and given only to a very limited number of specific persons. Fia sat back on her heels, still trying to understand or to guess how a king's ring came to be in Iain Dubh's belongings.

He came from the lowlands. He could read and speak like a nobleman. He carried a symbol of the King's protection with him.

What and who was he?

Realising that she was taking too long, sitting there and wondering about all this, Fia folded and placed everything back in the bag as best she could remember. Tempted to keep the ring in her possession, she instead tied it back into place. She would wait for the right time to face him with what she knew.

When she was summoned from the cave, it was Martainn who escorted her to the clearing. The men were eating all the extra bannocks she'd made the previous day to break their fast. Micheil would go hunting for supper, she was told. The small, agile man was probably capable of chasing down all manner of creatures of the forest.

'The men hiv need of yer skills, lass,' Iain Dubh said as she approached. A pile of garments lay in a heap before her. 'Ye can sit here and enjoy the day out of the cave while ye mend them. Or ye can take them back wi' ye while we wait on Micheil's bounty.'

She needed to get a better idea of the condition of the surrounding area for when the time came, so she nodded. 'Here in the light would be best,' she said. Her gaze moved back to him every few seconds as she tried to take notice of his movements and discover more about him through the rest of the hours of daylight.

Micheil returned with several rabbits and she prepared them to eat. The sun remained shining brightly as though apologising for being absent these last days and it felt good to be out of the cave for so long. With her skill of doing one task while listening and watching others, she learned that none of them knew who Lundie was meeting with. Also, they were simply in it as long as the gold continued coming.

Hired men, every one of them. Though he made sure to match their accents and coarse words, it was so clear to her that he was something different and more than the rest. The King's ring in his leather bag simply confirmed all the suspicions and caused more questions to swirl in her thoughts.

The winds grew chill as the sun set and the men began to ready themselves for the night. A couple of them went back to the cave to sleep, preparing the protection from the winds that sleeping out in the open did not give them. Without her cloak, it became too cold to remain and she asked to return to their shelter. Iain nodded and Martainn followed her to make certain she did not stray.

She entered and gathered together what she would need for her escape and the days it would take to get back to Drumlui and its village. Why Brodie's men had not arrived yet, she knew not. The obvious answer was the weather. Only the foolhardy or daft would risk travelling in a Highland storm. Or, had they, the outlaws, covered their path so well that no one suspected they were here? But Brodie would send someone to rescue her, of that she had no doubt.

If they did not arrive soon, she would be forced to rescue herself.

Niall watched as she left, Martainn close on her heels to see her back to the cave. Something was wrong, very wrong, but he had other matters to arrange now. Accustomed to lying to each and every one of the men in this endeavour, it felt very strange to prepare to tell the truth. It must be done carefully and in the correct order for it to work. These villains must be convinced to leave the possibility of gold behind and to do it soon, without hurting the lass.

To make that happen, he feared he must do exactly that. Would she play along with his act or expose him? From the way she'd studied him all day long, Niall believed she suspected he was not a simple outlaw. Though he'd like to share that truth with her, he dared not. Not until the others had left and she was freed to go back to her home.

When Conran and Iain Ruadh did not leave the fire as quickly as the others, Niall took the opportunity to plant the seeds of distrust and fear. Holding out the flask of *uisge beatha* to them, he waited for them to drink. The spirit was strong and bitter but favoured by the locals. Then he leaned back against the tree behind him and shrugged.

'The lass was quiet,' he said. 'Did ye see her glancing at the path all day? As if she expected someone's arrival.' He let the words hang out there for a few moments.

'She did seem to be distracted. Kept looking off in the distance,' Iain Ruadh said in agreement.

'I wonder if she kens who was here before.' Niall tried not to smile when Conran picked up on that.

'This place? Aye, there are signs that others have used this place all over it,' Conran added. 'Do ye think it was her people?'

'There are stories about Brodie Mackintosh hiding out in the hills from his cousin. 'twas many years ago, but everyone kens about it,' he said, nodding at them. He let them think about it for a minute or so and then jumped to his feet.

'Good Christ! Do ye think he will bring his warriors here looking for the lass?'

The two stood up as well, looking from one to the other and then at him. He tried not to smile. They were accustomed to following orders and not thinking for themselves.

'The damned woman has not told me the truth, but I wi' get it from her,' he said, making his hands into fists and flexing them several times. 'She wi' tell me what I want to ken.'

He strode off then, walking to the cave and passing Martainn on his way back without a word. Niall heard the other Iain and Conran telling him the rest. Arriving outside the cave, he pushed the flap open and went in. Fia stood in the middle of the chamber and he kicked a box in front of the flap as he grabbed her. Fear shone brightly in her eyes and she backed away several paces as he advanced.

'Ye hiv not been truthful wi' me, lass,' he yelled loudly enough that those following him would hear it. 'Does Brodie Macktinosh ken aboot this place?' he asked. 'Tell me now!'

Niall raised his hand and aimed at her face. At the last moment, he whispered to her.

'Drop!'

Chapter Thirteen

She fell at his command, but Niall felt her cheek under his hand. She'd not been fast enough to escape his blow completely. With a hand held against her face, she stared up in fear at him.

'Aye, he knows,' she said. 'We lived here for months.'

'Will he come here a-looking for ye?' he called out again, kicking several items across the cave as he did. 'Ye wi' tell me what I want to ken!'

'Aye, he will come. He will bring his warriors to find me!' she cried out.

The lass scrambled on hands and knees now out of his way, gathering up the length of her gown so she could move faster. He followed and reached down for her, grabbing the back of her gown and her braid in one hand. 'Beg for mercy,' he whispered.

'I pray you, mercy! Mercy!' She cowered under his anger. Exactly what he needed.

'Who are ye to him?' he shouted now, as he tugged on the buckle of his belt and loosened it. She screamed in true terror now, fighting her way free and crawling as far from him as she could. Niall stalked her across the stone chamber until he stood over her. 'I asked ye, who are ye to the mighty Mackintosh?' He took the buckle of the belt and the end together in one fist.

'What are ye to him?' he yelled at her as he slammed the belt down on the sacks lying there.

She cried out, raising her hands and arms before her to shield herself from the coming strike of the belt, never realising she was not his target. Fear was in control now so he gave her the word he needed her to say.

'His ward? His bloody ward?'

'Aye!' she screamed, tucking her head down behind her arms. 'His ward.'

At this point, she would say whatever he wanted. Before he could ask anything else, Anndra's deep voice echoed in from outside.

'Iain Dubh,' he said. 'Come out here now and leave the lass be.'

So, he or they could kidnap her, have their way with her but they objected to him using his hands or belts on her? He wanted to laugh at the absurdity of it as he walked to the opening.

'Ye wi' stay there until I come back,' he said so they could hear. 'I amna done wi' ye, lass.'

He kept the belt around his fist for good measure and walked out to talk to them. Primed as a pump and ready, they were, from the looks on their faces. Niall nearly burst out laughing at their expressions, but he held his merriment in check for now.

Every one of these men would kill anyone of their choosing if they needed or wanted to. They would lie, cheat and steal to get their way—and they had. For the last several months. With him. Now, their scruples were being raised for the lass. Good. This might work for all of them.

''Tis what I feared,' he said, dropping his leather-wrapped fist to his side. 'This was the Mackintosh's camp back when he fought his cousin. He kens this place,' he explained. They stared at him and then Anndra became the one who spoke for them.

'Did ye hiv to rough up the lass like that?' he asked, crossing his massive arms over his large chest and glaring at Niall.

'Aye, there was no call for such a thing,' Martainn added, matching Anndra's stance. Niall needed to bring this under control before they took over.

'Do ye understaun' what is going to happen?' he asked, glaring at one after the other while they thought on it. 'She is Brodie's ward. Close kin. No some village girl he cares no' for.' They blinked then, so Niall continued. 'He is coming for her,' he said, pointing towards the cave and the lass within.

'And if'n we let her go now?' Anndra asked. 'Send her home before he gets here.'

'Do ye think he will let us go off unscathed? We burned his villages. We kilt that old man. Now, we hiv taken his ward,' Niall asked.

'Ye took her,' Micheil said. 'We just wanted a little fun wi' her.' As though he was absolved.

'If we hiv her when he arrives, he wi' kill us and ask her later. I amna interested in waiting for that to happen.'

'So, ye wi' leave with the lass and get away?' Conran asked.

'Nay,' he said, shaking his head. 'I think we should leave her here and go off to find Lundie.'

No one spoke then. Niall suspected that one of them knew more than he did, especially more about where Lundie went. If not the specifics of whom he met, then at least the general direction.

'Lundie never tells us where he goes,' Micheil answered. 'And he has our gold. If we leave here, we wi' not get paid.'

The others joined the argument, all unwilling to risk the coming gold. But Iain Ruadh said nothing. And the man would not meet his gaze. He knew where Lundie was.

'Iain kens,' Niall said softly, nodding at him. 'Just tell us,' he urged. 'We can leave the lass here and ride to him.'

'I canna,' Iain Ruadh said, holding up his hand to forestall any further pressure to reveal his knowledge. 'Besides, if The Mackintosh was coming here, why isna he here yet?'

'For nigh on three days, the storms would have kept him close to home. Now that they hiv moved on...'

Knowing what he knew about the man, storms from hell would not stop him from seeking those who'd injured or harmed his people. 'twas only a matter of time before he sought vengeance for the attacks. Once he understood The Camerons were not behind them, he would pay whatever it cost to find out the truth.

'Iain Ruadh,' Anndra said, turning to face the man. 'If ye ken where he went, even the direction he rode, ye need to tell us.' The big man nodded at Niall now. 'I would rather we ride to meet him than wait here for our own deaths.' The others now joined in urging the man to share his knowledge with them.

'We canna go anywhere this night. 'tis the dark of

the moon and we would kill ourselves trying to leave here in the pitch-black of the night,' Niall said. 'In the morn, if Iain canna *tell* us anything, then we can just follow him when he leaves.' Iain met his gaze then and watched him through narrowed eyes. ''Twould no' be his fault if we followed him.'

One by one they nodded in agreement and Iain seemed content with handling the matter in this way. He would not speak about it and could not be blamed, yet no one wanted to be here to face death at the hands of a furious Brodie Mackintosh.

'We can meet up wi' Lundie and let him decide the next step,' Niall said, strategically acquiescing to Lundie's *rightful* leadership.

'And the lass?' Martainn asked.

'We leave her here wi' enough food to last a few more days. If she's here, The Mackintosh might let us be.' They all nodded and Niall turned to go back to the cave.

'Iain Dubh?' Anndra spoke his name. 'I think it would be best if'n ye leave the lass be. No more beating on her and no more of the other either,' he advised.

Now he must be the one to nod and accept their advice.

Walking back, he considered how much and what to tell Fia. Niall wondered what his reception would be when he entered.

She threw the cold water in the bucket at him as he entered. And now empty, it became another weapon of protection against him. As he wiped the water out of his eyes, she swung it in a wide circle to keep him from getting close to her.

'You…you…conniving bastard!' she said. The thud when the wood hit him was satisfying. It lasted only a few moments and then he tore it from her grasp and tossed it aside, wiping across his eyes with the back of his hand and sleeve.

He'd hit her. And he'd taken off his belt to beat her. And tossed her to the floor. Right now, he stood there staring at her with water dripping off his wet hair and shirt. Her sides heaved with anger as he watched her.

'You played your part well, Fia,' he said. 'I beg your pardon for…that.' He nodded at her cheek.

'My part?' she asked. He pushed the hair back out of his eyes and shook his head.

'Aye. I needed you frightened and reacting and not thinking on each thing I said. There was no time to explain and no guarantee you would follow my lead.' He took a step closer and she took one away. 'Does it pain you there?'

He reached up as though to touch her cheek and dropped his hand when she pulled back even more. Only the clothing on her back separated her from the cold stone of the cave's wall.

'Aye, it hurts,' she said. His eyes darkened then, turning the deepest shade of blue she'd ever seen. He truly did regret hitting her. 'You could have told me,' she said. Though…

'And risk you not reacting as I needed you to?' He shook his head. 'Nay. It played out how I needed it to. Now, we will leave here in the morning and—'

'We are leaving?' she asked. Where would they take her next? She would need to hurry her escape plans rather than be taken from here to another unknown place. At least here…she knew a way out.

'If you would give me a chance to explain,' he began. He lifted the box he'd kicked aside and placed it before her. 'Sit.

'I have convinced them to leave you behind. I expect that your chieftain will send men out for you now that the storm has cleared,' he explained. She nodded. 'They will find you.' He smiled then. 'Or you will find your way down to them.' Fia did not deny it now.

It made sense to her. When Brodie did get here, and she had no doubt that Arabella would have him handling it himself, he would unleash hell on these outlaws. Oh, her kidnapping was one reason, but these dastards had attacked *his* lands and *his* people. No one, no one, did that and lived to tell.

The only thing that could keep them alive would be the need for Brodie to find out who was truly behind this all. He suspected it was not The Camerons. If they, if Iain, cooperated and helped Brodie in finding out his enemy's identity, Brodie might let them go.

Or let them live.

She studied him then and realised two things. The first was that Brodie would never let them live. The second was that she did not want him dead.

Oh, she should, but she did not.

'Why did you do that?' she asked.

'Ah, lass,' he said softly. 'Cannot even an outlaw have a moment of good conscience?'

'You are no more an outlaw than I am,' she said, making her accusation aloud. Those eyes darkened once more and his jaw snapped shut, grinding teeth on teeth. 'You speak as one when you are with them, but not when we are alone.' Fia wanted answers now, especially if he was leaving in the morning.

'Haud yer wheesht!' he whispered furiously.

'Ah, there it is,' she said. 'Your false tone and speech.'

He approached her then and she felt as though a dangerous animal was stalking her. His movements were filled with the masculine grace and ease of a fighting man—she'd seen it with Brodie and Rob before. When threatened, their bodies shifted and became weapons. It was happening here before her eyes.

Outlaw, my arse, she thought.

'Have a care for what you say, lass.' His warning was spoken low, his deep voice whispering it softly, but she did not miss the message.

He was leaving in the morning. The worst he could do was tie and gag her to keep her from telling the others. But she needed to know the truth. If the result of this whole debacle was for naught except to point out the silliness of her romantic dream and to destroy her life, then she would have the truth from him.

'What outlaw carries a book of hours in his bag?' His eyes widened and the shock of her question made him choke as he tried to get words out. 'And what outlaw has a king's signet among his possessions?'

Murderous. If she had to use a word to describe his expression, it would be that one.

Without another word or glance at her, he rushed to the pile of bags and supplies, searched for the one he'd hidden away and pulled it out. He turned it on end and dumped everything out. If she had not been watching closely, she might have missed the brief touch of his hand on the wrapped book before he sought the other thing she'd mentioned. His hand slipped into the hidden pocket and a look of relief covered his face before he glared at her.

'You have no idea what you've done, lass,' he said.

'Tell me then,' she said. From the tone of his voice and the dark expression on his face, Fia suddenly wondered if she should have remained silent. 'Who are you?'

'There is so much more to this than I could ever say. Let that suffice,' he warned again.

'You are not Camerons, yet you all play the role to incriminate them in these attacks,' she said. 'Tell me.' She needed the truth. His words had revealed more than she'd expected. So, he was not an outlaw. Was he a nobleman as she suspected?

'All I can say is there is more here than you can ever know.'

'Iain Dubh!'

The thunderous voice stopped them as they stood. Anndra kicked the flap and yelled again. 'Get yerself out here now!'

He closed his eyes for a moment, almost in reverence, before meeting her gaze. Guilt, resignation, anger were all there.

'What will they do?' Fia asked as he stood.

'If I can convince them, they'll leave you alone and leave me to face the Mackintosh,' he said.

'And if not that?'

'I suspect you will survive,' he said. He had the ring in his hand, turning it over and over in his grasp. She nearly missed catching it when he tossed it to her. 'Hide that. Send it to the King if you can.'

The King?

God in Heaven, he was truly involved somehow with the King!

'What else can I do?' she asked. If she'd not been curious, if she'd not pressed him for answers, no one would have heard them.

'Run!' he whispered just before he did the same thing.

Not questioning him this time, she grabbed up her cloak and did just that.

Chapter Fourteen

Niall did not pause after telling Fia to run.

He barrelled out of the opening, intent on taking as many of them down to the ground as possible. Oh, he had no hope of defeating them on his own. He simply needed to distract them enough to let her slip away.

One of them held a torch, for it was full dark now, and it threw enough strange and moving shadows that should have given Fia more than a good chance to get away. He prayed she was as prepared as he suspected as he knocked three of them over. When he saw something move in the shadows along the path, Niall took off running in the opposite direction, hoping to draw the men away.

And they followed.

Without the benefit of a torch or the moon's light, Niall stumbled through the camp until he knew she'd gotten away. The lass knew her way around this place and knew the ways out, and, he did not doubt, hidey holes in which to take shelter. He heard Conran call out that she was not in the cave then. To keep their attention on him, he stopped and turned and threw himself into those behind him.

They became one tangled heap of bodies before the fighting began. Then, he just kept giving and getting—punches, kicks, elbows to the gut and face—whatever blows he could land on one of them. He heard the crunch when his nose broke. The pain of several kicks to his ribs and in his back that told him he would be pissing blood for days. It mattered not. Niall let out all the frustration and anger and loss that had filled him for years in that fight.

And he needed to give Fia enough time to get away.

He'd dragged her into this muddle after all. If he'd played the outlaw instead of the gawping man, she would not have been in the midst of his hunt.

Then, one of the men, Micheil he thought, got an opening and Niall felt his head snap back from the force of it. He smiled a bit as the back of his head smacked into someone's nose and broke that from the sound of it. Not unconscious, but dazed and confused, Niall fell to his knees and then landed on the ground. They did not stop then, using his inability to fight back to their own advantage. By the time someone—Anndra, mayhap?—called a halt to it, Niall could barely breathe.

'Bring him,' Iain Ruadh said. 'To the cave.'

Lundie's confidant. The quiet man who knew more than he said.

They dragged him to his feet and along the path back to the cave. And they took no care of further injuries as they did. When he was tossed to the ground inside the cave, he passed out for a short time before being shaken and kicked awake.

'Where is she?' Iain Ruadh asked.

Good then. They'd not found her. He said nothing which earned him another kick. That rib and several others were well and truly broken.

'It matters not now,' Anndra said. 'I heard what I heard.'

'Tell us again what he said,' the other Iain said.

'I only went after him to make certain he was no' beating on the lass again,' the big man explained. 'As ye said I should do, Iain.' Ah, the other Iain had already begun taking control.

Niall struggled to open his eyes in spite of one being swelled shut and blood from his nose and other cuts kept running into the one that wasn't shut. He tried to roll to his side so the blood could drip on to the ground, but they forced him back and someone held him there with their foot—their heavy, booted foot.

'And what did ye hear?'

'The lass said something about The Camerons to him. And he said there was more than he could say.'

Someone arrived behind him, but Niall could not turn to see. He only hoped that they had not caught Fia.

'No sign of her,' Conran said. 'Like she vanished into the night air.'

The pressure on his chest suddenly increased and Niall could not even draw in. Iain's face appeared before him.

'Does she know we are not Camerons?' he asked. A nod brought on more pain. 'What did you tell her?'

'Nothing,' he whispered, clenching his teeth against the pain.

'Search his things,' Iain ordered.

Niall could hear them climbing around, tearing apart bags and boxes. They would not find anything now, not if Fia took it with her. If he died here and now, and if Fia returned the ring to his godfather, mayhap the King would grant a boon of mercy to his sister and mother? He'd have died in service to the King after all.

'Nothing but this,' Anndra said. 'A book?'

They'd found his mother's book of hours. The last time he'd seen her, she'd given it to him with a mother's admonishments of seeking a prayerful rather than sinful life.

'What is this?' the other Iain asked him.

'I stole it,' he rasped out. 'To sell.'

''Twill do us no good,' the red-haired man said. 'We canna read and we canna sell it now.' Niall thought he heard him toss the book.

'So what do we do wi' him?' Anndra asked. The big man surprised Niall. He was using this to get rid of a competitor. 'Take him to Lundie?'

'Nay,' Iain Ruadh said. 'I think we leave him here to face the Mackintosh. He wi' be dead afore he can utter a word against us.'

'And fewer to split up the gold,' Anndra said. He really was surprising Niall.

'And the lass?' The shuffling of feet told of a new arrival.

'No sign of her,' Martainn said, out of breath from chasing the lass.

'Tie him up and gag him.'

Niall could not fight back. Soon he was trussed up tighter than a goose readied for the oven. They tossed him back on the ground and moved away from him.

'At first light, or sooner,' Iain ordered, 'we ride.'

He could barely see them leave, shadows of feet scuffing across the packed floor, raising dust and dirt in their wake. He breathed slowly to avoid coughing. Coughing, well that would be painful.

'Take anything ye think we wi' need,' Iain ordered. 'Get his coins and, Martainn, take the first watch.'

Niall realised that he'd found only one of his two purses in the bag. One was gone already… The lass! She was a canny one.

'But he is tied and gagged,' Martainn protested.

'Aye, and I still want a guard outside this cave.'

No one argued and soon the cave grew quiet and dark, for they'd taken or blown out the lantern. He heard Martainn mumbling under his breath for some time but Niall found it hard to concentrate.

His head ached, his chest hurt, his ribs burned and his leg screamed. After a while it all blended together and he could feel himself losing awareness. He drifted in and out of consciousness, plagued by ghosts and sins from his past. Was this what happened when you were about to face God and answer for your failings? Shivers racked his body and then ripples of pain became torrents racing through every part of him.

It continued for some time until he wondered if it would ever cease. Dying was more painful than he'd thought it would be.

The only good thing he'd done was get the lass free. She was smart and confident and would get herself off this godforsaken mountain and back to safety. He laughed at all the food she'd been stuffing in her cloak and then paid the price in pain. Hapless Dougal had better stand up and be a man in this. The lass deserved some happiness in spite of the muck she would be dragged through because of him.

The darkness began to claim him then and Niall knew it was nearing his end. The sound of a bell ringing softly once must be his call to judgement. And from the sound of the foul language after the bell, he knew his destination for eternity.

Fia winced as she said the words and slammed the iron girdle against his head. Only knowing what half of it meant, she could guess at its meaning. She remembered Eva's reaction when Rob had spoken them and knew it was bad. Still, being in this situation certainly must grant her some dispensation to use such words and phrases.

Martainn slumped over, falling but still blocking the opening to the cave. Now, she must move him to get inside. After checking to see that he yet lived and offering a prayer of thanks to the Almighty for that, she took no chance that he would wake and turn on her. She used the rope she'd found and tied his hands and feet first and then rolled him over several times. He landed off the pathway and in the low bushes there.

'Twas not something she was proud of or wanted to do for the man had not been particularly unkind to her. But since the others had ridden or walked out of the encampment in the dark of night, Martainn's horse was the only one left. She wanted to curse when she watched them take Iain Dubh's horse as they left. Now, the other men's fear of being captured made this one expendable, too. They'd left him behind without a word of warning or farewell, probably so they could steal his share of the gold Lundie promised to bring back.

It had taken her hours of watching from the hiding place before she'd felt ready to search for Niall. Brodie had made certain that everyone knew where to go if the camp was attacked and, lucky for her, those places of safety still existed. The one nearest the cave was open though she had to force her way through the overgrown branches that covered it.

Hiding there, she had planned to wait until they left or until Brodie arrived. With the bannocks and dried meats, she could last for days. If they left, she could search for more amongst what remained once they fled. Then, crouched safely in the dark, behind a tree and out of their view, she watched as they dragged Iain back to the cave. Badly beaten and unable to walk on his own, he could not fight them off.

Fia wanted to creep forward and hear what went on, but dared not. He'd done that—distracted them and then taken that beating—for her. To give her a chance to escape. And she would not render his sacrifice for naught. Then, some time later, Martainn had taken up his post and the others returned to their places around the camp.

Moving carefully, she watched as they each, save Martainn, quietly gathered up their belongings and followed Iain out of the camp. Because of the steepness of the path and their inability to see the edges of the road and the cliffs, they did one intelligent thing— they walked their horses down the mountainside.

The hours passed quietly as she thought about what to do.

She could remain here and wait for Brodie. Aye,

that was one choice. But that would leave the one who'd risked his life for her to face Brodie's wrath and judgement, if he yet lived. Now that she knew there was something more to this, to him, she did not think that the best choice.

She could leave the mountain herself, making her way through the hidden pathways that led down to the southern side of it, nearest to Glenlui and home. Martainn would realise his fate soon enough and escape on his own come morning. She even suspected that he would free Iain before he left, if Iain yet lived, though that would be the aid he offered and not before he was on his way. Fia could give the signet ring to Brodie to sort out since he was her chieftain and should see to matters of such importance as that. That was the best choice for a woman in her situation.

Somehow, even in the hours of waiting, she could not convince herself to simply walk away. Especially as she did not know if he would survive. And it was as she thought about what he'd said and done that she realised what he'd done.

Other than his hand hitting her cheek when she did not fall away fast enough, he'd not hurt her at all. Her fear made it seem worse than it had been. He'd yelled, he'd kicked things around, he'd even grabbed her and tossed her aside. And, when faced with exposure, he had trusted her with his most valuable possession. Her discovery of the prayer book had surprised him, but it was the ring that caused him the most concern.

Just before the sun began to rise, in the time when the sky stopped darkening but the light was not there yet, Fia made her decision. Skirting around the camp, she'd made certain they'd left and then worked her way to the centre. The pot, she knew, was too heavy to use effectively, so she'd picked up the flat girdle and crept back towards the cave. Using a side passageway, she'd approached Martainn and lifted her arm. With a quick prayer for forgiveness for the action, she'd swung it down. She had to offer another prayer after she'd uttered the offensive words as well.

Now with him securely tied and out of the way, she pushed against the flap and entered. The cave had been sacked, everything that had been organised and neatly placed now lay strewn across the floor. She'd picked up the lantern from next to Martainn and now held it up higher before her. She gasped at the sight of him there.

His face did not have a spot that was not bruised, cut or bleeding. One eye was swollen shut and his nose was broken and off to one side. They'd tied his hands behind him and he lay half-twisted on the ground. She took notice that, although tied together at the ankles, one of his legs did not look…well.

He made no sounds other than a shallow, raspy breathing. She searched within her cloak for the dagger she'd pilfered and found it. Though not as sharp as she'd like, it would have to do and she set to work slicing through the ropes to free him. Only when she moved him, turning him to lie on his back, did he stir at all.

With no assurance the villains would not return here to finish their task begun, Fia knew she must get him out of there. Must get them out of there. First though, his serious injuries must be tended to if he was going to be able to ride at all.

'Iain,' she whispered as she touched his shoulder.

'You must wake up now.' She shook him a little harder then and he groaned. 'Wake now.'

'Ah, 'tis you, lass. I thought with the vile cursing that I'd gone to hell for eternity.' He lifted his head then, or tried to, turning in her direction. 'You should go.'

'I am going nowhere without you, you daft man. They've left, every one of them, in the night. Cowards!' she said loudly.

He began to sleep again, but she shook him. 'They may be back if they find Lundie close enough. We must move.'

Though he groaned a noise that sounded like agreement, he did not rouse completely. Deciding instead to take measure of his injuries, she brought the lantern closer.

Over the years, she'd helped Margaret, Rob's sister, in her duties as village healer. Fia had carried her basket, sought supplies and helped her as she went about in the village, seeing to those in need. During their exile here, she'd watched Margaret care for the wounded. So, injuries and blood did not make her squeamish as it did others. Ailean, Arabella's Cameron cousin and companion for many years, passed out at the sight of blood. But not Fia.

Taking a deep breath, she leaned over and began to gently probe for broken bones. She'd watched Margaret fix a fractured nose before and, though not difficult, the sound of it did turn her stomach. Do it quick and push it hard, Margaret had said as she did it. Fia wondered if she dare try it now. Before she could convince herself not to, she reached over, slid her fingers across the bridge of his nose and pushed it hard back where it should be.

Shuddering, she slid her fingers over his face and cheeks and was thankful when everything else felt fine. She did not tarry over his injured eye for fear she would worsen the swelling there. Through his clothing, she could feel no breaks in his arms but the bone near his left shoulder was not even. The moan when she pressed on his ribs and then lower on his belly was not a good sign. Then, when she stroked down his leg, especially his right lower one, she found a huge swelling and signs it was broken. Tugging up the edge of his trews to examine it more closely, she saw the bruise and swelling spoke of a fracture in the bone.

Damn! He would not be able to walk or ride with such an injury. It would need to be set by someone who knew how to do it. The best, the only thing she could do would be to bind it with supports to keep it steady until it could be seen to. Moving quickly now, she found the box he'd kicked out of the way and pulled its broken slats apart. Choosing two that seemed the right size, she looked around for something to use to wrap them and remembered his other trews. They would give her long strips when cut into pieces.

She set about her task, keeping an eye on her patient and an ear to the opening for signs of anyone returning. By the time the sun came up and day was upon them, Fia had done as much as she could to prevent further injury. His trews and her shift had been sacrificed for the material necessary to bind his ribs and splint his leg.

Fia left him there to get Martainn's horse. The man lay unconscious there by the path, breathing and alive.

Heaven smiled on her for the horse was saddled and ready to ride. Bringing it back to the cave, she tied it there and went in to pack up what they could take. A skin of ale, his sewing box and shears, the last of the bannocks, a few extra garments and his sword and scabbard were all she thought necessary. They'd taken his coins, but she still had the other bag hidden in her cloak.

As she carried the supplies out to pack them on the horse, she knew that she needed to find one more item among the chaos of the cave. She crawled around until she found it and tucked it inside her gown where the ring already hung on a length of leather lace, secure and hidden.

It took more time and more strength than she thought she had to get him up on the horse. Several tries and possibly more injuries, too. The sun was moving higher in the sky by the time they reached the drovers' trail at the bottom and she had to make the final decision about their destination.

To the left and east was the lands of Glenlui. To the south lay the lowlands and eventually Edinburgh, the city of the King.

All she needed to do to make that choice was remember what his last actions had been when things turned against him—he made sure she got away but not before trusting her with the signet. He'd said to get it to the King. He trusted her.

Touching her heels to the horse's side, she guided it south, following the roads that they used to take cattle to market. He leaned against her, barely conscious and unable to tell her what to do. There were several villages along this road and she would seek a healer to tend to the injuries she could not. Then, she would find out the truth from the man she knew as Iain Dubh.

Chapter Fifteen

Days and nights passed in confusion and pain. No matter what he said or did, no matter how he begged or promised, they continued to ride. There was not a single part of him that did not scream in pain. There was not a moment when anguish was not his dearest companion.

Niall felt the fires of hell burning within him. His skin was too tight and on fire. He was racked, pulled and stretched until he screamed and could take no more. But oblivion was too hard to find and he kept returning to the pain.

Then the freezing of winter would strike, chilling him to the bones and making him shudder at its icy touch. Not even the warmth of the body that covered him could take away that cold.

Was this his punishment for his father's sins? His betrayal of his friend and King? Or had Lundie found him and was forcing him to reveal his true mission? Neither, for the devil that confounded and tortured him had soft hands and a gentle voice, urging him back to her every time he slipped into the darkness.

At first, for many days and nights, he wished she would stop and allow him to seek the darkness of death. Then, he came to crave her voice, her touch, her scent. Even her stern and forbidding voice when he failed her. But the worst was when she cried. The tears scalded him, burning his skin and tormenting his ears with the sound of her soft sobs.

Then, with the voice of an angel, she sang to him with soft words and tunes that eased his heart and his mind and his suffering. She would cradle him in her embrace and sing so gently it made him want to weep.

Niall did not know when he first came back to himself. It felt as though an early morning's fog burned off, bit by bit, until one day, one moment, he awoke and opened his eyes.

He took a few minutes to get his bearings and then realised he was alone. In a small chamber. That held a bed and a stool and not much else. He lifted his head, but the dizziness became so profound he did not try it again for a long time. Instead, he began by stretching each of his limbs to find out where the worst of it was.

Toes on both feet worked and moved without pain. Both feet could shift and circle on his ankles. The first bit of trouble came when he moved his legs and a searing pain tore up from his right one, taking his breath away. Slowly, he evaluated his body parts for possible injuries and discovered that his leg was most certainly fractured. His ribs, a number of them on both sides, were cracked and a bone near his neck as well.

Slowly tracing his fingers over his face, Niall felt the bump on his nose where it had broken and then been pushed back into place. Not the first time and most likely not the last. His eye swelled quite a bit but it opened a little and he could see clearly.

But as he thought about his injuries, he remembered nothing after the beating that caused them. How he got here, wherever that might be, was a mystery to him. Someone had taken care of him to keep him alive this long. When he heard a voice approaching the door, he knew then.

Fia Mackintosh.

The last vision he had of her was as she ran from the cave as he threw himself at the others. To protect her. Then, in spite of them searching the camp for her, she was gone.

As she spoke to someone outside the room bits of memory floated before him. Her standing over him saying things a young woman should never say. The touch of her hand on his burning skin. Her hair cascading over him as she bathed him with cool water. The other part of him seemed to be working well if he judged its reaction to his thoughts of the lass.

The latch on the door lifted and it opened slowly. She came into his view slowly and he realised she was trying not to disturb him. He watched through nearly closed lids as she pushed it open with her hip and carried the tray inside. After setting it on one of the stools, she closed the door just as quietly as she'd opened it. He savoured the moment when he could watch her before she found him awake.

She moved around the chamber at ease, now dressed in a plain but clean gown. Her hair lay gathered in a braid that swung from one hip to the other as she walked and put things down. She'd not looked at him yet so he supposed he'd been asleep for a while and had not been expected to wake at this time. Niall enjoyed seeing her in the day's light and without need for a lantern. He saw then the small, open window near the ceiling, its shutters thrown open to let in the light. Without meaning to, Niall moved his leg and the pain made him gasp, bringing her attention to him.

Fia met his gaze with a gasp of her own and then ran to kneel by his side…and burst into tears. She tried to speak and then got up and left the chamber, this time letting the door bang closed with a resounding thump.

Niall tried to follow her, forgetting about the extent of his injuries, and paid a terrible price. But he could use the one thing that still worked.

'Fia!' he yelled, holding his arms across his chest to keep himself steady when the urge to cough followed close by.

He heard footsteps coming down a corridor outside the door and then a woman spoke. Not Fia but an older woman from the sound of it.

'Weel, at least he didna die,' she said. 'Here now, dearie, dinna greet so.' The latch lifted once more and a woman almost the size of the doorway stood there with Fia. 'Go on in wi' ye, lass. He looks as worried aboot ye as ye are aboot him.' Fia stepped into the chamber, but now her easy manner and motion were replaced by hesitancy.

'Fia, are you well?' he asked her when he understood he could speak again. She nodded, almost shyly, at his question. 'Come here.' He patted the bed next to him and she crossed the room to him. When she glanced back at the woman, he knew she was nervous.

'I wi' bring ye something more filling than that

broth,' the woman said. 'Yer sister has been mightily worried about ye.'

'Sister?' he asked quietly after the door closed and the woman's steps faded down the corridor.

'I did not know what to say other than to claim kinship with you. Saying otherwise would simply raise more questions and consequences.'

Consequences like being married. For in the Highlands old customs still held sway, and some said that claiming another as your spouse before witnesses made the act indeed true. He smiled then, once more so impressed by her quick thinking and intelligence.

'Where is this place?' he asked, trying to sit up. His head spun so badly, he stopped and lay back down.

'Crieff,' she said. 'This is a small inn and Mistress Murray owns it.'

'How can it be Crieff? We were in the west, almost to the coast there and now we are...' With no recollection of travelling at all, he was struck dumb by it. How could he, she, they, have made it all this way? Especially with him in such a sad state. 'Tell me how you accomplished this.'

As she began her tale, Niall realised he'd never heard the lass talk so much. Her explanation of what had happened sounded much like the stories told in the King's court to entertain his guests. He also noticed that the entire time she spoke, she tended to him—holding a cup or the bowl of broth for him to drink, smoothing the sheet and blankets that covered him, helping him wash his face and hands and more.

If she was to be believed, she had knocked out Martainn with a girdle, tended to his injuries and helped Niall on a horse, ridden to the next village, stopped at a monastery to seek a healer, travelled with merchants and used their half-empty wagon to bring him this far.

Her face lit up during some parts of her story and darkened with worry at others. When she finished, he could not remember all of it but was astounded by what he did. Yet not once did she say why.

Why had she done this for him? Why had she risked her life and safety instead of simply waiting for her chieftain to arrive? Why was he even still alive?

'Why?'

He didn't mean to say it aloud, but once he had, he waited for her answer. He'd done nothing but drag her into the middle of even more danger than she'd been in during the attack on her village. He'd brought her into a clandestine hunt he could not reveal. She risked everything for…what? Who?

She seemed startled by his question. The only one he'd asked throughout her whole explanation. But, of all of it, all the people and places and the rest, it was the one he needed to know.

'Why?' she repeated, her green eyes wide.

'Why did you do this, Fia? You could have, nay, should have, left that mountain and gone back to your people. You could have just seen to your own protection and safety. Only a daft person would…do what you did.'

'You trusted me and saved my life. I thought I should save yours.'

The words somehow startled her and shocked the piss out of him.

For so long in his life, no one had worried over him. No one had asked for his trust and he'd given it to no one. He did not trust his godfather to fulfil his promises. He did not trust any of the men he'd worked with or those in the gang he'd joined. Then this woman had been plucked from her own life and yet remained when others would have run.

He had so many questions for her, but his head began to spin and his words slurred. Niall fought it. He wanted to speak with her. The ring? Did she yet have it? His body had other ideas for it dragged him down towards the darkness. The soft touch of her hand on his head eased his worry.

'You must rest,' she whispered against his ear. 'I will watch over you. And worry not for your belongings are safe.'

Fia watched as his eyes drifted closed and he fell back to sleep. This time, he'd managed to stay awake for longer than the four or five times before. As Mistress Murray and Glynis, her cousin the healer, told Fia, this could and would happen any numbers of times before he would be strong enough to remain awake and conscious. Injuries like he'd suffered could have serious affects.

She brushed his hair from his face with her hand and tucked the blankets up over his shoulders as he slept. He'd taken more of the broth and watered ale this time than the last and surely that must be a good sign. That he remembered nothing—again—could not be.

Fia had invented a story of ruffians attacking them, brother and sister they were, as they travelled to visit family in the south. She never mentioned Edinburgh or the King, only giving an unnamed destination. The village they'd found first were hospitable and the wise woman there helped her with his injuries. And sent her to the monastery on the road south for more help.

The good brothers kept Iain there for several days and nights seeing to the worst of things and stabilising his leg so it would heal correctly. When a group of merchants travelling south stopped there for the night, the abbot arranged for her and Iain to join them. All along the way, she used his coins to pay for what they needed. Crieff, a large market town, seemed the best place to stop and allow Iain to heal.

She'd not dared to send off that ring to the King as he'd asked. She would more likely be arrested for thievery herself if she tried. So, she kept it hidden away and waited for him to wake so he could decide about it. And, tell her about this connection with the King.

And all the while, she kept a sharp watch for any of the outlaws. She thought they would scatter now, afraid of being discovered, afraid of capture. Fia suspected that they would not pursue the two of them into a market town so close to Edinburgh like this and risk being identified by her.

He sighed in his sleep and then mumbled words she could not understand. Fia sat on one of the stools and watched him for several moments. Nay, he was not waking again. When she heard footsteps down the corridor, she rose and opened the door, not wanting anyone to knock and disturb him.

'Lass, how is he?' Mistress Murray asked in a whisper. Peeking her head in the door, she nodded. 'Puir mon…he does need his rest.'

'He drank the broth and took some ale as well this time,' Fia said. 'Let me get the bowl.'

Fia gathered up the bowl and spoon and cup and followed Mistress Murray back into the kitchen. She greeted several of the servants along the way, now knowing all their names. Without pausing, Fia washed the dishes in the large bucket used for that purpose and left them to dry.

'Och, now, lass,' Mistress Murray began. 'I hiv told ye that ye dinna hiv to do that. Ye are a paying customer and 'tis no' right for ye to do the work of servants.'

'I am deeply in your debt for everything you have done for us,' Fia said. 'If not for you and your help, Iain would not have survived.'

It was true. A fortuitous meeting with the woman had yielded a place to stay that was clean and safe. Mistress Murray called in her cousin who was as experienced and talented as Margaret Mackintosh was, to Iain's benefit.

'Weel, now that he is on the mend, it should be no time at all before you can travel to your family. In the south, did ye say?'

Mistress Murray, like most people, liked to gossip. As an innkeeper in her own right, a widow who kept her late husband's business after his death, gossip was as valuable as coins for trading amongst the other merchants in the town. The one who knew what was happening was valued. And Mistress Murray made it her role to pry into the lives and goings-on of her customers. Fia watched as the woman took her hand and patted it.

'Would ye be going to Edinburgh or even further into the borderlands?' The woman turned away to a task as though the information did not truly matter. She was good at this. Almost as good as Fia's own mother. 'I will keep an ear open if I hear anyone travelling south who could accommodate ye. I am certain ye've no wish to travel alone after what has happened.'

'Nigh to Kelso,' she said. That was where Iain said he was born. She'd given the name in the prayer book as theirs when asked. Iain and Fia Corbett, late of Inverness, on their way home to the borders. 'I would appreciate your help when the time comes.'

'Peigi! Get a bowl of that stew!' the innkeeper called out to one of the servants. 'And the fresh bread.'

A few moments later, a steaming bowl of thick, aromatic stew sat before her with a chunk of still-warm bread. A crock of butter arrived just after it.

'Go on wi' ye, then!' she said, handing her a spoon. 'Ye look like death yerself. If ye dinna rest ye wi' be the next one stuck abed, lass.'

Fia could not resist the smell of the stew. It had been the one joy of staying here after those days at the camp, cooking only what she had to use. This inn, the best one in Crieff the merchant's wife had told her, was known for their food and clean beds. And, as she dipped once more into the stew, worthy of every one of Iain's coins she spent to secure them a private chamber with meals included.

Mistress Murray never stopped moving even as she talked with Fia. The woman ordered the servants around, called out to other customers in the public room and cleaned and arranged dishes, pots and pans. All without losing her place in their conversation and all without pause. Fia appreciated being around people again, just as she was in Drumlui. And sitting in the kitchen, amidst the bubbling pots and busyness, was always one of her favourite places.

'Hiv ye been out to walk yet, Fia?'

'Nay, not today, Mistress,' she said. She liked to walk the town, even running some errands for her landlady while Iain slept.

'Get out there afore the rains arrive,' she advised. Rubbing her shoulder, the woman tsked several times. 'Rain is coming. Go, enjoy the sun while it deigns to show itself.' When Fia would have refused, the woman shook her head. 'I wi' look in on him. Dinna worry.'

'Have you anything for me to do?' she asked. She always asked, for the woman had been a godsend to her these last days.

'Nay, lass,' she said with another shake of her head. 'Just enjoy yer walk.' When Fia would have washed this bowl, Mistress Murray waved her off, trying a stern expression this time.

'My thanks, Mistress,' she said. Grabbing her cloak, now emptied of all its treasures and supplies, from a peg next to the back door, Fia left the inn and stood for a moment to gain her bearings.

The day was a sunny one, warmer than in the Highlands at this time in the spring, so she stood with her face lifted to the sunlight for a moment. Then she made her way along the lanes, looking at goods for sale and speaking to several merchants about their wares. She guarded the coins she had as she sought out and purchased a few garments that Iain would need now that he was awake.

She walked for about an hour and when she arrived

back at the gate that led to the inn she was proud of herself. Fia had managed to not think about his disturbing question and her untruthful answer for that whole time.

Chapter Sixteen

He was trying to figure out how to handle private matters when the door opened and the woman who'd been here with Fia entered. She took one look at him and stepped back to the open door.

'Tomas! Munro!' she called out loudly. The scurrying footsteps in answer to her call came quickly.

'Aye, Mistress?' they said in unison.

'Help the lad,' she said, with her knowing gaze on him. 'See to things.' The two lads, both of them tall and strapping, entered the room and came at him.

'Here now,' she called out, stopping them. 'First, let's get him oot of bed and to a chair.' They approached each side of the bed and reached for him. 'Gently, lads, gently.'

No matter gently or not, it hurt to sit up and to move at all. The dizziness grew stronger as they lifted him to sit first and then it became something worse and more noxious. It hurt to breathe. It hurt to piss. But, under the innkeeper's vigilant gaze and experienced hands, everything was seen to in a brisk, impersonal manner and done speedily. She called out orders better than most clan commanders did and her lads were quick to respond and carry out her wishes.

A chair appeared and he was placed there, his bad leg supported during the move and now positioned with the stool and a pillow beneath it. At her call, a maidservant rushed in carrying fresh bedding and, between the maid and her mistress, the used sheets and blankets were removed and new ones placed. Niall's head spun for a different reason as he watched the burst of tasks being done through the room.

'I hadna wanted to bother yer rest these last few days, so the room hasna been swept or cleaned weel,' the woman explained.

'My thanks, Mistress…?' He could not remember her name though he was certain Fia had told him.

'Murray. Mistress Murray,' she said.

'My thanks for your consideration and all your help,' he said with a nod. A slow one that did not bring on the queasiness. 'You have been very helpful to Fia during this time.'

'Yer sister is one of the sweetest lasses I hiv met,' she said. 'The burden she has borne these last weeks after yer injuries! Most women would never manage through such things!'

'Aye, she is a remarkable young woman,' he said. The innkeeper's sharp gaze touched him as he spoke. The tone of his words did not reflect a brotherly attitude, nor did he feel one towards her. He felt… He cleared his throat and nodded. 'I am just sorry that she has had to see to all of this on my account.'

'Weel, ye are on the mend now and will be back on your feet soon enough to begin seeing to things.' Mayhap Mistress Murray did not think that unattached young women should be in charge of things? 'Peigi! Bring some hot water and soap.'

He was left alone a short time later with a bucket of steaming water, a cloth for washing, a cloth for drying and a small crock of soap. It took all his strength to do it, but soon, he was clean and dry for the first time in…months. Only his hair remained unwashed but that would have to wait until he could move more freely.

So much activity so quickly took its toll and he found himself dozing as he sat. Wrapped only in a blanket, he leaned his head back against the wall and rested. He laughed then at his deplorable condition— weak as a bairn and unable to stand or move much without help. And that's where he was when she entered the chamber.

There was some colour in her cheeks now and she did not look so drawn and worried. Tired, though. She did look tired. Small dark smudges laid beneath each eye telling of her lack of rest. He studied this woman who had indeed saved his life. And her reasons for doing so were a complete mystery to him.

She stared at him even as he watched her and he knew there was so much he wanted to say to her. Yet, the words disappeared from his thoughts and he could only watch her as she came in and closed the door.

'I brought you these,' she said, holding out a pile of clothing. 'I fear your others did not survive the journey.' She laughed then at something and her face lit and her eyes shone brightly. ''Twas your coin that bought these.'

'So, you found more than the book and the ring then when you searched my belongings?' She nodded. 'How long had you been planning to escape?' he asked. Now that it was over, it felt a safer topic than some others he wanted to bring up to her.

'From the beginning of it, though once I comprehended you were not Camerons, I knew I needed to get that word to Brodie.'

Smart.

Fia walked over and handed him the shirt. He let the blanket drop to his waist and struggled his way into it. When he could not raise his arm high enough due to the pain, she was there, easing it over his injured shoulder and then holding it as he got it on. A tunic followed the same route and was soon in place over the linen shirt. That left the…trews. She held them out to him and blushed.

'Did you see to my care while I was unconscious?' he asked, accepting the garment. There had been no one else, he suspected. She turned and walked to the other side of the raised pallet in the middle of the chamber without answering. He smiled that she was not shy or intimidated by anything about him.

'Aye,' she said, safely away from him.

'Tell me again how we got out of the camp,' he said to distract her from her discomfort. 'I remember nothing of what happened and little of what you told me earlier.' He wanted her talking. He wanted to hear the voice that had called him back from darkness now while he could see her. 'And, if you would push the trews over that, I will see to the rest.'

His leg, broken indeed, was wrapped in some contraption consisting of wooden slats and linen or cloth strips. A short but wider piece sat under his foot and all of it was tied somehow together, keeping his leg straight. But there was simply no possibility of him leaning over and manoeuvring the garment over it.

'Here,' she said. 'I took out the seam so that it will fit over that. Mistress Murray's cousin Glynis told me how.'

It did work as expected and he was able to put his other leg in and pull them up into place. Exhausted now, he asked her again. Her telling would give him a chance to rest before anything else was expected of him.

'So, how did you get me out of there?'

'Do you remember nothing of it?' she asked.

'I remember trying to distract them by charging them as you ran. I remember the worst of it and them worrying over your escape and the Mackintosh's possible arrival. A few more kicks and nothing.' He touched his head and face. 'I thought my nose was broken. And I could not see out of one eye.'

'Aye, 'twas broken.' She'd pushed it back in place. Would her wonders never cease?

'I hid until everything settled down, then made my way around the camp to see what they were doing,' she explained. 'One by one, those cowards left in the night, walking out quietly so Martainn did not know.'

'And Martainn?' he asked. If the man had been left behind, what had happened to him? From the guilty expression in those bright green eyes, he had his suspicions. 'Not the cooking pot?' He laughed then. 'Poor Martainn.'

'Poor Martainn, my ar...' she began and she stopped. 'The pot was too heavy to wield well, so I used the girdle instead.'

He doubted that any of them stood a chance against

her once she set her mind to something. He'd not or else he would have resisted that urge to see to her safety. He should have simply seduced her and abandoned her when the time came, as an outlaw would have. As he should have. To protect his own mission. To save his family.

But once he'd seen her and then when she kissed him in the night, Niall knew he would not be able to do that. Lured in by those eyes and that mouth, tempted by her innocence and intelligence, he had found— at the worst possible moment in his entire life—the woman he'd dreamt of finding.

For, as smart and self-reliant and confident and resourceful and caring as she was, Fia Mackintosh was not a suitable bride for Lord Niall Corbett of Kelso. He could not have both her and everything promised by the King. 'twas one or the other and sadly he knew what his choice must be. When the time came, he would see her back to her family and be eternally grateful that he'd found her.

'It only took one time and he slept,' she was saying then. 'I knew we must get out of there, so I packed up what I could. Getting you on the horse took the longest time.'

'I must have been a dead weight to you? How did you do it?' Resourceful again.

'You were awake for part of it,' she explained. 'I just did it. I decided that I would get you out of there and you could return that ring to its owner.' She reached up and touched the neckline of her gown. 'I have kept it safe for you. And the book of hours, though I have been reading that each night.'

The thought of her holding his mother's book tore

at his heart. More, she'd known it was important in spite of his refusal to reveal anything about it to her. In spite of that, she'd found it and brought it along.

'I am glad that it is being used.' He smiled at her. 'And I hope you are praying for my wicked soul as my m—' He managed to stop himself before he revealed anything more.

'I am,' she said, smiling back at him then.

'And what of Martainn?' he asked. 'Must we pray for your soul as well?'

'You might find this something that is difficult to believe, sir,' she said, standing and walking over to the door. 'Before I met you, I neither cursed nor hit people with pans or pots. I was a well-behaved young woman in service to a lady. So, I must blame my sins on you,' Fia said. 'Clearly you are the cause.'

Before he could respond, she pulled open the door and walked out, returning a few minutes later with young Tomas and Munro. She stood back while they aided him in returning to the bed. This time, he insisted on sitting up.

'You should not fight on this. Give in to what your body is telling you.'

She'd spoken those words like the true innocent she was and all Niall could do was sit in silence while observing the smirks on the faces of young Tomas and Munro. Inappropriate or not for a brother and sister to say, the lads picked up on the tawdry double meanings of words even if she did not. The devil was on his own shoulder and he nodded them out of the chamber before replying.

'If you order me to bed, lass, I would never argue the point,' he said, watching her face for the expected becoming blush. 'I hope you will join me as you did that last night we had in the cave?'

'You must be feeling better if you can jest like that,' she whispered, adjusting the covers in spite of his suggestive words. He noticed that she could not stop herself from helping him.

Jesting took his strength and instead of pithy reply, he yawned loud and long. She laughed right in his face then and, especially to hear such a thing after so much danger and trouble, he loved the sound and sight of it. He loved...

Niall searched her face then, staring at her beautiful green eyes, and knew the truth—he had fallen in love with the one woman he could never claim.

He did not fight the exhaustion and let it claim him then.

Fia sighed as he fell into sleep's grasp. He'd given her the strangest look just before his eyes closed then. The man truly had no idea of what had happened over the last fortnight.

She'd slept at his side every night except the ones they'd spent at the monastery. There, he was left in the care of the brothers and she was given a room in the area outside the gates reserved for lay people who visited. And when they travelled with the others, she kept a distance but was with him. Once here at the inn, separated only by a blanket, she held him through the night.

She picked up the drying cloths and buckets to return them to the kitchen. Within a few minutes, the chamber was straightened and he was snoring softly. Seeing him awake just then, sitting in that chair with that wicked smile had made it so clear to her that she'd almost lost him.

He'd almost died several times. When the fever caught hold of him, sending him into convulsions from the heat, she knew he would die. And he did not. Then when he would not wake, the brother at the monastery told her he would simply slip off life's hold and pass into death without ever opening his eyes. That was when she took him from there. The brothers must have thought her mad, but they did arrange for their travel.

So when she saw him sitting there, she wanted to cry. Though worn out and thinner, his beard scruffy and his hair a tangled mess, she understood he would live. She'd made all sorts of bargains with the Almighty during those long, dark nights and she wondered which one He'd accepted.

The one in which she promised to never disobey her parents again?

Or the one when she said she would never utter a bad word or impolite phrase again in her whole life?

Or the one when she vowed to never look on him in a wanton and sinful way or to kiss him ever again if he lived?

Knowing what was preached by the church, she suspected it must be that last one, but she could not help the way she felt when she was near him. Even in his deepest sleep, when he could not know she was there, he would gather her close and whisper to her. A few times, Fia thought him awake and speaking to her. Only when she saw that his eyes were closed and he could not be roused did she understand.

Trying to sort out her thoughts, she retrieved the book of hours and opened it. Fia felt guilty, reading from such a fine, expensive and personal gift as this was. Not many people could afford to own such a book let alone commission one made for them. She'd been permitted to read any book that Arabella or Brodie owned and understood what an honour and privilege that was. But to sit here and hold this one was special and she knew it. She smiled then as she saw the name once more. Elizabeth Corbett.

His mother, she knew now. Iain had slipped twice in referring to the owner of this book. Who must be or have been a wealthy woman. Or she could have received it as a gift from someone wealthy. Fia sighed, knowing that she would understand nothing until or unless he revealed his identity to her.

The rains did come as Mistress Murray had predicted, but these were calm and quiet when she compared them to the wild Highland storms they'd had. After she'd helped with chores in the kitchen, against the woman's orders, she crept back into the chamber to find him yet sleeping. Fia removed her shoes and stockings and slid on to the bed next to him as she did each night.

When he shifted his arm, she lay closer, resting her head on his chest where she could listen to his heart beating. Strong and calm now which eased her fears even more. Some time in the night, his arm gathered her in and she moved closer, carefully resting her arm over his chest. Almost asleep, his whisper surprised her.

'Why, Fia? Why did you save me?' he asked.

They'd spoken several times over the last days and after he'd slept, he remembered nothing of the conversations. Part of her needed to tell him, to tell him a secret of her own even when he would not share his. She'd lied earlier. Her reasons had nothing to do with his actions and were completely about her.

Her needs. Her dream. Her imaginings.

She would say it and get the weight of it off her soul. He would sleep through it and never remember. Mayhap then she could deal with him rationally and return home when the time came?

'I saved you because I wanted my dreams to come true, Iain. I'd dreamt of being swept up by a handsome rogue, falling in love and finding my future with him. As Arabella did. As Eva did.' She took in a slow breath and let it out on a sigh. 'I wanted that, too.'

He did not move or react so she knew him to be asleep.

'If I saved you, mayhap you could love me. If you loved me, my silly, girlish dreams could come true. If…'

She'd closed her eyes against the tears that came. Tucking her head down, she let sleep claim her then.

So she never saw him watching her as she spoke or saw the pain in his gaze when he realised he would kill those dreams very soon.

Chapter Seventeen

Alan realised he'd made a serious mistake when he'd discovered the camp empty.

He'd found the tracks of men and horses all along his path up the mountainside and the area at the top was a disaster. They'd left in a hurry. They'd left separately. They'd left in two different directions. He found signs of all of those things. But as he went from cave to cave, he'd found nothing to tell him if Fia was alive or dead.

There was blood and signs of a struggle involving a number of people. Broken things and chaos. But no sign of Fia. He knew from his previous time here and from what Brodie had told him that there were hiding places to ensure his people could escape from an attack. Well, this had looked like there had been an attack in several places around the camp.

He'd searched and then began calling for the lass, thinking that she had taken cover and might yet be there. Nothing. No one.

Then, ten days later, he thought he might finally be back on her trail.

After doubling back on the tracks, he'd realised that

one single horse had left the camp using the southern trail. Following that had taken him out of Mackintosh lands along the paths used by the cattle drovers at the end of the summer as they guided their herds to the markets in the south. Since the roads were usually the clearest, most passable roads, they were used by many others the rest of the year.

What he did not understand was why she was going south and east instead of Drumlui? Then, when he'd found more blood along the trail, he worried that she'd been injured and was confused and travelling without direction. He would never forgive himself for leaving her behind and not following Brodie's instructions.

He'd come upon the small village and stopped at the village well. A few coins spread around and he'd found out the truth—'twas the man he'd seen at the camp who was injured, and Fia was taking him to the monastery for help. Completely confused over this development, he'd followed along until he reached that holy place.

Each place along the trail brought more surprises about Fia and this man. At the monastery, she'd claimed him as kin when the monks treated his extensive injuries. He'd caught up to the merchants whom the abbot said had taken them on travelling on the road to Stirling only to find that they'd been left in Crieff. Now, almost two weeks and many miles later, Alan stood in the main square of the market town looking for them.

He'd been here once before very close to the time when the cattle were brought in for the yearly tryst and he was gladdened that it was not then. With a dozen or more head of cattle for every human resident of the town, there was more dust and dirt and shite than could be borne. And fights, murders and deaths as the raucous visitors from the outlying islands and Highlands often found cause to use their fists and swords to settle or cause disputes.

Now though, it was a more pleasant version of itself, and its wide streets were filled with travellers on their way to other places. Unfortunately for him, the inns and places where visitors could take rooms were spread all over the town and not concentrated in one section or another. He wandered the streets, listening and looking in pubs and market stalls for any sign of the lass, all the while trying to sort out why she would yet be with the black-haired man.

If the man even lived. The monks said they'd done what they could and did not expect the man to wake. And that his 'sister' insisted on returning him to their family. Alan shook his head over that bit every time he thought on it.

After three days without a sign of Fia, Alan was ready to admit defeat and return to face an angry Mackintosh chieftain. The only good thing was Alan's knowledge of who was behind the troubles rising between their families and that might save him from the shame of failure. And once Alan reported back to Brodie, he had no doubt that every available warrior and every possible connection and ally would be used to find the girl.

If she had returned once she escaped, her ruination could have been handled. But now, with witnesses reporting her staying with her kidnapper and even helping him escape, it would be more difficult to manage the shame that she would face among their kith and kin.

Then, without warning, he spotted her in the square as she crossed the street. Alan was so certain he would not find her that he nearly missed her, but she appeared to be making her way to the butcher's shop. He knew where she would be.

Though Niall remembered little of the time when he was in the worst pain from his injuries, it did nothing to ease it now as he began to recover from them. After lying abed for all those days, no part of him wanted to move with ease or strength. His leg was the most serious injury and the only good thing about it was that the bone had not broken completely or through his skin.

Glynis assured him he would walk without a limp once the healing was complete. And she insisted that the wooden brace be worn until such a time as she was pleased with his progress. He did not tell her that when he needed to leave for Edinburgh he would go, whether or not she approved.

But, he did appreciate her care. And the way that Mistress Murray had taken Fia in and watched out for her while he could not. Not that he'd ever truly been good at that. Niall stood at the doorway to the kitchen, quite proud of his progress, and watched as the innkeeper ordered everyone about their chores. The lass was in the middle of it and never seemed happier.

Niall had not let on that he'd heard her words or remembered them. 'twas just as cowardly as the outlaws who'd left one of their own behind in the dark of the night. Even admitting to knowing her reasons or her dreams would hurt her more.

He could be on the threshold of being able to reclaim his heritage and his honour. The King would see that his attempt to do his bidding made him worthy of his godfather's favour. He might not have succeeded, but with the clues he had picked up, he could continue to investigate.

Or mayhap the King would show mercy to his mother and sister in response to his heretofore efforts? He rubbed his hands over his face and then caught himself before he stumbled.

As he watched Fia helping there, he could not help but realise that, if he did not please his godfather, there was one good thing to come of it. Her. He could go to Brodie Mackintosh himself and explain his involvement. In confirming that 'twas not a Cameron plot and with the King's signet as proof, Niall might be able to find a place there and keep Fia as his own.

His heart wanted that. His soul did too. She smiled and he knew it. At the sound of her laughter, as one of the servants tried to balance bowls and dance, he needed to claim her. She glanced over at him at that moment and he saw the expression in her gaze.

It made him want to drop all pretence and expose his every secret to her. It made him want to beg her forgiveness. It made him want her as he never had wanted any woman in his life.

What made this ever worse was that he read more than the frank desire in her eyes. She wanted him. Oh, but it was nothing as simple as lust in her gaze. He saw a dangerous combination of wanting and... loving. The nobleman within him urged him to leave now, to make his way to the King and end the charade. The rogue he was now could not have left even if he tried. Every moment with her now was a step towards complete and utter disaster.

Mistress Murray thankfully broke the moment when she stepped between them, on her way down the corridor in which he stood. As he shifted to let her pass, her constant smile disappeared and she whispered so that no one else could hear her.

'Ye are no more brother to her than I am,' she warned. 'If ye hurt that lass, ye'll be answering to me first.' Niall stumbled back against the wall at the vehemence of her words. 'Finish yer game and let her be.'

Did the lass engender the same fierce protection from everyone who met her? He wanted to laugh then, but this was serious. Mistress Murray saw more than Fia did and she was the centre of gossip and talk in this town. Though she used it, he'd noticed, as entertainment, he understood the weapon it could become.

He nodded without saying a word. Arguing would make things more difficult. She knew their story was a fraud and knew he was one as well. But that much, Fia knew. He sensed that the innkeeper knew even more. Her eyes flared when he looked at her.

'Ye talk in yer sleep,' she said. With a glance towards the kitchen, she nodded. 'Finish it.' She walked away, raising her voice and warning him not to stumble.

Niall needed to find a way to get a message to Edinburgh and arrange his return and a meeting with the King. It was a thing that could customarily be arranged through an inn such as this one, with people travelling to and fro, into the King's city on any given day. But, he could not entrust such a message to Mistress Murray now. He had no doubt the woman would read every word of it and raise questions he'd not even thought of then.

He remained out of bed the rest of the day, pushing himself harder than he had. There was so much to do and he must be on his feet to do it all. First, he would find a way to send his message. Then he would seek out a way to get to Edinburgh and make his case to the King. He was tired of the subterfuge. Tired of the constant lying. Tired of deceiving the one person who'd given him his life back.

Mostly he was tired of not having a life to live. Nearly a decade of jumping at the King's commands, doing any nefarious deed he wanted done, was too long. Too much. It needed to be over.

Exhausted in every possible way, Niall lay on the bed later, thoughts and plans and other plans tumbling in his mind. Within days, he needed to set his plan into action. No matter what happened, he would see to the lass. She did not deserve the changes wrought to her life by Iain Dubh or the man he used to be. He rubbed his face and waited for the lass to enter the chamber, ever mindful of Mistress Murray's very credible threat.

Fia had noticed the conversation and encounter between Mistress Murray and Iain and knew the woman saw through their lie. She had a keen eye for seeing through concocted stories. She must have heard thousands of made-up excuses and fabrications while she tended to her guests and customers here. So, it surprised Fia little that the woman had seen through theirs now.

After helping with some of the preparations for the

morning when the inn would be filled with hungry travellers wanting to break their fast before leaving, she tugged off the handkerchief from her hair. No matter how cold it might be outside, a kitchen like this with its huge hearth and oven always lit held the heat within it. She walked to the doorway that led outside and let the cool night air pass over her, easing her as the woman sent her servants off to bed.

'I told ye that ye dinna hiv to do chores like this,' Mistress Murray said.

Holding out a mug of ale to her, the woman motioned to the chairs next to the huge table where most of the kitchen work was done. Fia accepted it gratefully and drank some before sitting down as directed.

'I feel better keeping busy. At home, I am accustomed to helping when I can.' Fia pushed her hair back and, without needing to think about it for her hands were so used to the task, she braided her hair under control again.

'And where is home, Fia?' She'd fallen right into the woman's well-set trap. Before she could think of something to say—for it was more difficult to lie to this woman by the day—Mistress Murray shook her head and patted Fia's hand. 'We both ken yer no' a lowlander named Corbett. Yer a Highland lass by my best guess.'

Fia could not voice another untruth to this woman. She nodded without saying a word.

''Tis no' my intention to pry,' she began. In watching this woman over the last days, Fia understood that her most ardent prying would begin now. 'But are ye in some kind of trouble?' She leaned in closer and spoke softly. 'Ye and yer *brother*?' She winked as she said *brother*, telling her in clear terms that their pretence was over.

'Nay,' she said as confidently as she could. 'We are not in trouble.'

'Then why are ye no' at home? Why are ye travelling wi' him?' She nodded her head in the direction of the chamber Fia shared with Iain.

Fia thought before she answered the question. And then thought again, not willing to give out knowledge about him or even how they'd met, since it could get him in trouble. So, finally, she shrugged.

''Tis quite complicated, Mistress. I will return home, soon I think, but first there is something I need to see to the end,' she admitted.

She'd spoken the truth. No matter how things began between them, she knew in her heart that there was something more now. She saw it in his gaze and heard it in his words. And that was why she would learn his truth before she returned home.

'Dinna be stubborn, lass,' the woman advised. 'I ken yer mam would greet ye wi' open arms no matter what.'

There it was. Stubbornness.

She was too stubborn to let this go. If her whole life had to change, and it would indeed, she wanted to know why. Why had he been there? What did he know? Why did he have to make her fall in love with him? Why could her silly dreams not come true?

Fia knew the answer to the last one and it taunted her every day. Dreams were not meant for the likes of her. Oh, high and mighty Highland lairds and ladies might see theirs come true. But for a simple Highland village girl, no matter the company she kept, it was simply not meant to be.

'Aye, Mistress,' she finally said, standing and washing her mug out in the bucket. 'My mam will welcome me home.'

'But yer no' going yet?'

'Nay. Not yet,' she said, with a shake of her head. Fia glanced down the corridor towards the chamber she shared with him and then back at the woman who was trying to help. 'But soon. Very soon.'

She made her way quietly down the hallway and lifted the latch. He lay on his back on the pallet, his one arm stretched over his head and the other across the pallet as though waiting for her. He mumbled in his sleep constantly, when he was not snoring, but she had understood little of it now.

It had been worse when the fever took control over him. When his body was racked with pain and heat, he did not mumble. He cried out loudly and spoke to the demons that troubled him.

Dishonour. Treachery. Exile.

Terrifying words that were part of the mystery of him. She'd remembered what he'd whispered when she'd asked him what he was—*I am a man who had sold his honour to the one who will pay the most*. What had he done and to whom had he sold his honour?

The strangest thing was the way he said these things in the middle of the night. Pain and remorse filled his voice with every declaration he made. With every name spoken. With every prayer uttered.

Now, since Glynis gave permission to remove the brace at night, he'd been sleeping more soundly.

And spoke little of the things he only remembered in dreams.

Fia stood watching him then and thought of what was coming. No matter how stubborn or curious she was, she knew there was no way to stay here and avoid trouble.

Days. Two, possibly three days were all that was left to them here. A place where she did not ask all the questions she wanted answered. A place where he turned to her in the night and sought and offered comfort. A place where she could pretend everything would work out for them.

Once his leg was stronger, he would travel to Edinburgh and she would lose him. Even though he gathered her in close to him and kissed the back of her head and neck when she settled there, she could not see a way in which she could keep him.

Worse, she suspected that learning the truth would make her want to leave him behind.

Chapter Eighteen

Like the time in the cave, it all began in the middle of the night with a dream.

His kisses had stirred her more than she'd ever admit to him and she'd been thinking about what love play might be like. The women in Drumlui—married, widowed or those with lovers—made no secret of the pleasures that could be had with a man during a long winter's night. Or even a short summer's night.

In her curiosity, she noticed things. Things between men and women. In that first dream, they had done some of those things. She wanted to touch him, so she did, stroking his skin and touching his chest as she'd had a wont to do since watching him undress from his wet clothing. And when she wanted to taste his mouth as he had hers, she did that. All of it happened only in her dream. Until she opened her eyes and realised it was real and her hand was inside his shirt, stroking him.

But this time, it was different. She would not wait for a dream so she could blame her lapse in virtue on something or someone else. Nay, this time she would touch him and kiss him because she wanted to…she wanted…him.

Niall blinked a few times as his eyes opened. His body had reacted to her caresses already for the flesh between his legs swelled and hardened against his belly even now. Meeting his gaze, she pressed her hips closer to him and noticed that flesh surged in size and rigidity against her. Her skin burned now, the fabric of her shift irritated her and she wanted to touch him, her skin to his.

In the dim light of the lantern left burning low, she was watching him as she touched him. He'd taken to wearing his shirt and trews to bed, to keep up the pretence of their kinship should anyone enter without warning. But she wanted them gone now.

'Fia…' He whispered her name and she knew he would try to stop her. But she would not be naysaid in this. She touched her hand to his mouth and shook her head.

'You owe me a boon, Iain Dubh, and I will claim it before we are parted.' His eyes filled with some unknown emotion and then took on the wicked gleam she'd seen before. His body shifted towards her, but he might not have even known that. 'Now, must I take my boon or will you give it freely?'

His mouth moved against her hand, but no sound came out. She smiled then, pleased at rendering him speechless, with his own words and without his usual quick retort. She lifted her hand. 'Well, 'tis your choice.'

'Take your boon, lass,' he whispered. 'Take what you want.'

Fia leaned up on one elbow and just studied him.

Given the choice, given the power, she wanted to touch him…everywhere. So, she got up on her knees at his side and began lifting the edge of his linen shirt. He eased his body up off the bed a bit so she could remove it and then he laid back.

His body was impressive, even now after the injuries. He would give even Brodie a good fight with his strong chest and arms. She lifted her hand and stroked with one finger from his shoulder to his neck and then down, following the whorls of black curls on to his chest. When one finger was not enough, she spread her fingers out and slid them into the hair there. When he jolted as she touched his dark brown male nipple, she smiled.

When his breathing changed and he began to pant in shallow, quick breaths as she circled the sensitive areas, she did what she wanted to do. Taste him. Crouching up on her knees, she kissed along his jaw, skimming her lips over his several times. He grabbed her head and pulled her against his mouth and opened to her tongue.

Her body shook as she swept her tongue deeply into his mouth, seeking and finding and suckling on his. The place between her legs began to throb and grow wet. Her breasts ached and the tips hardened much like his flesh had. She pulled away at the thought and watched as it moved within his trews. She'd seen it when he'd changed his garments in the cave, but not enough to satisfy her curiosity well enough.

'Nay, lass,' he warned, seeing her intention. He reached out to grab her hand and she shook her head.

''Tis my boon to take as I please.'

'Lass.' One word, elongated into a sound that almost sounded as though he begged for something. Was he begging her to touch him or not to?

At first, she outlined the shape and size and hardness of it with her fingers. It moved to her touch and his hips thrust with each caress. He barely breathed now, gasping with each inch closer she moved. Fia tugged at the laces, loosening the front piece, and then she slid her hand inside. The curls there were tighter, springier, than the ones on his chest. And then she found his flesh and wrapped her hand around it. Hot. Smooth and hard. His manhood pulsed against her palm as she stroked its length. He hissed and reached down to take her hand.

'Did I hurt you?' she asked. She lessened her grip and stroked the length of it gently.

'Nay.' His voice was hoarse and more like a groan.

'Should I stop?'

His answer was to thrust his hips once more, sending his flesh surging into her palm. Still grasping him, she set about to explore all the other interesting places on his body. The muscles of his chest and stomach rippled at every caress. She tugged his trews out of her way, pushing them down to expose his hips and thighs to her view. The lines and ridges that led from his hips to his manhood drew her gaze and her fingers and soon he was gasping and moaning.

'Stop, I beg you,' he said, covering her hands with his. 'Or I will shame myself.' He took several slow, deep breaths, holding her hands still while he did. Fia eased her hands from him and slid from the bed.

'What are you doing?'

She knew she had him at a disadvantage. He still needed some help getting on and off that pallet and his leg did not move easily yet without pain. He was trapped there and she liked it but she truly did not know what to do next. He smiled the wicked smile of a rogue and held out his hand to her.

'Come back here,' he whispered, drawing her down to his side once more. 'Lie here.' He entwined their fingers and pulled her next to him. He slid one arm under her and shifted until they lay facing each other. He reached behind her head and loosened her braid. 'That is something I have wanted to do since I saw you in the village.'

The touch of his hands as he used his fingers to shake the braid apart sent a tingling through her whole body. He gathered much of it in his hand and brought it over her shoulder, spreading it on his naked chest. Then, he leaned down and kissed her mouth. In one moment, it was gentle and easy and in the next he took control and took her mouth with relentless attention. She lost herself in the heat of his mouth and the caress of his hands.

Niall smiled against her mouth. Once more she'd surprised him. First in demanding her boon and then in being the one to control the passion that flared between them. There was a second when he thought she meant to put her mouth on his erection and he nearly passed out from the anticipation of it. Now though, the bigger surprise was that she once again put herself into his hands.

She shifted next to him, pressing closer and closer until he lifted her and laid her across him. Guiding her leg over his hip, he loved the pressure on his hardened flesh. He gathered the edge of her shift and slid it up, caressing her thigh and then cupping her bottom as he moved. The scent of her arousal spread around them as he turned and opened her thighs wider around him.

Now he made her gasp, returning the intimate touches to the most sensitive place on her body. She met his gaze as he slid the back of his hand along the inside of her leg, closer and closer to the curls there. He stopped less than an inch from the damp folds of flesh he longed to touch, to kiss, to suckle. He held still until she moved, thrusting her hips forward against his hand. Turning it, he parted the curls and delved into the folds, sliding one and then two fingers along them.

Her open-mouthed breathing excited him. He pressed deeper, using his thumb to find the small, raised nub that would intensify her pleasure. When he did, she pulled her hips back from the intense, exquisite caress.

'Too much?' he asked, not moving. She nodded and then shook her head and then shrugged, confused and surprised, he thought. 'Come back to me.' A few shallow breaths and then she slid her hips back to his hand. His thumb pressed against that place but he let her choose to move. Soon, she was allowing him to stroke her there.

Her head fell back and he felt her body tightening around his fingers. Her own fingers tried to find purchase on his skin and she raked her nails over his chest. Pushing in deeply, Niall slid one finger inside her, and then another, watching her reaction to each. A low, soft moan began from deep in her throat and he knew what would happen.

'Rock your hips, lass,' he whispered. There was so much more he wanted to do then, so many places he wanted to taste and pleasure, but this night was not for that. His bollocks tightened too, aroused to bursting at the sight of her melting against his hand.

Niall shifted more to his side, opening her up to him, and increased the pressure against the nub that now hardened like his flesh did. With one finger, he slid back the hood of flesh and touched it directly, just as could be done to his erection. She gasped and then her body shuddered and trembled against him. He did not stop rubbing and stroking and plunging his fingers into her until her body surrendered and collapsed against him.

He held her in his arms then, sliding her leg down and tugging her shift back to cover her. She was not even aware of him then, for the pleasure had overwhelmed her. So, he lay there, with her in his arms, feeling quite noble. His prick was not happy, it lay there on his belly hard and unsatisfied, but Niall would hold to his decision about her.

He might not be able to keep her, but he would not take her virtue. He might have pleasured her, he might even have seen the first time she was aroused and reached satisfaction, however, hapless Dougal would be in for a surprise when his bride proved to be a virgin in the marriage bed. Something deep within Niall, some feeling from the days when his family yet lived together and he was being groomed as his father's heir, unfurled inside him and made him think he was not a complete and utter failure.

Chapter Nineteen

Fia watched as he walked unaided across the yard before the inn. It was the most level place for him to practise. He held his walking stick, procured by Mistress Murray's cousin for his use, but refused to rely on it. For most of the last hour or so, it stood up, stuck in the dirt like a strange plant, where he'd put it.

It pleased her to see him so improved, even while her heart broke with each passing day. She'd not gathered up enough courage to ask him for his story. When he'd touched her with such passion and such caring, she could almost believe he would not leave her. His restlessness as he improved in strength and endurance each day simply pushed the truth ever closer. Fia understood that when he finally asked her to turn the ring and prayer book back to him, it would be time.

For now, she was determined to enjoy every moment with him so that she could savour the memories even into her old age. As he passed her by, counting aloud for the number of times he'd crossed the yard, he smiled and touched her hand. Though the day was fair with a bit of spring chill in the air, he was sweating from the effort. After he made it across and back one more time, she stepped in front of him.

'This is enough, Iain. You should rest before you tire yourself out completely.'

He accepted the mug of ale from her and drank it in two long swallows. When he handed it back to her and turned, she stopped him, her hand on his arm.

'You just rose from your sickbed not five days ago. Do you wish to return to it so soon?' she asked.

'You sound like a nagging fishwife, Fia.' Standing in the middle of the yard, surrounded by animals, travellers and dust, with her hands on her hips now, Fia thought she might be one. He smiled then and nodded. 'You have the look of one as well.'

'I think I have been listening to Mistress Murray too closely,' she admitted.

'And you like to be in charge of things,' he said. Though he teased her, she knew it for the truth it was. She did like to say what, where, when and how things should be accomplished. He walked to her side and leaned in closer. ''Tis a failing of yours I have noticed lately.'

'Twas true—she did not like to sit around and be told what to do. Oh, that was exactly what she did within the household of the chieftain, but the trouble she got into usually involved matters of control.

'Make no mistake,' he said softly now, catching her gaze with his. 'I cannot complain about your tendency to take over matters, for if you had not, I would have died.' He reached out to take her hand and she gave the tiniest shake of her head to warn him off. Their pretence still stood in place. 'I will be grateful to you for ever, nagging fishwife or not.'

'Fia, lass!' the innkeeper called out to her. 'Can ye pick up my order at the butcher's? 'tis small enough for ye to manage.'

'Aye, Mistress,' she said. 'Do you feel strong enough to walk with me? You have seen nothing but the inn and this yard. 'tis no more than three streets up and two over.' He looked fit and strong standing before her.

'I will need my sword and bring along our purse,' he said. She smiled when he called it that. She'd spent whatever coins she'd needed from his.

Within a few minutes, they were walking slowly away from the inn for the first time since they'd arrived there almost a sennight ago. Once they turned the corner and were out of sight of the building, Iain stopped for a moment.

'I need to find the bailiff's house,' he said. 'Do you know where it is?'

'Aye.' She only knew because she'd witnessed a fight in the streets one of the first times she'd walked out and the perpetrators had been dragged away by the bailiff to face punishment. 'When we turn left to the butcher's, the bailiff's is to the right.' She did not ask. She would not ask.

'I need to send a message to the King's minister and the bailiff would be the most trustworthy in that task.'

It began now. The first step in the journey that would see them separated. It surprised her how much it hurt. All she could do was nod and take a deep breath to let the pain subside. As they walked, Fia felt him slip his hand around hers in between their bodies where it would be hidden from the sight of others.

She tried to talk as they walked, pointing out various merchants and people of interest to him that she'd met or heard Mistress Murray gossip about. Crieff was a large and busy market town and there was so much to see as they walked. Iain did not ask or add much to her conversation and she could see he was deep in thought. When they reached the crossroads she'd mentioned, she stopped and nodded to the right.

'The bailiff's is that large house, the third one on this street,' she said, pointing to it. 'Shall I wait for you?'

'Nay, go on to the butcher's and I will see you back at the inn, Fia,' he said. She turned because she did not want him to see the tears that burned in her eyes. He grabbed her hand and tugged her back to face him. 'I wish, I have prayed that there would be a different way to handle this and there is not. I will explain it all when we get to Edinburgh.' She nodded, praying the tears would cease gathering. 'One more thing.' Fia looked up at him, waiting. 'I need the ring.'

'Twas his ring, so why it should bother her so much to give it back, she knew not. She lifted it out from beneath her gown and over her head. Gathering up the leather strip she wore it on, she placed it in his hand. He closed his fist around it and stepped back.

'I will see you at the inn,' he said. Then he strode off in a slow, measured gait, avoiding horses and people across the street. He changed somehow as he walked away, he carried himself differently, became someone different.

In those moments, she felt the first cut in the tenuous fabric that bound them together. At first, she could not see her way for the tears, but she soon brought herself under control and wiped them away. Fia found the butcher's street and turned towards it. As she passed by the opening of a small side lane, someone grabbed her and dragged her into the shadowed passageway. She was pushed up against a wall with a large, masculine hand over her mouth before she could take a breath.

'Fia!' The voice sounded familiar but only when the man pushed the hood back off his head did she recognise him.

'Alan Cameron?' she asked, searching his face. 'Why are you in Crieff?'

'Come away here,' he urged as he tugged her deeper into the darkened alley. 'We need to speak.' She followed him without resistance and he stopped a short distance further. 'Brodie sent me, Fia. He sent me to find you.'

His words shocked her. It did not make sense until she considered it for a minute…or two…or three. Alan was the best tracker in both of their clans. He had, from the time he was a child, been able to find anything lost or stolen. He'd found Arabella when Brodie had kidnapped her. At the camp in the mountains.

'You went to the camp?' He nodded. 'You followed them to the mountain?' Another nod. 'When?'

'It matters not.' He brushed off the rest of her questions. 'I will take you home now.' He glanced towards the main street. 'Before he comes back.'

'He? You mean Iain?' she asked.

'Aye. I know he kidnapped you from the village and took you to the mountain camp. I was there when the storm hit. Then after I followed one of the men when he left the camp to his destination, I came back to get you out and you, and everyone, were gone.' He pushed his hair back and rubbed his face. 'God Almighty, I thought you must be dead when I saw all the blood!'

'I am well, Alan. Truly,' she said, hugging him. Brodie had sent help as she'd expected. 'You came alone?'

'Aye. Brodie wanted to keep it as quiet as possible. To avoid…avoid… Oh, hell, Fia, he wanted to protect your reputation as much as he could.' Even under the dirt on his face, she could see the faint blush fill his cheeks. He raked his hair back once more and shrugged.

'So now?'

'Now, we leave. I have secured two horses and they're waiting for us on the other side of the town. He cannot move quickly so he'll have no way to follow or stop us.' Alan slid his hand around her arm and began to walk. 'I have coin enough and credit on Brodie's name for whatever you need for the journey. We will head south to Stirling and then west from there to home.'

The answer to every problem stood before her with a plan, a good plan, to see her home safely. She would never have to see Iain again. Never have to face him walking away from her. Never know the truth that drove him.

'I cannot come with you, Alan.' She stepped back, pulling her arm free.

'I do not know what he has done to you, Fia. Why you would want to see to his care and bring him here and then stay with him. But Brodie gave me orders and I will take you home.'

'I will return home, but not yet. I need another day or two. He is not what he seems, Alan.'

'Fia! He is a murdering, thieving outlaw. Even if he was not the one ordering the attacks, he took part in them.'

'He is connected to the King, Alan. There is more going on here than you know,' she said. The similarity to Iain's words was not lost on her.

'The King, Fia? The King? He is leading you on a merry dance. Using you, lass, for his own purposes. I saw you at the camp. The two of you.' He grabbed her by the shoulders and forced her to look at him. 'He was seducing you, lass. Using you for his own purposes. Even now, even here, he uses you.'

'He has the King's signet,' she said in a furious whisper. 'He seeks a meeting with his minister now.'

'Anyone can make a signet, Fia lass. Would you know a real one if you saw it? But, come now. Before it is too late,' Alan said, once more pushing her along the alleyway towards the road.

Fia tried to stay calm, but she knew she could not go with him. If she did, she would never find peace and she would regret and mourn the man she loved. So, she did the only thing she could…she ran. When she got to the street, she shouted for help. When Alan got there, he was besieged by people trying to help her.

Surprised for only a moment, he stared at her in disbelief and then took off running. No one could catch him, so Fia knew he would be safely away without harm. She watched as he disappeared around the corner, heading towards the other side of Crieff.

The butcher waved her inside his shop, offering her ale and a place to sit while she waited for Mistress

Murray's order. He complained loud and long over the increase in these petty street crimes. Guilt assailed her over what she had called down on Alan's head, but she'd made her decision many days ago. She'd been through Highland storms, a hellish journey, a life-and-death struggle, had found the man of her dreams and would lose him soon enough.

But she would see this to the end, though her foolish heart filled with its foolhardy dreams kept beating with hope of an outcome more to her liking. Damn her stupid heart and her silly dreams!

Alan scrambled through the back alleys, behind, around and through stores and shops and inns and pubs, and managed to escape the angry mob Fia had called down on him. Now, sitting inside the stables where the horses awaited him behind an inn at the edge of Crieff, he tried to figure out what had gone wrong. He had often heard his father and Brodie and other married men lament over the strongheaded women in their lives, but he'd never thought of Fia in that way.

He'd known her since she was a wee one in the camp. He'd barged in, intent on saving Arabella, and been captured by Brodie. He'd met her during the few days he'd been held, not unkindly, as prisoner until Arabella had freed him to escape. He'd continued to see the girl during visits over these last six years to Drumlui Keep and on her visits, travelling with Arabella, to The Cameron strongholds.

Now sitting here, pressing a cloth to the cut on the back of his head, he wondered if rescuing women was his strongest talent. Mayhap he should only search for lost animals or stolen property and leave the saving of maidens to others?

The only good to come from this startling encounter with Fia was that he knew their destination—Edinburgh. Whatever this Iain was doing, whatever he'd gotten into, he was taking that ring back to the King. If he'd stolen or fabricated it, the man would be facing his own death. Which made no sense.

Brodie and Alan's own cousin both had factors who lived in Edinburgh and waited on the pleasure of the King while overseeing their masters' business in the city. Large fortunes were traded there, goods of all sorts shipped from the city's harbour to ports all over England, Scotland, Ireland and the Continent.

Alan decided to seek out Brodie's factor and send a message to the chieftain concerning the whereabouts of his wife's servant. He would wait on further orders before trying to take the lass anywhere.

And he would seek out information about the man he knew to be behind the attacks. That was not the kind of information to trust to any message carried by any messenger that was not himself. But that would keep for now. If he could not get the lass away, he would still try to protect her as much as he could, even if 'twas from herself.

He left that day, not waiting to begin his journey to Edinburgh. If the lass was telling the truth, if the man was telling her the truth, they would get to the King's city not too far behind him.

Chapter Twenty

It took only two days to receive a reply to his message. The bailiff recognised the royal seal and could not help him enough in sending a messenger. Niall returned to the bailiff each day and was there when the messenger arrived with the answer to his request—the King would receive him privately at the guest house of Holyrood Abbey four days hence.

He took as a better sign the invitation to stay at the minister's home just outside the abbey's grounds the night before their meeting, *to prepare* the note said. Niall touched the ring that lay under his tunic and offered a prayer he would be successful and see his family reunited in their home.

Four days before he could make his argument to this godfather to return his status, his lands, his honour.

Four days before he would lose Fia.

He'd hired a small wagon to take them there, his leg not strong enough to ride a horse yet, and because it would give Fia a place to sleep if they could not find an inn. Now the drovers' roads that Fia had used to bring him from the mountains and to here became the main pathways from town to town. But even the sun, shining brightly on a clear, cool morning, did not brighten the lass's face as they took their leave.

'My thanks again, Mistress Murray,' he called down once he manoeuvred himself on to the seat and straightened out his leg. With the wooden brace back in place, it took some help from the lads to make it possible. The brace, he thought, would be removed at their first stop.

'Ye take care,' she called back, 'and ye see to our lass.' The dark glare in her eyes belied her good wishes. If she knew what he would do, she would not be trying to be polite to him. Nay, she would be beating him with the broom she kept by the kitchen doorway and chasing him away from *our* lass.

Niall watched as she bent her head down, whispering to Fia. Every so often the lass would glance at him and nod at the woman. He tried not to stare, but lost the battle. Then, though she thought he did not see it, the older woman reached into her skirt and tucked something in Fia's hand, closing her fingers around it so no one could see. More whispering followed before Fia threw her arms around the woman and hugged her. When a group of men arrived on horseback, Mistress Murray pulled away from Fia, smiled and waved her off.

The woman was, from the first to the last, a woman of business.

Niall reached over and helped Fia up on to the seat next to him. He'd noticed she'd slipped whatever the woman gave her into the convenient slit in her cloak before climbing up. Once she was settled, he shook the reins and guided the horse out on to the busy town streets.

She'd not asked any questions of him when he'd returned from the bailiff's. Nor anything at all during the last three days as he sought out a way for them to travel. And part of him wished she would yell and scream at him like a fishwife, using some of the terrible words she knew, rather than the quiet acceptance in her gaze.

The only time he'd been able to make her react was in the dark of night when she climbed into bed beside him and continued her exploration of things between a man and a woman. He never initiated it. He'd convinced himself not to touch her now that their paths would be going separately. He had used her for so much that he would not do this.

And each night, as she stripped off her shift and stood naked before him, he damned the only noble scruples he could find within himself. As his body screamed to take her, to spread her legs and fill her with his flesh, he would not. When his dreams showed him the ecstasy of claiming her, he refused to act on it. Then, after giving her as much pleasure as his hands and mouth could give her each night, he quietly saw to his own matters to avoid taking the only thing he had not taken from her.

'So, the road south?' he asked as they reached the crossroads.

'Follow this one to the edge of town,' she said, pointing to the next street they encountered.

'We will take the road south to Stirling, then on to Falkirk and Edinburgh.' He did have one question for her. 'What did Mistress Murray give you?' Niall nodded at the edge of her cloak.

'A purse with enough coins to return to her inn, if I need to,' she answered. Another person setting out to protect the lass. He shook the reins at the horse and they began the long journey ahead of them in silence.

The weather favoured them that day and they reached Stirling by day's end, even finding a place to stay. He used the time to ask about her family and her service to the Lady Mackintosh. She told stories of all sorts and he loved seeing the vibrant way she described the goings-on of her kith and kin. He'd missed all of that in the last ten years.

The second day, the rains were back and he was grateful that the lass had bought their supplies. Two lengths of good Highland woven tartan saved them from being soaked to the skin as they continued as far as they could along the muddy road. But talking was difficult until they sought and found shelter in an old, unused barn for the night.

The knowledge that everything would change on the morrow hung in the very air around them as they finished their simple meal of cheese and bread and ale and settled in for the night. Niall knew her questions would not be held back now and, in a way, he wanted to tell her everything. Even now though, he could not. The King did not wish his secret spy to become known.

And hopefully she would never learn about his father's treason and the depths to which Niall had sunk or the nefarious acts he'd committed since then. Or the exile of his mother to a convent. Or the shame of a forced and inappropriate marriage that his sister had to bear, if she yet lived.

So, as the rain yet fell outside, he held her in his arms and allowed himself to consider whether all of what he'd done so far would be worth the reward he wanted. Whether loving her and giving her up after seeing a tiny sliver of the man he wanted to be was worth more to him than his goal. Whether she was enough to make him give up on his hopes of seeing his family reunited, whole again, after so many years.

If he reclaimed his life, she was lost to him. The King would, no doubt, have a suitable bride already in mind and to his own purposes. If he walked away, he could never claim her for he was guilty of so many transgressions and could do nothing to prove himself other than guilty. Niall would never make her suffer the life on the run as he had lived these past months and years. She deserved better than that. She deserved better than him.

Bloody hell, even hapless Dougal would be better for her than he would be! He laughed then and she turned in his arms to look at him with a frown.

'I was just thinking on hapless Dougal,' he admitted, though not the rest of it.

'Why do you call him that?' she asked.

'I watched him trying to convince you to accept his offer and could tell he had no chance,' Niall admitted. 'He seemed so mild-mannered and, well, hapless.' He met her gaze then. 'Will you have to settle for him?' He had not meant to ask it in that way, but it brought up the painful topic.

'Somehow I think he would be settling for me now, Iain.'

'And you would take him knowing that?' She would be tolerated. She would be a scandal. She would need to endure knowing what they thought of her…all because of him.

'I think I might enjoy a lack of adventure in my life,' she said. 'For a time at the least.'

'Fia, I am sorry,' he began. She put her hand over his lips once more.

'Why did you do it? Tell me why you took me from the village, Iain?'

She wanted the truth. She deserved something.

'Niall.' He looked at her. 'My name is Niall.'

Fia had no idea of what prompted this strange conversation except that this would be the last time they were truly alone together. And now hearing his true name she smiled. 'Niall then?' He nodded. 'Niall… Corbett? And Elizabeth is…?'

'My mother. The book belonged to my mother.' She let it go then, the sadness in his voice made her heart hurt for him and his loss.

'So, Niall Corbett, why did you take me from the village?' Fia sensed there were boundaries that he would not cross, truths he would not expose, but that did not mean she would not seek what she needed to know. He let out a sigh and gathered her closer.

'Anndra and Micheil had plans for you, lass,' he said. 'At first, when Lundie backed me on it, I was going to let you be. Then Anndra came back intent on having you.' He shifted and leaned on his elbow, looking down at her. 'He knocked you out and would have dragged you off into the woods, if I had not taken you myself.' He leaned over and kissed her then, a gentle touch on her mouth. 'I had no choice.'

So he'd never intended to ravish her, then. He'd tried to save her and ended up bringing her into the middle of this misadventure that would change her life for ever. And Lundie… Something tickled her memory about Lundie but she could not bring it to mind now.

'I thank you for that, Niall Corbett,' she whispered, stroking his chest. 'Why were you there? You have not done one roguish thing since I met you.'

'Oh, Fia.' He laughed, burying his face against her chest, laying kisses all over her. Even through the layers of clothing, it made her tingle and ache for more. 'I think I have been roguish to you lately.' She grabbed him by the hair and lifted his head up so she could see his face.

'I am certain that I took advantage of you, Niall.' His gaze softened as she spoke his name. His true name. 'You were in your sickbed and I slaked my lustful feelings on you.' She smiled. 'You could not escape me.'

He laughed then and she joined him. It felt better to be light-hearted than morose and crying. There would be time for that later, when he left her.

'I found myself on the wrong side of the King's judgement,' he said. She watched his face for signs that he was jesting. 'So when he wanted someone who could find the cause behind these recent problems between the Mackintoshes and The Camerons, he sent me to join them.' He rolled away from her, lying on his back and staring off into the dark corners of the barn.

'So you became an outlaw.' The words stayed there between them and she realised that, though he might have saved her for some reason, he had been part of all the attacks on her clan.

'Aye. Now I must return with the news that I failed.'

'What will happen?' She leaned up now and put her hand on his chest. He covered it with his, entangling their fingers. 'What had he promised in return?'

'To save my family. My mother. My sister.'

'Oh, Niall,' she whispered. 'What will happen to them now?'

'I plan to throw myself on his mercy and hope that he has some. There are some details I can give him. I hope they are enough.' He lifted her hand to his mouth and kissed it. ''Tis that uncertainty and more that forces me to let you go.'

His tone was intractable, the words his final decision. And she could think of no way to change his mind or change the course of things. So Fia offered him the only thing she had to give.

'I love you, Niall Corbett. I just need you to know that when tomorrow and the days after come.'

She had hoped he would tell her of his love, but he did not. He pulled her close and kissed her, letting her feel his longing. Then he turned her on her side and lay behind her, tucked close with her.

The rest of the night had passed in silence as did the early morning when they rose and began the last part of their journey together. With each mile they crossed, Niall became less and less like Iain Dubh and by the time they rode through the West Port gate into Edinburgh, the man at her side was someone she did not know. He'd told her only that he would be meeting the King at Holyrood Abbey the next day and that they had a place to stay for the night near that place.

As they made their way down the crowded and

busy street called Cowgate, she marvelled at the sights
around her. The castle stood above them on an ancient mountain with a ridge before it that led down
to the town of Cannongate and further to the abbey.
Tightly packed buildings nestled on either side of the
ridge halfway down to the abbey. They rode by and
Fia found herself fascinated by the sights and sounds
of such a huge city.

They continued along the rural road, leaving the
castle and city behind and riding towards another crest
of mountainous crags that rose to twice the height of
the castle's rocky platform. And there, at the foot of
these crags, lay the abbey of the Holyrood, founded
by the King's ancestor of the same name. The abbey
held all the lands around it, including the park and
loch and more. Fia had to keep reminding herself to
close her mouth and keep breathing.

She thought the Highlands and her home were
beautiful, and they were, but this city appealed in
many different ways. As they turned on to a small
road near the entrance to the abbey's lands, Fia knew it
was time. Niall stopped the wagon near a stone house
and waited. Servants immediately came out to assist
him down from the cart and aided him in walking up
the steps at the front of the house.

When she looked up, a man of powerful bearing
stood there in the door, waiting for him. Niall bowed
deeply before the man and waited. The man touched
his shoulder and then pulled him into an embrace and
towards the door. Niall stopped then and turned to
face her.

'This is Brodie Mackintosh's ward. See to her comforts,' he said in a voice that commanded obedience.

And then he left her behind, walking into the fine house with the other man.

It was over. Well and truly over.

Now all she needed to do was convince herself and that damn silly heart beating rapidly in her chest that it was done.

Chapter Twenty-One

'Yours was the last face I thought to see here, Alex,' Niall said as he followed his cousin along the hallway. 'I thought you were still in France.'

'Ah, not now,' Alexander Lindsay, Earl of Struthers, answered. 'While I am here, the King asked me to see to this matter with you.' His mother's sister had married, a second time, to Alex's father, making them more kith than kin. He waved Niall to one of the chairs and motioned to one of the waiting servants. Once they both had glasses of wine, Alex asked, 'So what the hell is this matter I must see to?'

Niall downed the wine and held out his glass for more. If the servants thought that a filthy-looking, unkempt man should not be sitting here with the earl drinking this costly wine, they kept it to themselves. But Niall noticed a few unguarded glances aimed his way before they looked away. As though they expected him to attack their lord and rob the house of all its costly items.

'Did the King not explain?' he asked. Better to know what Alex knew before sharing too much.

'Some Highland problem between two of their clans or such,' Alex said. 'You were to find the source of the trouble.' Before he spoke again, a manservant entered and whispered to the earl.

'A bath is ready for you,' he said, nodding to the servant. 'And clothing as well. You cannot appear before the King like this,' his cousin said, pointing at his condition. 'See to his care,' he ordered. 'I will see you at supper.'

Niall decided that clean clothes would not be a bad thing, nor would a hot bath considering how his leg pained him. So, he handed the glass to the waiting servant and followed the other towards the doorway and stairs.

'Niall, is the girl truly the Mackintosh's ward or is she someone you wish me to get rid of for you?' Alex watched him closely, waiting for his answer.

'She is as I said, very dear kin to the chieftain and his wife. If you would, see her clothed and cared for before she is taken to his factor's house here in Edinburgh,' Niall said.

'Very well. A clean break is best in these situations.' But Alex was not done. 'And will there be complications when she is sent there?' A polite way of asking the impolite.

'Come now, Alex. There are always complications when it comes to women,' he said, trying for a lighter tone than his current mood. 'But, nay, her return will be welcomed and without bloodshed.'

He walked out and followed the servant up the staircase to the next floor. His leg ached badly with each step taken. Though he kept watching for some sign of where they'd taken Fia, he saw none. Niall turned himself over to the servants and found himself scrubbed to within an inch of his life, his hair cleaned and clipped and his beard groomed from that of a wild Highlander to a more dignified length and shape.

Then, when the warmth and the wine should have lulled him comfortable, he was struck by a deep restlessness instead. His first thought was to ask Fia to walk with him and see the abbey just up the road. He stopped before taking a step towards the door of the chamber.

For so many weeks he'd come to rely on her and to enjoy her company. He turned to her day and night to talk or ask questions of. When he was in pain, she'd eased it with her soft caresses and words. When frustrated over his leg's slow healing, she had soothed his mood. Even when he'd wanted to do his worst and seduce her, she'd cleverly guided him out of that. And when he wanted to leave her untouched, she'd insisted he not.

Now, he would leave her and everything she was and everything she gave him behind and seek a new life without her. Niall turned away from the door and stood by the large window that gave him a view of the abbey's buildings and park. That was his future. In that place, the King would decide on his petition to return his lands and titles. On the morrow, he could be returned to his status and his earldom once more.

The evening crawled by and Niall was aware of every passing second. Supper with Alex was a pleasant thing, with good food, better wine and stories of his cousin's adventures in France on the business of the King. No mention was made of Fia at all. 'twas as though she'd disappeared from his view, much like the servants did when their duties were done.

When he sought his chambers, he listened for some sound of her. Passing a number of chambers, Niall tilted his head waiting for some noise or the sound of her laughter…or tears.

He was still listening when the sun rose, breaking through the fog and making the dew on the park shimmer in its light.

'Twas like she could not be seen by human eyes.

One moment she was conversing with Niall and then next she became a thing, shuffled around by the servants, fed, bathed, clothed, provided with whatever comforts or care she needed. She never left the very luxurious chamber after she entered it. A maid brought her news and instructions.

Housed somewhere on the lower floor of the three-storey house, she understood. She understood her place now. She'd been told that someone would arrive to take her to Brodie's house in the city after she'd had a chance to eat and pack up whatever she wanted to take with her. Everything from their cart had been brought into her chamber and placed there for her perusal.

Other than the clothing in her bag, there was nothing else she wanted to claim. All of it, any of it would remind her of him. And once she left here, she knew it would take every ounce of willpower and strength she had to forget him. 'twould be better to leave everything behind.

The maid arrived to tell her that her escort was waiting outside and as Fia turned to leave the chamber, she saw it. The book of hours. He'd guarded it for so long and it meant so much to him that she knew she could not keep it. But she would not simply leave it there for him to find. She would have a final word with him.

Pushing by the maid, Fia walked down the hallway where he'd gone on his arrival here. She'd heard the deep voices of him and their host as they talked in a chamber off in this direction. Though the maid tried to stop her, she continued on, listening for the same voices. The manservant in front of the closed door shook his head. She stepped around him, opening the door and stepping into a dining chamber.

'My lord,' the man called out. 'I tried to stop her…'

The man who'd greeted Niall yesterday came to his feet and waved the servant off.

'I beg your pardon, my lord,' she said, curtsying to the nobleman. 'I wanted to return this to Niall before I left.' Glancing around the room, she noticed another man sitting with his back to her. 'I did not mean to interrupt your meal with your guest,' she said.

All she could see was the black hair of the man's head over the chair where he sat. When he stood, with a grace of one born to nobility, and turned to her, she gasped. In the fine clothes of wealth and groomed to meet a king, she would not have recognised him if they'd passed on the street outside.

He looked magnificent. She noticed the expensive clothing that matched the other man's and was suitable for the court of the King. No longer Iain Dubh, the Highland rogue, or even Niall Corbett, the King's spy, this man was…no one she knew. Only when he glanced at the book in her hand did she break free of her stupor and speak.

'I did not want to leave and not return this to... you.' Her voice shook and there was simply no way to control it.

'My thanks, la... Mistress,' he said, taking it from her.

He met her gaze and she searched for something of the man she knew, the man she loved, there. The silence grew uncomfortable and lengthy until the other man interrupted.

'Your escort is waiting outside for you,' he said. 'See her there.' The manservant was at her side now, waiting.

Niall said nothing else to her, nodding slightly and then stepping back. Letting her go.

Fia gathered herself and walked out of the room, trying not to lose control. She stopped just outside the door, motioning the servant she would follow. They began talking before the door even closed and she heard everything.

'I can see why you kept her. A fine piece in bed, was she?' the other one said.

'Aye, she was that,' Niall said, laughing. 'I did not plan on her being part of my work, but I was not about to refuse her when she begged me to touch her.'

'Will she cry of love and promises to the Mackintosh, Niall? 'tis important that there be no problems or complications now.'

'Nay. She understood it from the first.'

'You could arrange to keep her, if the King grants your petition.'

'Do you think he will?' Niall asked.

'I suspect that you will be Niall, Earl of Kelso, before the end of the day, my friend,' their host said. 'The King has been trying to teach you a lesson. With what you've done, I think he will grant his godson's plea for mercy.'

She turned to the door and could see in the small opening. Niall met her gaze then and nodded.

'Once my titles and lands and my monies are returned, why would I need her?' He smiled—not the wicked one that had teased her heart, but a cold and calculating one. 'I could arrange for a woman as my leman if I need one.'

'If the King plans to marry you to Sinclair's daughter, you will want a leman to warm your bed and your privy bits, Niall. She is a cold-hearted bitch.'

'I care not as long as she brings me that dowry,' he said, now closing the door in her face.

Fia stumbled back into the wall before she walked quickly down the hallway. Who was that man? How could he have said such things about her? He'd not done this to save his family, for he'd never once spoken of his mother or sister to Lord Lindsay. He spoke not of honour restored, but wealth and position.

She had been such a fool to believe a word of what he said. From the start, he had lied to her. While he had busily fooled the outlaws into believing he was one of them, he'd fooled her into thinking he was noble in his purpose. And she had gone along with all of it. Worse, she'd fallen in love with him.

Fia wrapped her cloak around her shoulders and walked from that house, never looking back. She'd learned her lesson well this time.

Alan stared at her as she came down the steps towards him. His narrowed gaze told her that he saw and knew more than she wished he did. She looked away as he helped her on to the waiting horse and then followed at his side back up the main road towards the city.

And away from him for ever.

Niall clutched his mother's book so tightly that the leather made imprints in his palm. The shock on her face as he disavowed her, denied her, was horrible to watch. Now, as he peered through the window out on to the street, he noticed how she carried herself with such dignity and grace.

'Here, you need this,' Alex said, handing him a glass.

Niall swallowed it without ever looking at it. The strong spirit burned a path down from his throat into his gut. He held it out for more.

'I would say you succeeded. The young woman does indeed hate you,' his damned cousin said.

'A clean break.'

'Aye. She will not look back.'

Though his cousin was not looking out of the window, he was correct in both ways—Fia never turned her head towards the house and she would never be tempted to return to him.

'So, enough of that,' Alex said, lifting the thrice-filled glass from his hand. 'We must prepare for your audience.'

'Do you think he will listen? If not for me, then for my mother and for Mary?' He pushed his hands through his hair. 'Good God, I have not seen Mary since they took her from my mother and sent her off. I have no idea where she is, if she yet lives.'

'And your mother remains in the convent? Has she taken vows?'

'Aye, but she has refused that step. But I was turned away three years past when I tried to see her.'

'The King has been solidifying his control after decades of turmoil and a lack of a sound treasury. That is why he wanted to solve the problem between those two clans. They are both powerful and wealthy. And, to your benefit, he has been placing men loyal to him in control of the areas near the borders. He does not wish to see England coming here again in his lifetime.'

'So, you think there is a chance?'

The discussion went on for a while more as Alex reviewed his story and advised his approach. He would throw himself on his godfather's mercy to save his mother and sister. The only thing that would assure his success would be the identity of the one behind the plan to disrupt the western Highlands.

And that was the one piece of the puzzle he did not have.

Chapter Twenty-Two

She'd never been to The Mackintosh house in Edinburgh before. Well, she'd not been to the city either. Now, Alan led the way through another gate, the Nether Bow, and right up the main road towards the intimidating castle at the top. Though the King chose to stay at the abbey for comfort or even at Dunfermline across the firth where his father was buried, most state business and matters of importance to the kingdom were handled at the castle. So, those having business with the King's court maintained houses within the city for the ease of conducting those matters.

Alan kept glancing back at her and she tried to ignore his sympathetic expression. He'd tried to tell her. He'd tried to help her and she had refused him. Good Lord, she sent an angry crowd after him!

'Alan,' she said. He slowed and came to her side. 'I beg your pardon for what I did in Crieff.'

'Ah, Fia, do not worry over it,' he said. Knocking on his head, he laughed. 'I have a hard one like my da says.'

Soon they came to a street, or a *wynd* as they called

it there, and Alan directed her to a narrow but tall house in the middle of a block of similar structures. She'd never seen anything like it. But, here in the city, houses looked pushed into every nook and cranny possible. And unlike a keep made of stone, most of these houses were built of wood.

A servant came out and took hold of her horse so she could climb down. Alan did the same and then led her inside. Glancing around, she was welcomed by a woman whom Alan said was the housekeeper. In many ways as the woman showed her through the house, she reminded Fia of Mistress Murray. She also took Alan, though a Cameron and old enough to see to himself, under her wing and sent him to the kitchen to eat.

It was as he passed her in the narrow corridor leading back to the kitchen that a memory struck her. Forced to move against the wall, she remembered back to Crieff when he had pushed her against the wall and argued for her to accompany him. He glanced at her and apologised then as he moved on. But she was trying to force the words back into her mind.

I followed one of the men when he left the camp to his destination.

Fia followed Alan to the kitchen and just watched him, hoping the rest would come back to her. He accepted every morsel that he was offered and he smiled often.

I followed one of the men when he left the camp to his destination.

'Alan, I need to speak with you,' she said. He would remember the rest of it, but somehow he knew that another was behind the attacks. He'd said that, too, even though Fia had ignored it. He shoved a hunk of meat in his mouth and washed it down with ale before following her to the front chamber near the door.

'Are you well, Fia? You look a bit peaked.' Then he blushed and mumbled, 'Never mind, I should not have said that. After all you have been through, you must be exhausted and heart-sore.'

How could men be so thickheaded and nice at the same time? Shaking her head, she thought about what she should do. He was correct—her heart hurt. She would never be with the man she loved. If he stood to be an earl if the King restored his title and lands, he would be above her in status and be out of her world for ever. If he stood high in the King's favour, everything would be his. And he would not, could not, be hers.

If he did not, and she did believe his words to her on their last night together, his family would suffer. His callous words to her in front of his kin did not have the sound of truth to her. 'twas like he was doing whatever he could to push her away from him.

'Alan, you said something to me in Crieff and I cannot remember it clearly. Did you say you got to the camp and followed someone out of it? Did you follow the man called Lundie?'

Alan stared at her and then nodded.

'Where did he go?

'He went to Keppoch and met with Alastair Mac-Donald.'

'Of the Clan Ranald of Lochaber?' she asked. 'Are you certain?' At his nod, Fia nodded, too. 'You know what that means?'

'Aye. Clan Ranald is behind the troubles.'

The proof Niall needed was in her hands now. And

Alan's. But would he help the man who'd just broken her heart? Would she?

'I need you to speak to Niall and tell him what you know. He was sent by the King to find the culprit behind it.'

'Niall? Niall Corbett, who kidnapped you and who… I beg your pardon, Fia. I cannot believe you would even want to think about him, let alone let him seem the hero before the King and Brodie.'

'He needs to complete the task the King set for him.'

'Why the hell do you care if he succeeds? You should be cursing him to hell and the Highlands right now. I heard, you know. I heard and saw him with you. I know what he wanted from you.'

'Alan. You can still tell Brodie all of it.'

He was correct—she should be hating Niall and using every one of Rob Mackintosh's bad words to curse his fate to the heavens and anyone who would listen. But, she loved him. And she had faith in him that his heart had spoken the truth to her. He needed to save his family. With this information, at least one of them would get their dreams fulfilled.

'Oh, God, Fia!' he said, staring at her then. 'I saw the two of you and how he looked at you. You love him, do you not?' She nodded. 'And he loves you.' She nodded again, certain of it.

He spat out a word that made the housekeeper gasp in horror and Fia laughed. Then he nodded and trudged out of the house.

A very strange feeling filled her then and Fia knew she had done the right thing in this. Relief. Satisfaction. Done. She would go home now. It would all work itself out and her life would be her own now.

It was over now.

He'd thought the night before had passed slowly, and it had. But this day moved at a slug's pace. Niall understood it was the anticipation of meeting the King. Alex told him that they would sup with the King privately, to discuss this family matter. If anyone could convince the King to mercy, it would be Alex.

The fact that Alex had not done so before was more about his attention to other matters of state over in France for the last decade. And, he supposed that men who held that much sway over the King must pick and choose their causes well or lose influence. And clearly other matters had priority to Alex over his mother's sister and niece.

Niall's leg was tormenting him as well. The days of travel had allowed it to stiffen. He needed to stretch it, as Glynis had told him, and he needed to walk or he would be immobile by the time he was summoned for the meeting. So, with some time before even the noon meal, Niall decided to walk to the abbey gates and back.

He'd only got around the corner from his cousin's house when he was grabbed and dragged into an alley. If he'd been steady on his feet or had remembered the damn walking stick, no man the size or ability of his assailant would have succeeded. Fearing he would fracture his leg the rest of the way through the bone— as Glynis said another fall would—he did not fight back. Oh, his fists would work well once they stopped.

He swung once, losing his balance as he did, and soon found his face shoved up against the wall of the building next to him and a knee in his back to keep him there. The man made no move for the purse tied inside his tunic and did not attack him further.

'Who are you? What do you want?' he asked.

'I am not here to take anything from you,' the man said, turning him around to face him. 'She sent me.'

Niall could not think of whom that could be. He had no ties to any woman in the city. Except the one he'd just sent away...

Fia.

'Alan Cameron,' the man said. 'Brodie sent me to find the lass.'

'She is here, hale and hardy,' he explained.

'Aye, I know that. But she wants me to tell you something.'

Niall took a breath. Why send a message through this man? A Cameron at that. 'Tell me then.'

'I am a tracker,' he said. 'I find things. I find people. I found Fia at the camp.'

'You were at the camp? When?'

'Just as the storm hit. I waited it out and then came up the mountain.' He'd been there? 'I left and followed your man, the one Fia said was called Lundie.' The man shook his head and looked up at the sky. 'I thought she was safe enough. I saw how it was between the two of you.'

'And you followed him?' Niall asked. If he'd tracked Lundie, he might know who was behind it all. Could he?

'I do not think you deserve the knowledge, but Fia

asked me to tell you.' He glared at Niall and then shrugged. 'Your Lundie met with Alastair MacDonald of Keppoch.'

Niall could not breathe. He could not think. Was the chief of the Clan Ranald of Lochaber the one plotting to break the alliance between the Mackintoshes and The Camerons? It all fell into place. The Ranalds of Lochaber had been contesting Mackintosh ownership of some lands near their borders. But, they'd been unwilling to challenge both the Chattan Confederation and The Camerons, too.

'So tell your king and I am certain proof will be found. I will be telling Brodie as soon as he arrives in the city.'

With that, the man let go of him and turned to leave. His thoughts muddled just then with both excitement and confusion.

'Why did she send you? Why tell me now?'

Alan Cameron did not speak, he glared at Niall, waiting for him to figure it out. 'She did it for me?' His throat tightened at the truth.

'Aye, you daft prick! She did it for you.' The man walked away, muttering all manner of rude comments to himself.

Niall stood there, shocked by her gift to him. In sharing this with him, she'd made it possible for him to regain everything he'd lost. In spite of his ugly words and denial of her, Fia had given him his future and restored his past. Even knowing that it would separate them for ever. He stumbled his way back to Alex's house to ready himself for what would now be a successful meeting with the King.

* * *

Hours later, he stood as the Earl of Kelso, high now in the favour of the King, his godfather. As the King raised a cup to his good fortune, Niall knew he'd never felt so empty as he did at that moment. For in gaining everything he desired, he'd lost the one thing he loved.

Chapter Twenty-Three

Fia kept her head down as she embroidered the fabric in her hands. The vibrant threads would remain bright and visible when the tapestry was hung on the wall behind the dais in the hall. Arabella had been planning it and all three of them—the lady, Ailean and Fia—had been sewing it for weeks now. Well, since her return to Drumlui and the Mackintoshes.

She smiled at something Arabella said, not truly listening now, and continued her part of the scene. It would depict a hunt in the woods with a huge antlered stag and Mackintosh warriors. The colours favoured in their tartans were there—red and blue and green.

'Ailean? Would you see if the cook has more of those cakes that were at table last evening? I fear I have this strange desire for one,' Arabella said.

'I will go, my lady,' Fia said, carefully placing the embroidery aside. 'twas her task to see to the lady's needs and comforts and not Ailean's.

'Nay, Fia,' Arabella said with a shake of her head. 'Ailean?'

Ah, so this was to be the time, then? Five weeks had

passed and now Arabella would get to it. Fia watched as the lady's cousin left the room as ordered to fetch a non-existent cake. A mere pretence to prepare for the questioning. Truly, she admired the lady's restraint in this. Five weeks with nary a question other than the one asked on her return.

Are you well, Fia?

Fia understood what was being asked and wanted to scream out so many things, but she did not. She simply nodded and went with her mother back to the village. Even her mother avoided asking too many things and chose to ask about the places Fia had seen, since Bradana had never left the area around her village during her entire life.

It was a comfortable topic. Fia spoke of Crieff and Edinburgh and had her mother laughing over Mistress Murray and her lads. She even managed to never mention *his* name during all of it.

She was home with her parents for only a day when her father said what was on his mind and most of it involved hunting down and killing the outlaws himself. Only at her mother's pleading did he let it fade into silence. The chieftain, her mother assured him, would see to the matter. Two days passed before she was summoned back to the keep.

Oh, Fia understood what they—Brodie and Arabella—were doing. By bringing her back into their household and to her former place, they were telling the rest that she was valued. Still, it did not stop all the gossip or the prying glances or sly questions and comments around her. But, no one would insult her openly when the laird and lady had welcomed her back.

Her life was returning to its usual pace now. She

found peace in her work and keeping her hands and mind busy. It was only the nights that tormented her now. Her mother did not ask why she woke crying. Her mother did not tell her it would be better. Her mother simply held her and let her cry as though she understood more than she could know.

Now though, she would be held to account for the time away from here and the things that had occurred during her captivity. Arabella watched as the door to the chamber closed, but waited until Ailean's footsteps could no longer be heard before speaking.

'My cousin has asked Brodie's permission to speak to you, Fia.'

Confused by the topic when she expected something much different, she frowned. 'Your cousin?' The Camerons had almost as many cousins as the Mackintoshes did and Fia had lost count when she'd reached sixty of them.

'Alan. He will be visiting in a few days and wishes to speak to you.'

The man felt guilty that he did not follow Brodie's orders and get her out of the camp sooner. His decision had solved one huge puzzle but created more problems...for her.

'I have told him he owes me no apology, Arabella.' Fia stood up and walked to the small table where pitchers of ale and wine sat. Pouring some watered ale in a cup, she offered it to the lady before filling one for herself. 'He helped me in many ways.'

The lady's smile, a slight lifting of one side of her mouth, warned her of her mistake. She had never considered what other purpose he could have...

'Alan wishes to *speak* to you, Fia. I gave him my

blessing.' Arabella watched her expectantly and nodded when Fia understood. *Speak* to her. *Blessing?*

Alan wished to offer her marriage.

She swallowed down the ale and filled the cup with the more potent wine there. Two mouthfuls of that went down quickly and then Arabella touched her arm.

'Does his intention disturb you? Is he somehow not suitable? Or it is any thought of marriage?' Arabella watched her closely, waiting for her answer.

Though Dougal had not shunned her upon her return, neither had he pressed her for an answer to his suit. He'd eased his way back into her life, showing up at different moments and making her aware of him. Some quiet words spoken during one encounter told her that he would not withdraw his offer.

And—God forgive her!—all she could think of was the word 'hapless' whenever she saw him. No matter that memory, Dougal was kind to continue his attentions to her considering…

The lady observed her in this pause for a few more moments before taking her hand and pulling her over to the cushioned bench near the window. Then it was Arabella's turn to pause before speaking her mind.

'My husband would like to set things right for you. He wishes to find a suitable husband and provide you a dowry, Fia.'

'A generous offer, lady, but—'

'Nay. 'twas his plan before…any of this happened. We spoke of it before we left for Achnacarry.' Arabella leaned in towards her and lowered her voice. 'He has charged me with the task of finding out if you have objections to marriage because of…anything…that may have happened.'

Fia smiled at the concern in her lady's voice. And at the lady's discomfort at breaching her privacy over what had or had not happened to her. Arabella retrieved their cups and waited until Fia had another sip.

'Were they cruel to you, Fia? Did they…harm you?'

Fia stared off in the corner, remembering many, many things that had happened to her during those weeks, and shook her head.

'Nay, lady. They did not.' Arabella let out a breath.

'I am glad then,' she said. 'I would not wish that an act that can hold such joy and pleasure be tarnished for you in that way.'

Fia could not help but smile then, memories of the joy and the immense pleasure he'd given her made her skin feel too tight then. And the heat in her blood as she remembered his mouth on her caused her to blush then, and perspire. None of that reaction was missed by the lady.

'So you are not opposed to marriage then?' The lady was as relentless as her husband could be, though her outward appearance and demeanour hid it well.

'I am not opposed…' Fia began, shaking her head. 'I just do not wish to consider one now.'

'I told Brodie I was right and he would not believe me.'

'Not believe you, lady? On what matter?' The laird accepted the lady's counsel on most every matter, even some that other men thought she should not have a say about.

'I told him that you did not mourn virtue lost, but a love lost.'

Fia should not be surprised at the lady's ability to

see through her, for she herself had been kidnapped and forced to return to an unwanted marriage.

'I just need some time.' She did not wish to explain further or think of it, of him.

'Very well,' Arabella said, patting her hand. 'I am here if you wish to speak on matters of a delicate nature, but I will not press you again.'

Very much like Mistress Murray and her denial of prying, Fia knew Arabella wanted to do nothing as much as she wanted to press about this.

'Ah, here is Ailean,' she said, walking to the more comfortable chair as her cousin opened the door. No sweet cake was left after all. Arabella's wink confirmed it had been a performance to give them privacy.

'Lady, what brings your cousin to Drumlui now?' she asked once she'd taken up her needle and thread.

'Some dispute over lands, as usual. The King wishes it settled before war breaks out in earnest.'

Fia's mouth went dry. Was this the matter that had caused the attacks? Would that mean Niall would…?

'If my husband wishes my counsel, he will ask for it,' Arabella said. 'God Almighty knows I would never give it without being asked.'

It took only a moment before they all laughed, knowing full and well that there was hardly a matter the lady did not speak to.

Four days later, as they sat continuing their work on the tapestry, a huge contingent of men arrived in the yard. Arabella urged patience and only a short time later, the lady was summoned to the hall by her husband. Though Arabella assured her there would be no talk of marriage from Alan, Fia dreaded seeing him.

She followed Arabella and Ailean down the stairs to the main hall, now filled with dozens of men it seemed. She recognised some of the Camerons and noticed several of the warriors wearing a clan tartan she did not know. They opened a path to allow someone to approach Brodie just as she and Ailean took their places off the side of the dais, close enough to assist the lady if need be but out of the way of things.

Though they did not stand on the formalities held to at the royal court, Brodie's steward could certainly do the task when needed. Greeting family or other neighbouring clans or allies was done simply. But this visitor seemed to need more. Fia watched as Fergus puffed out his chest and called to his chieftain.

'My lord Mackintosh, may I present the special emissary from the King's Justiciar of Lothian, Lord Niall Corbett.'

The world before her began to spin as the man she thought to never see again walked up the steps and bowed to Brodie. And then he swept his gaze across those present, meeting hers for the briefest of moments before returning to Brodie. Lucky for her, she was sitting on a chair or she would have fallen over for certain.

So, he had given the King the information and had taken his place among the nobles of the land. He wore the garments and symbols of a lord of the realm and was now a 'special emissary' of an even greater man—the one who oversaw justice in the Kingdom and carried out the wishes of the King.

'My lord Mackintosh, I bring greetings from both the King and Sir Robert de Lauder of Bass to you,' he said in voice she did not recognise. 'Lord Alastair

MacDonald and the Cameron come, with the King's blessing, to discuss a matter of great and grave importance to your clans and to the King's justice.'

Fia was trying to control the trembling that had begun the moment she saw him and she was losing that battle. She must get out of here. Looking up, she knew there was no way to leave unnoticed now. Then, Brodie moved and drew everyone's attention.

When he should have formally accepted the greetings presented to him from the King, he instead walked down the three steps separating him from Niall and punched him in the face. Silence reigned momentarily and then the confusion really began, as the men who'd accompanied Niall began to rush forward and The Mackintosh warriors charged with the safety of their chieftain moved to intercept them. Other guards stepped close to the lady, ready to protect her.

From one instant to the next, this had gone from diplomatic meeting to armed camp. She'd never seen the like.

'Stop!' Niall shouted at his men.

He rubbed his jaw where the blow had landed as he climbed to his feet. Brodie nodded and his warriors moved away. Now face-to-face, everyone held their breath to see what would come next.

'Aye,' Brodie said, crossing his arms over his massive chest. 'There is much we have to discuss.'

'Just so,' Niall said.

'Clear the hall!' Brodie called. 'My lady, if you would remain?' Arabella nodded, as though she would have left if he'd said so. 'Everyone else is dismissed.'

She stood, shaking from the shock of seeing Niall and the dangerous tension in the room, and began to follow Ailean out. It happened rarely, but when Brodie ordered them out, they left the lady's care to him.

'Fia?' Brodie said.

Though he spoke it in a quiet manner, her name seemed to echo loudly across the hall. She met his gaze and waited. He canted his head a bit and then gave her one sharp nod.

It had been for her. Brodie knew more than she'd told anyone if he knew the connection to Niall.

Fia nodded back and left the hall without ever looking at Niall.

Niall rubbed his jaw as The Mackintosh looked over at Fia. He understood the action better than anyone. Now acting as the King's emissary, Niall could not be punished publicly for what he'd done. But Brodie would not let the insult to his kin go unnoticed even if his involvement began at the command of the King.

And, if these Highlanders behaved the way he knew they would, there would be more than one punch in his future for what he'd done—to their kin and to their Fia. She left, pale and trembling, without ever looking his way. He and the few others allowed to remain waited for quiet to be restored.

The chieftains took places on opposite sides of the table, in what looked like a masterful chess match. Lady Mackintosh sat at her husband's side and a little away from the table, giving it the appearance that she would only participate if her husband allowed it. From Fia's stories, Niall knew that was not the way of it here.

The lady called servants in briefly to bring wine

and ale and food and then, they were left to sort out the mess begun by Alastair Macdonald's grab for lands he did not own and could not claim legally.

The King made it clear, as did his Justiciar, that three powerful Highland clans would not be permitted to go to war. It was up to Niall to sort it out and make the King's offer, or rather, make them agree to his plan.

Nigh to three hours later, an agreement was reached between the chieftains over the lands and the punishment for Clan Ranald of Lochaber for the attacks on Mackintosh lands.

As the others were led off to chambers for their stay, Niall walked over to Brodie and his wife. If his plan, the true reason he'd talked his way into handling this though by rights it should have been handled by the Justiciar who oversaw the northern half of Scotland, was to succeed, he needed both of them on his side.

'My lord? My lady? I would speak to you both.'

Niall waited and received only a curt nod. The lady whispered something to her husband before they led him off the dais and back to a small chamber. From the rolls of parchment and books, this must be the steward's room for handling the business affairs of the laird and his clan. As the laird waited for his wife to sit and then closed the door, Niall realised that the rest of his life would be decided in the next few minutes.

Chapter Twenty-Four

Any sense of peace disappeared when he arrived. For the hours after she left the hall, she paced the length and breadth of the upper floors trying not to fall apart. Fia knew what she would do—she would leave the keep, pleading illness if necessary, and go to the village. She could stay with her parents in their small cottage tucked safely away in the heart of the village.

As long as he remained here, as an emissary of the King would, and she did not leave there, she could avoid the terrible pain of seeing him again. Once this matter between the clans was settled, he would ride out of Drumlui and out of her life for ever. When Lady Arabella returned to her chambers, Fia met her, ready to ask for leave to go. With a nod, Ailean was dismissed.

'So that was him? The man who kidnapped you?'

'Aye.' She did not have the strength to do this now. To be picked apart with questions and made to dwell on the subject and the man she wished to not have to think about again.

'Come now, Fia,' Arabella said softly. 'I do not

think he looks like an outlaw at all.' She turned and walked to the chair. 'But then my husband did not see fit to share his knowledge of this matter with me.'

'I pray you, Arabella. I do not wish to speak of this. Or to see him again.' She could feel her control beginning to shred and knew she would break down soon. 'With your permission, I would like to stay with my parents while he is here.' She met Arabella's shrewd gaze. 'I beg you to give me leave to do so.'

She'd never asked something so strongly of her lady before. Arabella was not mean-spirited at all. Fia did not understand why the woman hesitated at all in granting her request.

'I have no wish to see you so upset, Fia. Certainly you may go to your parents.'

Fia nodded. Getting her cloak from the alcove near the door, she paused and looked at Arabella. 'My thanks, lady.' She lifted the latch on the door and opened it before the lady spoke again.

'Do you love him, Fia? Whether outlaw or lord, do you love him?'

Unprepared for such a frank and revealing question, Fia took in a breath and gave the truth she wished was not so. 'Against all reason and sanity, aye, I do.'

No one spoke to her as she left and if it was strange to see her running from the keep, out the gates towards the village, no one stopped her to say so. She was out of breath by the time she reached her parents' cottage. Their empty cottage.

They returned later without a word of explanation and Fia fell into the usual way of things when she stayed here. She helped her mother prepare their evening meal and they ate together. No one seemed to want to talk and it was a quiet supper.

She did not rest well that night, knowing he was so close and yet so far from her made it impossible to sleep. When she did, the dreams came again. Of him. Of them. Of some future that existed only in her dreams. The morning found her exhausted and awake.

Only when she watched the entourage of warriors and chieftains leave Drumlui Keep and ride away towards the south at midday did she feel relief. And sorrow. And pain. And loss. But now, she told herself as she finished having a good cry by the stream, now she could get her life back.

Her parents never asked when she would return to the keep, so she decided to stay another day in their company. Her mother subscribed to the belief that idle hands found their way to trouble, so she sent Fia on errand after errand, giving her chores to do until Fia decided the keep would not be such a bad place after all. She finished up folding the washed clothes and took her leave.

As she walked up the path towards the centre of the village and the well, he was there. The breath within her stopped and she stared at him. The refined air and garments were gone. Before her stood Iain Dubh looking much as he'd looked the first time she saw him here. Her hands itched to touch him and when he smiled that wicked smile she loved so much, her mouth went dry.

'I stopped to parch my thirst but I canna seem to find the dipper, lass,' he said, in the voice of a Highland rogue. 'Hiv ye seen it, mayhap?' He took a step towards her then and she shook her head.

'Why are you here?' she asked when she could get words past her lips. 'Why?' She clasped her hands tightly in front of her and tried to think. Her body betrayed her when he stepped closer and blocked her escape down the path.

'I am here to do what rogues do,' he said, his voice seductive and enticing. Another step closer. 'I am looking for a Highland lass to kidnap, seduce and plunder.' He reached out to touch her face and she shuddered. 'Are ye willin' to be kidnapped, Fia? I could even let ye hiv yer way wi' me?'

'Go. Now. Away from here,' she repeated the words he'd said to her in this place. If he left now… If he turned and walked away, she might not lose control.

'I tried, Fia. Truly I tried,' he said softly. The rough accent gone, he spoke not as an outlaw or a courtier but as just a man. 'The King was quite pleased with what your cousin found out. He offered me my choice of rewards. My title, lands, all of it.'

'So you have everything you ever wanted,' she said. 'So go back to it all.'

'Ah, lass. It must have been your prayers for my wicked soul, for once I had everything in my grasp, I realised that the one thing, the one person I wanted most, was lost to me.' He reached out to stroke her cheek with his hand, sliding it until he cupped her face.

'He wants me to marry. He wants me to continue my *excellent work* as his man, so he can order me to wherever he needs someone to see to his interests.' He smiled then. 'I did not reveal Alan's part in discovering the truth behind the attacks, but Brodie knows and will offer him an appropriate reward.'

'So who does the King wish you to marry?' she asked in spite of telling herself not to. This would not end well and would lead to pain and heartbreak for her.

'My cousin Alex was right—Sinclair's daughter is frightening, so I refused. But I told my godfather that there was the perfect woman for me. One who tried to knock me out with a cooking pot when I tried to seduce her. One who stole my purse and my dagger. One who listened when I needed to talk and prayed for my wicked soul. One who eased my pain and saved my life. One who loved me...'

He stepped closer and smiled, taking her hand in his and kissing her fingers. 'Well, the King said then I'd better stake my claim and marry her before someone else did. He especially liked the part about the cooking pot the best, I think.'

She laughed in spite of herself and in spite of the tears pouring down her face now. Then she looked at him, meeting his gaze for the first time and seeing the love there.

'So, my love, which will it be? Do I kidnap you, seduce and plunder you until you agree to marry me?' He leaned in to whisper to her, 'I promise to make the plundering very pleasant for you.' He leaned back.

She began to speak but he shook his head and put his finger over her lips. Fia loved the merriment in his eyes and in his temperament. She'd wondered if it was only him acting the rogue before, but now recognised that it was part of his true nature. At his words, that damned unrelenting hope within her heart stirred, waking up those silly, girlish dreams once more.

'Or do we go to the chapel and marry first? I might live to get to the seducing and plundering part that way.'

He touched his eye and she noticed the bruise there. If Brodie had landed his blow on Niall's jaw, how had his eye been injured? At her frown, he said, 'Your father felt 'twas his place to answer my previous insult to your honour. I did not think he would do it so vehemently.'

'I saved you once, my black-haired man,' she began. 'I do not want to see my hard work go for naught. If everyone decides to protest your ruination of me, you may not survive it.' She watched the love in his gaze grow. 'And I have yet to be truly and completely ruined.'

'I could see to that for you, Fia.' She laughed at his offer.

'I think I will take marriage, then ruination.'

He stared at her without speaking or breathing or moving and a seed of doubt entered her thoughts. Then, he grabbed her and kissed her until they were both breathless.

'I thought you, as the good, obedient lass you are, would take that choice. Come…' he mounted the horse she had not even seen and held out his hand '…they are waiting for us.'

'And your mother? Your sister? Are they well?'

'Aye. Better than I knew. You will meet them soon enough.'

He pulled her up behind him and touched his feet to

the horse's side, urging it on. Fia slid her arms around him then, laying her face on his back. Could this be happening? Could they truly be together?

As it turned out, aye, they could.

He was more nervous now than when he'd asked her to marry him or when they spoke their vows. Hell, he was more nervous now than when he'd demanded the King allow him to marry her.

Now, he stood in the doorway of the chamber and stared at…his wife. Beautiful, intelligent, thoughtful, funny, loving, headstrong Fia was now his. And those damn scruples that had kept him from claiming her could go to hell now.

'You look nervous,' she said, smoothing the bed-covers over her legs. Though the sheets were pulled up high, he knew she wore nothing under them. His cock rose, knowing the loveliness of her curves, the taste of her skin and the sounds she would make when he pleasured her.

And, oh, he planned on pleasuring her.

'I am a bit,' he admitted as he walked in and closed the door behind him. The chamber smelled of heather and roses from the preparations made by Fia's mother and Arabella. 'I have never plundered my wife be-fore.' She smiled, a wicked one by his measure, and one brow edged up.

'Does this plundering take long?'

He laughed then. Niall had never expected to find such joy in his marriage bed or even marriage. He loved seeing the frank desire in her gaze as she looked at him. He loved that she did not hide it from him.

He loved…her.

'If you wish, it can take as long as you'd like,' he offered. 'As long as you do as I say.'

'Then, Husband, come in and let the plundering begin.'

She lifted the sheets and exposed her naked body to him. His flesh ached to be within her. When she opened her legs, he gave up trying to be noble and patient. He dropped the long robe he wore and climbed on to the bed. Fia reached out to touch him and he shook his head.

'Nay. If you touch me, 'twill be over.'

'Niall?' she asked, sliding on to her knees before him. 'I may have promised to obey and submit, but I am not sure I can do that.' She reached out and touched his flesh, sliding her hand around him and stroking him.

He tried to say something humorous back to her and could not think of a single thing. So, he leaned over and kissed her as he'd wanted to do for the last month.

She softened under his lips and he pulled her into his arms, their bodies touching, his flesh cradled by her belly. Fia opened to him as she always did, fully welcoming him. He eased her down on to the bed and knelt over her, kissing her mouth, her face, her neck, her shoulders, her breasts and down and down until he reached the curls at the juncture of her legs.

Her body trembled and shifted beneath his attentions until she relaxed her legs and he moved between them. Lifting one over his shoulder, he pressed his mouth against her most intimate flesh, tasting the very essence of her and stroking her until she thrust her hips in rhythm with his tongue.

She tousled his hair, tangling her fingers in it and

holding him there. She was close, very close, to finding satisfaction and he wanted to within her, to feel her body tighten and then shudder its release.

'Fia,' he said, sliding up her body and kissing her mouth. 'I want to be in you.' All she did was gasp against his mouth with each touch.

He moved his hand where his mouth had been, stroking and rubbing, harder, faster, deeper each time. Then he placed his flesh there and moved into her. Pushing slowly, he eased in and slid back. She was tight, so very tight, and her woman's flesh held him snugly. Niall lifted her knees and slid his hand beneath her hips.

'I love you, Fia Mackintosh,' he whispered as he seated his flesh all the way in her, making her his and his alone. He paused, controlling the urge to thrust again until she became accustomed to him there. When her hips shifted, he pulled back and thrust in again.

It was killing him to wait but he would do whatever he must to ease her way.

'Why did you stop?' she whispered, wrapping her hands around his buttocks and pulling him in close.

He gave up the fight and took her. With a hand under her bottom, he guided her movements, allowing him in as deep as he could get. Shallow quick breaths told him she was near to her peak. She matched him now, thrust for thrust until he felt her tighten around him. Her body arched and she moaned out as her release was upon her. Niall kissed her, open-mouthed, tongue teasing tongue, as he felt his cock harden and thicken in readiness.

And then, his release began, his seed filling her depths and his own body reaching satisfaction.

'Twas some time before their breathing slowed and their bodies relaxed. Niall remained within her, rolling them to their side and holding her close.

'Are you well?' he asked quietly, kissing her forehead. 'Was I too rough?' Though he had pleasured her before, he had never entered her like this.

'I am well, though a bit sore,' she admitted. Leaning back, she met his gaze. 'I had not realised how much more there was to this plundering. I might not have threatened you with the cooking pot if I had known.'

He laughed then and held her close. She softened against him and her breathing became slow and even. Just when he thought her asleep, she whispered once more.

'I might have even plundered you back.'

Lucky man that he was, she did just that for him later in the night.

Epilogue

Crieff, one year later...

'Hurry, lads!' Mistress Murray called out to Tomas and Munro. 'Clear the yard and be quick aboot it!'

A man came ahead and said his master and mistress, wealthy persons, he said, a lord and lady travelling through Crieff, needed a place to eat and freshen themselves on their journey to Edinburgh. He offered her coins, gold ones, if she would have a room and a meal ready for them. Said they'd heard of her inn and her food and wanted to see it for themselves.

Shock quickly turned to excitement for her as she realised what this could mean to her business. If she were known to the wealthy and noble travellers, her inn would never be empty. Her purse would overflow. This was her chance.

'Peigi, is the stew hot? The bread in the oven?' she called out as she walked through the dining room once more, cleaning the tops of the tables with her apron and searching for the broom for one more sweep.

'Aye, Mistress Murray,' the girl called out. 'When will they be here?'

'They will be here when they get here,' she answered, accepting the spoon of beef-and-vegetable stew from the maid. She blew on its several times and then tasted it. She took a pinch of this and a little of that and tossed it in the pot. 'Stir it and keep it warm now,' she directed. 'And dinna let the bread burn!'

The sound of horses and people arriving in the yard brought her rushing to the door. The lads ran to grab the bridles of the horses while the lord helped the lady climb down.

They were dressed in fine clothing, gowns and tunics like she imagined the nobles wore to meet the King. The lady's long hair was braided and dressed with ribbons through it. The lord held out his hand and escorted her to the door. Mistress Murray dropped as far down as her bad knees would allow to greet them.

'My lord,' she said nodding at the man. 'My lady. Come and be welcome at The Hen and The Loaf.' They followed her within and she led them to the best table in the inn. 'Would ye like ale or wine mayhap while I bring yer meal?'

'Aye, Mistress Murray,' the lord said. 'That would be fine. Fia, would you prefer wine or ale?'

Fia? Why, that was the name of the lass who'd stayed here a year or so before, tending to a man she'd claimed was her brother. Brother and sister, my arse, she'd thought when they arrived. And, she was right.

'Ale, if you please,' the woman answered, placing a hand on her belly. Her pregnant belly.

She looked up at them now and gasped. 'twas them!

Here in her inn, dressed as fine as she'd ever seen. How could it be?

'Mistress Murray, how do you fare?' the lord asked. His name was…was…Iain. And when they'd left he was most certainly not a lord.

'I am well, my lord,' she said, still trying to figure this out.

Peigi carried the bowls of stew and steaming bread in from the kitchen then. Mistress Murray stood back and watched as they sat at the table and Peigi placed everything before them. She poured ale into her best mugs and placed them where they could reach them.

'Niall,' the lady said. 'Tell her.'

'Twas definitely the couple who had stayed in her back chamber, while he recuperated from a terrible beating. He nearly died, he did, and she had helped the lass nurse him back to health.

'I know you had your suspicions when we stayed here, but you were always kind to my wife,' he said. Reaching inside his cloak, he took out a purse. 'We came to bring this back to you,' he explained as he handed it to her.

When they'd left, she'd worried over the lass. So, she'd gathered a few coins and gave them to her in case she needed to escape him. Now, the purse was filled and not just with copper or silver coins, but gold ones.

'You saved my life, Mistress Murray,' he said. Lifting the lady's hand, he kissed the back of it. 'And you gave comfort and protection to my wife when she had no one else. For that, I am grateful.' She held the fat purse in her hand, estimating how much it contained.

'You gave us refuge when we had none,' the lady

said. 'If you have need of anything, send to us in Edinburgh.'

'Thank ye, my lord, my lady,' she said, overwhelmed by their generosity and her good fortune. 'Yer man asked aboot the room?'

'Could the lads see to my men? Food and drink for them while they wait?' the lord asked.

Then, he guided the lady to her feet and escorted her back to the corridor and to the room they'd shared. Did they mean to rest? The bed linens were clean, put on just before they'd arrived so they could. She followed them part way down and then stopped when he closed the door behind them.

Laughter echoed from within the chamber and she could hear them talking. Then, the sounds became something else and she went back to the kitchen, shooing the lads and Peigi in front of her. She put stew in wooden bowls and had Peigi take them outside to the men who escorted the couple.

It took some time, about as much time as it took for the lord and lady to return from the chamber down the corridor. Her hair was different than when they left, the ribbons gone from her braid and her laces looser than before. His cloak was askew and his hair a mess.

They laughed all the way out into the yard and, when he lifted her back on to her horse, the lord stopped and kissed the lady thoroughly on lips already swollen from other kisses, she could tell.

'My thanks for such a good meal and for such a warm and inviting place,' the lord said. She smiled at the way he said it loud enough that her neighbours and any travellers on the road could hear it.

'Thank you, Mistress Murray,' the lady said. 'For all you did for my husband and me.'

They began to guide their horses away when she called out.

'Your names, my lord? My lady?' She only knew them by the false names they'd used a year ago.

'This is Lord Niall Corbett, the Earl of Kelso, Mistress Murray,' their man said as he handed her another purse in payment for their meals…and use of the room. 'And his wife, Fia Mackintosh.'

'Good day to ye both,' she called out as they left. She and Peigi and the lads watched as they rode off towards the south road and then she turned to go back inside.

Husband and wife, eh? Lord and lady? Mistress Murray tucked the purse inside her tunic and thanked the Almighty for her good fortune.

'Brother and sister, my arse,' she said aloud.

* * * * *

If you enjoyed this story,
you won't want to miss these other
great reads in Terri Brisbin's
A HIGHLAND FEUDING *mini-series*

THE HIGHLANDER'S RUNAWAY BRIDE
STOLEN BY THE HIGHLANDER

COMING NEXT MONTH FROM

ⓗ HARLEQUIN®

ℍISTORICAL

Available October 18, 2016

ONCE UPON A REGENCY CHRISTMAS (Regency)
by Louise Allen, Sophia James and Annie Burrows
Uncover three Regency heroes in disguise with these three magical
Christmas novellas to warm your heart!

UNWRAPPING THE RANCHER'S SECRET (Western)
by Lauri Robinson
Sparks fly when Crofton Parks, the stepbrother who heiress Sara Johnson
believed was dead, returns to Colorado to claim his inheritance...

THE RUNAWAY GOVERNESS (Regency)
The Governess Tales • by Liz Tyner
When runaway governess Isabel Morton is rescued by handsome stranger
William Balfour, she decides to save William in return...by becoming his
bride!

THE QUEEN'S CHRISTMAS SUMMONS (Tudor)
by Amanda McCabe
Lady Alys Drury's gaze lands on a familiar face. Why is Juan, the Spanish
sailor she nursed back to health, at Queen Elizabeth's Christmas court?

Available via Reader Service and online:

THE WINTERLEY SCANDAL (Regency)
A Year of Scandal (spin-off) • by Elizabeth Beacon
As the daughter of wild Pamela Winterley, Eve lives in the shadow of
scandal. Meeting Colm Hancourt is sure to get society's tongues wagging.

THE DISCERNING GENTLEMAN'S GUIDE (Regency)
by Virginia Heath
Bennett Montague, sixteenth Duke of Aveley, is seeking the perfect bride.
He knows exactly what he wants, but will the arrival of Amelia Mansfield
unravel all his plans?

REQUEST YOUR FREE BOOKS!

HARLEQUIN®

HISTORICAL

Where love is timeless

2 FREE NOVELS PLUS 2 FREE GIFTS!

YES! Please send me 2 FREE Harlequin® Historical novels and my 2 FREE gifts (gifts are worth about $10). After receiving them, if I don't wish to receive any more books, I can return the shipping statement marked "cancel." If I don't cancel, I will receive 6 brand-new novels every month and be billed just $5.69 per book in the U.S. or $5.99 per book in Canada. That's a savings of at least 12% off the cover price! It's quite a bargain! Shipping and handling is just 50¢ per book in the U.S. and 75¢ per book in Canada.* I understand that accepting the 2 free books and gifts places me under no obligation to buy anything. I can always return a shipment and cancel at any time. Even if I never buy another book, the two free books and gifts are mine to keep forever.

246/349 HDN GH2Z

Name	(PLEASE PRINT)	

Address		Apt. #

City	State/Prov.	Zip/Postal Code

Signature (if under 18, a parent or guardian must sign)

Mail to the Reader Service:
IN U.S.A.: P.O. Box 1867, Buffalo, NY 14240-1867
IN CANADA: P.O. Box 609, Fort Erie, Ontario L2A 5X3

Want to try two free books from another line?
Call 1-800-873-8635 or visit www.ReaderService.com

* Terms and prices subject to change without notice. Prices do not include applicable taxes. Sales tax applicable in N.Y. Canadian residents will be charged applicable taxes. Offer not valid in Quebec. This offer is limited to one order per household. Not valid for current subscribers to Harlequin Historical books. All orders subject to credit approval. Credit or debit balances in a customer's account(s) may be offset by any other outstanding balance owed by or to the customer. Please allow 4 to 6 weeks for delivery. Offer available while quantities last.

Your Privacy—The Reader Service is committed to protecting your privacy. Our Privacy Policy is available online at www.ReaderService.com or upon request from the Reader Service.

We make a portion of our mailing list available to reputable third parties that offer products we believe may interest you. If you prefer that we not exchange your name with third parties, or if you wish to clarify or modify your communication preferences, please visit us at www.ReaderService.com/consumerschoice or write to us at Reader Service Preference Service, P.O. Box 9062, Buffalo, NY 14240-9062. Include your complete name and address.

HH15

She would become the best songstress in all of London.
She knew it. The future was hers. Now she just had to
find it. She was lost beyond hope in the biggest city of
the world.

Isabel tried to scrape the street refuse from her shoe
without anyone noticing what she was doing. She didn't
know how she was going to get the muck off her dress.
A stranger who wore a drooping cravat was eyeing her
bosom quite openly. Only the fact that she was certain
she could outrun him, even in her soiled slippers, kept her
from screaming.

He tipped his hat to her and ambled into a doorway
across the street.

Her dress, the only one with the entire bodice made
from silk, would have to be altered now. The rip in
the skirt—thank you, dog who didn't appreciate her

trespassing in his gardens—was not something she could mend.

How? How had she gotten herself into this?

She opened the satchel, pulled out the plume and examined it. She straightened the unfortunate new crimp in it as best she could and put the splash of blue into the little slot she'd added to her bonnet. She picked up her satchel, realizing she had got a bit of the street muck on it—and began again her new life.

Begin my new life, she repeated to herself, unmoving. She looked at the paint peeling from the exterior and watched as another man came from the doorway, waistcoat buttoned at an angle. Gripping the satchel with both hands, she locked her eyes on the wayward man.

Her stomach began a song of its own, and very off-key. She couldn't turn back. She had no funds to hire a carriage. She knew no one in London but Mr. Wren. And he had been so complimentary and kind to everyone at Madame Dubois's School for Young Ladies. Not just her. She could manage. She would have to. His compliments had not been idle, surely.

She held her head the way she planned to look over the audience when she first walked onstage and put one foot in front of the other, ignoring everything but the entrance in front of her.

Don't miss
THE RUNAWAY GOVERNESS by Liz Tyner,
available November 2016 wherever
Harlequin® Historical books and ebooks are sold.

www.Harlequin.com

Love the Harlequin book you just read?

Your opinion matters.

Review this book on your favorite book site, review site, blog or your own social media properties and share your opinion with other readers!

Be sure to connect with us at:
Harlequin.com/Newsletters
Facebook.com/HarlequinBooks
Twitter.com/HarlequinBooks

JUST CAN'T GET ENOUGH?

Join our social communities
and talk to us online.

You will have access to the latest
news on upcoming titles and special
promotions, but most importantly,
you can talk to other fans about your
favorite Harlequin reads.

Harlequin.com/Community

Facebook.com/HarlequinBooks

Twitter.com/HarlequinBooks

Pinterest.com/HarlequinBooks

THE WORLD IS BETTER WITH

Romance

Harlequin has everything from contemporary, passionate and heartwarming to suspenseful and inspirational stories.

Whatever your mood, we have a romance just for you!

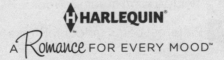